SWEET LIKE SUGAR

SWEET LIKE SUGAR

WAYNE HOFFMAN

KENSINGTON BOOKS
www.kensingtonbooks.com

KENSINGTON BOOKS are published by

Kensington Publishing Corp.
119 West 40th Street
New York, NY 10018

All Kensington titles, imprints, and distributed lines are available at special quantity discounts for bulk purchases for sales promotion, premiums, fund-raising, educational, or institutional use.

Special book excerpts or customized printings can also be created to fit specific needs. For details, write or phone the office of the Kensington Special Sales Manager: Attn. Special Sales Department. Kensington Publishing Corp., 119 West 40th Street, New York, NY 10018. Phone: 1-800-221-2647.

Kensington and the K logo Reg. U.S. Pat. & TM Off.

ISBN-13: 978-0-7582-6562-3
ISBN-10: 0-7582-6562-X

First Kensington Trade Paperback Printing: September 2011
10   9   8   7   6   5   4   3   2   1

Printed in the United States of America

For Mark,
my apple tree

Acknowledgments

First and foremost, thanks to my editor, John Scognamiglio, and my agent, Mitchell Waters, for getting this book published, and for all their guidance along the way.

I never could have finished the project without the support and helpful advice of Carolyn Hessel, Alana Newhouse, Don Weise, and Andrew Corbin.

Several people provided me with the physical space I needed to write: Stacey Hoffman and Victor Ozols; John Nazarian and Robert Reader; and Sarah Thompson and Diane Stafford at Poor Richard's Landing. My colleagues at the *Forward* and Nextbook Inc. allowed me the time I needed to write, which is no less important. And my friends in the Catskills helped preserve my sanity, such as it is, amid all the *mishegos* of writing and revising: David Nellis (and Pearl); Neil Greenberg and Frank Mullaney; John Murphy and Hal Moskowitz; and the entire Greynolds family. I couldn't have done it without all of you.

There are also, unfortunately, people who didn't live to see this book's completion. Allan Berube and Eric Rofes—my beloved mentors and friends and much more, two gorgeous and generous and brilliant men—were both taken too suddenly and too soon. Jim Merritt also died after a long illness, but not before his difficult final months inspired a large chunk of this story. And my remarkable great-aunt, Irene Wolfe, passed away in 2009, but she read an early draft of the novel, so she knew that her name and a piece of her spirit would endure.

My eternal gratitude to my parents, Marty and Susan Hoffman, for being much more wonderful and supportive than Benji Steiner's parents. And to my partner, Mark Sullivan, for his love, wisdom, honesty and, above all, patience.

SWEET LIKE SUGAR

CHAPTER 1

I was looking at Internet porn when the rabbi opened my door.

It wasn't as sordid as it sounds. I wasn't some yeshiva boy caught performing an unholy act. And he wasn't even *my* rabbi. Just *a* rabbi. An old, white-bearded man who had other things to worry about.

Still, I was startled when my office door opened without a knock and even more surprised to see the rabbi. He stood on the threshold, hand on the doorknob, breathing slowly and deliberately, wordless. I glanced down at the picture on my screen, a young shirtless guy—his hair thick and black, his teeth large and white, his eyes filled with devilish desires; his posture suggested complete confidence, his physique total vanity. I glanced up at the rabbi: ashen, hunched over, weak on his feet; his belly was bloated, his hair thin and dull, his expression a museum of sadness. One a man, the other also a man. I looked down again and switched off the monitor.

As I stood up from my desk, I saw Mrs. Goldfarb behind the rabbi. She craned her neck and peeked over his shoulder.

"Benjamin," she said to me, "I'm sorry to bother you, but Rabbi Zuckerman is feeling a bit faint. Do you think he could lie down on your couch for a few minutes?"

Nobody had called me Benjamin for years. I'd gone by Benji since junior high. But Mrs. Goldfarb still thought of me as one of her second-grade Hebrew school students, and to her, I'd always be Benjamin.

"Of course," I said, although this was a somewhat odd request. The rabbi owned the Jewish bookstore in the front of the shopping center, where Mrs. Goldfarb worked as the manager. But in the six months since I'd opened my office in the back of the shopping center, neither of them had ever stepped inside. Mrs. Goldfarb at least waved if she walked by my window on her way to the parking lot and she'd say hello if we bumped into each other at lunchtime in the sandwich shop several doors down. The rabbi had never given me more than a passing nod. Even now.

Mrs. Goldfarb gently nudged him forward, and I took him by the elbow, lifting his hand from the doorknob and leading him slowly toward the sofa. He lowered himself onto a cushion and then, with a labored groan, raised his legs onto the couch and turned his body to lie down on his back, his black lace-up shoes still on. He closed his eyes, one hand on his chest clutching his silver-framed spectacles, the other at his side holding his black knit yarmulke.

"I think he's just overheated," Mrs. Goldfarb said to me. "Our air-conditioning isn't working so well and the store gets very hot on a sunny afternoon. I'm sure he'll be fine after he lies down for a few minutes. Is it okay if I leave him here with you?"

"Sure," I said, not seeing any choice.

Mrs. Goldfarb turned to the rabbi. "You just relax here. I'm going back to mind the store, but I'll come check on you in a little while. Tell Benjamin if you need anything." Without opening his eyes, the rabbi feebly waved her off.

Mrs. Goldfarb walked out the door, and I followed her onto the sidewalk.

"Are you sure he's all right?" I asked. "He looks awful."

"Rabbi Zuckerman is a very stubborn man," she said, pausing to light a cigarette. "He started feeling dizzy about an hour ago. I told him to go to a doctor, or at least go home, but he wouldn't. Then I remembered seeing a couch in your office, right in the window, and I thought maybe he'd agree to lie down there. He didn't at first, but when he lost his balance and almost knocked down a whole bookshelf, I insisted."

"What should I do if he gets worse?" I asked.

She took a deep drag and exhaled slowly. "Just run and get me, Benjamin," she said. "I'll handle it. I don't mean to bother you—"

"Oh, it's not a bother. I'm just worried about him," I said, even though, truly, I was mostly worried that he'd bother me: snoring or throwing up on my couch, or simply, with his rabbinical presence, preventing me from surfing for more porn.

The porn, incidentally, was for a project I was working on. A legitimate, work-related project. A new bar called Paradise had opened in D.C. and the owners were looking for a graphic designer to create an advertising campaign that would make the place seem sexy. I was hunting for semi-naked photos for a mock-up ad I planned to pitch them. That's why, on an otherwise ordinary Monday in June, in my little suburban office, I was looking at dirty pictures. Until the rabbi appeared.

The rabbi didn't move when I went back inside. I switched off the overhead light and muted the sound on my computer.

He didn't move when the telephone rang, but I shot up from my chair with a start and grabbed it on the first ring. It was Michelle, my roommate.

"It's over, for real this time," she said, skipping "hello" altogether. "You will totally not even *believe* what he said to me this morning."

Looking over at the rabbi, who appeared undisturbed, I whispered into the phone, "I can't talk right now. I'll call you back later."

"Benji, I can't even hear you. What did you say? What's going on?"

"I can't talk right now," I whispered again, a bit louder. "I've got to go. There's a rabbi on my couch."

"A *what* on your couch? A *what?*"

I placed the receiver back in its cradle, turned off the ringer, and checked Rabbi Zuckerman. He was asleep.

When I turned my monitor on, the nearly naked man was still there. Glancing over at the rabbi, I closed that window and started working on a different job instead: an album cover for a friend's band, where everyone kept their clothes on.

"How long did he sleep?" Michelle asked that evening as we stood at the kitchen counter, scooping Chinese carryout onto her Corelle dishes.

"Not that long. Maybe an hour."

"That sounds seriously creepy, Benji," she said. "Some sick old man passed out on your couch. You don't even know him."

She was picking the water chestnuts out of her shrimp lo mein and putting them on my plate, like she always did.

"I know who he is," I said.

I cut the egg roll down the middle and put half on her plate.

"Yeah, but you don't really know him," she said. "It's just weird. You're not the school nurse. What if he died right there in your office?"

"He wasn't about to die," I protested. "I was just doing Mrs. Goldfarb a favor. It was no big deal."

Michelle stared at me with a cockeyed expression that said, "Give me a break."

"Besides," I said, "it's the closest I've gotten to sleeping with a man in months."

She cracked a grin and bit into her half of the egg roll.

We each grabbed a bottle of Amstel Light—we were watching our figures—and headed to the living room to finish our dinner.

Michelle spent most of the meal talking about the latest minidrama with her boyfriend, Dan. The current spat was over the Fourth of July: They'd made plans to spend the day together downtown, having a picnic by the Jefferson Memorial and watching the fireworks on the Mall, but that morning, scarcely a week before the holiday, Dan had invited a few of his buddies to join them.

"I told him I thought we were going to spend the day together," she said. "And he says, 'Well, we still are spending it together.' And I'm like, 'Yeah, together with your friends.' And he's like, 'What's wrong with my friends?' I mean, is he for real?"

"What *is* wrong with his friends?"

"God, not you, too. Don't you get it?"

"I get it, he's being dense."

"He's just being a typical guy. I didn't think Dan was like everyone else I dated, but maybe they're all the same once you get to know them."

"Them?"

"Guys," she clarified.

"Hello? I'm a guy, remember?"

She gave me that cockeyed look again. "You're not a guy."

I raised an eyebrow.

"Oh, shut up, you know what I mean," she said.

I did know what she meant. And, unfortunately, she was right about guys as far as I could tell, which explained why, five years after we graduated from the University of Maryland, Michelle and I were still living together in the suburban apartment we'd only planned to share for one year, tops. That's why, even though we were both what most people would consider attractive—no gruesome disfigurements, no missing teeth or fingers, no prominent warts—neither of us had managed to hold on to a boyfriend for more than four months. That is, until Michelle met Dan, who had lasted nearly eight months so far, and actually did seem different from everyone else she had dated, meaning that he was the first one I honestly liked.

She vented about Dan while I ate my lo mein; my role in these situations was simply to listen and nod sympathetically until I was prompted for a response. I had cleaned my plate by the time she was done talking.

"Sometimes I wonder if it's even worth it," she said, working toward some kind of conclusion. That was my cue.

"I think Dan's pretty great," I offered.

That was all it took to set Michelle off on a new speech, recounting Dan's many virtues: He likes football, he's open to foreign films, he's a great kisser. Soon she was taking back most everything she'd said just moments before and vowing to work out some kind of compromise for the Fourth of July.

"Do the picnic with his friends during the day," I suggested, "but make it just the two of you for the fireworks at night. That's the only part that really seems like a date."

She pondered this for a second.

"That sounds like it'd be okay," she said. "You're always so good at figuring this stuff out."

"Then why am I still single?" I asked.

"Nobody's good enough for you," she answered. She stood up, leaving most of her dinner on the coffee table, and walked toward her bedroom. "I'm going to call Dan right now and see what he thinks about your idea."

"I'll see you later then," I said. "I'm going out."

She stopped and turned to me. "Got a hot date?"

"It's for a job. I'm going to Paradise, that bar I told you about. I'm working on an ad campaign for them and I want to see what the place looks like at night."

"All right, but not too late," she said, pretending to be my mom. "You've got work in the morning."

* * *

Artists and theologians have offered many different visions of Paradise, but none, to my knowledge, has involved vertical blinds. Nonetheless, vertical blinds were the defining feature of this newest interpretation, located just north of Dupont Circle on Connecticut Avenue.

Looking at the full-length front windows from the sidewalk outside, I could only make out fragments of men between the white plastic strips: a tattooed bicep framed by the sleeve of a clingy T-shirt, pale legs sticking out of the summer's most fashionable drawstring shorts, a face bearing the sloppy smile that comes from too many two-for-one shots of Absolut Citron.

Inside, the pieces came together. Dance music pumped at a volume just quiet enough to have a conversation, but loud enough to keep an older crowd away. The lights were dimmed to a flattering level, but still allowed patrons to check one another out with some degree of discrimination. The place smelled of beer and new plastic and CK One.

An inexperienced observer might have called the crowd homogenous: Men in their twenties and thirties—there were no women, none—milled about alone, or in groups of two and three. Haircuts ranged from short to very short; waistlines all seemed to be between thirty and thirty-two inches; clothes were casual yet uniformly neat and unrumpled; everyone was clean-shaven except for four men with identical soul patches. Three bartenders—all shirtless, hairless, and ever-so-slightly gym-sculpted—were nearly impossible to tell apart. And the crowd was overwhelmingly white, despite the fact that Washington was an overwhelmingly black city.

But someone like me, more familiar with D.C.'s gay bar scene, could see the room's diversity—a pierced eyebrow here, a leather armband there. A group of deaf boys signed to one another in the corner, near a bank of televisions showing music videos. One young man's wrinkle-free black T-shirt said "Support Our Troops—Impeach Bush" in white letters, while another man's white T-shirt bore a caricature of Hillary Clinton—the odds-on favorite in the 2008 presidential election, which was still more than a year away—and said "*Another* Clinton? Just Say No." People's shoes were sure indicators of who lived downtown (funky black shoes) and who lived in the suburbs (tan workboots), who worked by day as a personal trainer (scuffed sneakers) and who was a congressional aide (same sneakers, no scuffs). It was a veritable melting pot, albeit in a very limited, D.C. kind of way.

I stood against a black brick wall in my cuffed jeans and tan workboots, sipping a rum and Diet Coke, taking mental notes about the space and the crowd, while I waited for Phil.

We'd been friends for years. Bar buddies, actually, meaning that we only ever saw each other at bars—I'd been to his studio exactly twice, briefly, and he'd never ventured across the District line to visit me, or for any other reason as far as I knew. But we were good companions: We kept an eye out for each other, each making sure the other wasn't too drunk, too lonely, or being hassled by some loser. We were well suited for this kind of relationship, because we liked each other but weren't attracted to each other, had similar taste in bars but different taste in men.

"This is an unexpected surprise," he said, clinking his beer bottle against my glass. "Out? On a school night? You?"

"I've got homework," I said,

"If this is your homework, I can't wait to help you cram for your finals."

I could always count on Phil to meet me for a drink, no matter what night it was; he lived in the middle of Dupont Circle, so for him, going to a bar usually involved a three-minute walk down the block. When I'd called him at the last minute to say I was headed to Paradise, he didn't hesitate. "Sounds heavenly," he said. "See you in an hour."

We stood side by side, both surveying the crowd while we chatted without making eye contact. Phil told me about the new guy he'd been dating.

"I just saw you a week and a half ago," I said. "When did you meet him?"

"Three nights ago," he said. "But it's serious."

I'd heard this before. But I listened again, knowing I shouldn't bother committing the guy's name to memory for at least another week.

"And how about you?" Phil asked. "Any new guys?"

"Nope," I said.

He gestured at a man standing at the bar. Blond, cute, wearing an Izod shirt and sipping something pink from a martini glass.

"Get a load of that one," said Phil.

"I thought you and this new guy were serious."

"Not for me, dummy, he's not my type," he said. "But he's right up your alley. Blond, just the way you like them. And he's checking you out."

Phil was right. And, like a good bar pal, he quickly made himself scarce so the blond at the bar could come over and talk to me.

"Do you go to Washington Sports Club?"

That was his opening line.

"I'm sorry, what?" I asked.

"The gym up the street," he said. "Have I seen you there?"

I didn't belong to that gym, and he probably didn't, either, but it was an easy enough way for him to start a conversation. It worked. Within twenty seconds, we were facing each other, talking about things other than the gym. Out of the corner of my eye, I saw Phil give me the thumbs-up from across the bar and then he slipped out the door.

I had to work in the morning, and I lived a half hour away in Maryland, so this was just idle flirtation, not a pickup situation. But we spent the next hour talking about Mister Izod's job (paralegal), his recent move (from North Carolina), his last boyfriend (a pothead with bad credit). We didn't get around to me, somehow; I'm better at listening and he didn't ask many questions.

He did walk me back to my car, though. Before I got in, he gave me his phone number and e-mail address. And a kiss. And a promise to chat later in the week.

The traffic lights on Sixteenth Street are perfectly timed: If you go above or below the speed limit, you'll hit red lights at least a dozen times, but if the street is clear and you travel precisely at the limit, green lights will greet you at every intersection. I set my Corolla's cruise control to coast at thirty miles per hour and let my mind wander as I rode the hills of Northwest Washington, past the churches and Rock Creek Park and the stone-fronted homes.

When I started the drive, I was thinking about Mister Izod, what we might plan for the upcoming weekend, and what I'd wear.

But for reasons I can't explain, by the time I reached the suburbs and turned onto Georgia Avenue, there was another man on my mind: Rabbi Zuckerman. No words, no feeling, only his image stuck in my memory—eyes closed, glasses in hand. He stayed with me as I pulled into the garage under my apartment building and rode up the elevator, then tiptoed past Michelle's room. And when I finally lay in bed after midnight, drifting toward dreams, I saw him still. He, too, was sleeping, breathing slowly but deeply, his chest rising and falling.

I dreamed I was a kid again, and Grandpa Jack was leading the Passover seder. Grandma Gertie, of course, was yelling.

"If you children have any questions about what we're doing, just ask," Grandpa said.

I looked at my big sister, Rachel, then back at my grandfather, nodding. I had lots of questions: Who gets to drink Elijah's wine if he doesn't show up? Why are we talking about the Soviet Union on a holiday that takes place in Egypt? Why is everyone so excited about the afikoman when it's just another crummy piece of matzoh?

"Don't ask anything!" my grandmother loudly insisted, wagging her finger at me before I could get a word out of my open mouth. "We'll be here all night."

I closed my mouth.

My grandfather pretended not to hear her: "Do you have a question, Benjamin?"

Grandma Gertie looked directly at him, her wagging finger still out. "Jack! The only question anyone has is, When will this thing end? Just get on with it."

He didn't turn to face her, didn't lose his composure for one second. But he winked at me. Not at me and my sister—just at me. Man to man.

We got back to the seder, plodding through the Haggadah without skipping a page. Rachel, who was ten, had already learned most of the songs and prayers in Hebrew school, but they were still foreign to me. Grandpa Jack stopped periodically to explain in English, answering several questions I hadn't even asked yet, although I didn't quite understand some of his explanations.

When it was time to recite the Ten Plagues, I couldn't keep quiet any longer. I burst out: "I know a song about the plagues!"

Grandpa Jack looked up from his Haggadah. "A song about plagues?"

"Well, not all of them," I said. "Just about the frogs. We learned it in Hebrew school."

My sister piped in. "It's a song for babies," she told him.

"Rachel!" my mother scolded from across the table.

But I didn't respond to Rachel's remark. Taking a cue from my grandfather, I pretended not to hear what she said.

Grandpa Jack asked me to sing my song.

I had to stand up to perform it properly, since it had hand motions and I wanted to give the full effect.

"One morning when Pharaoh woke in his bed, there were frogs in his bed and frogs on his head . . ."

My mother was clapping along, my father humming; they'd heard this before. Rachel rolled her eyes. But I was only paying attention to my grandfather, who put down his book and watched me closely through his wire-framed glasses as I used my hands to act out a sleeping Pharaoh, a hopping frog, something on my head.

"Frogs on his nose and frogs on his toes. Frogs here, frogs there. Frogs were jumping everywhere."

My parents applauded. My grandfather beamed: "That was a beautiful song, Benjamin. Pretty soon you'll be sitting in my chair, leading the whole thing."

"Stop it, Jack, he hasn't even finished first grade yet," my grand-mother interjected. "Can we get back to the seder now? The children will starve if we don't get to the meal soon."

Grandpa got back to the Haggadah, distributing horseradish and matzoh and reciting more prayers. But when nobody else was look-ing, in the middle of a blessing, our eyes met and he gave me another wink.

The morning after the seder, while my mother and grandmother made marble cake, Grandpa showed me how to make matzoh brei, which is like French toast for Passover. After breakfast, we went for a walk through the park near my parents' house. He was too old for the teeter-totter, but he pushed me on the swing for a few minutes. When we got back home, he was ready for a nap. But he had nowhere to rest. Whenever they visited from Florida, Grandma and Grandpa slept on the foldout couch in the living room, despite my mom's insistence that they'd be more comfortable in my parents' bed-room. ("What, we're going to put you out of your own bed in your own home?" Grandpa would ask.)

"If you want to nap, you can use Benjamin's bed," my mother said, noting that the sofa bed had already been folded up for the day.

He went upstairs, leaving me alone in the living room. I was ex-cited by the chance to watch daytime television, to see what I'd been missing while at school on a normal day. But after watching a few *minutes of* Phil Donahue *and* Ryan's Hope, *I was already bored. I wondered: Aren't there any cartoons on? I headed up to my room to play with my Transformers.*

I grabbed the plastic action figures off my desk, careful not to make a sound and wake Grandpa. He was asleep on his side on top of my Bugs Bunny bedspread, his glasses inside one of his shoes next to the bed. He was facing me, but his eyes were closed. I watched him napping, breathing deeply and snoring softly, his shirt still buttoned, his belt still buckled, like sleep overcame him before he could even put on his pajamas.

He seemed all wrong in this setting, a grown man in a child's room, his gray stubble scratching against my Daffy Duck pillowcase. But there he was in my bed, my grandfather.

I put the toys back on the desk and climbed into bed with him, squeezing into the sliver of space between Grandpa Jack and the edge. I tried not to wake him, but I accidentally elbowed him, and he opened his eyes.

"Here, Benjamin," he said, shifting over toward the wall to make more room. I nestled into him, my back to his stomach. He put a hand on my shoulder and then went back to sleep as if nothing had changed. I closed my eyes and tried to imagine frogs jumping on both of our heads.

When my mother opened the bedroom door a few minutes later, I kept my eyes closed and pretended to be asleep. "Isn't that sweet?" she said to nobody in particular, backing out and closing the door behind her. When she was gone, my grandfather kissed me on the back of my neck, his stubble tickling my skin, and I knew that he was only faking sleep, too. We were sweet deceivers together, Grandpa Jack and me, daydreaming silently side-by-side in my safe and narrow bed.

CHAPTER 2

"Drink plenty of water."

My mother. On the phone. At seven in the morning.

"You woke me up to tell me to drink water?" I asked, groggy.

"I just saw it on the news," she said without apology. "It's going to be dangerously hot all week. You've got to remember to drink lots of water."

"Fine."

"And wear sunscreen."

"Mom, I'm not a farmer. I work inside."

"They said on the news to wear sunscreen," she said. "The sun is very strong."

There was no use arguing.

"Okay, I'll wear it."

"And don't forget to put it on your face."

"I'm going back to bed now, Mom. I don't have to be up for another hour."

Instead of saying good-bye, she paused for a moment and said, "You're welcome."

Her weatherman was right: The heat wave showed no signs of letting up. Temperatures soared into the nineties before noon on Tuesday, with the sun streaming down directly on the shopping center's unshaded storefronts, bleaching posters taped in the windows and making every metal door handle too hot to touch. The humid air hung with an over-ripe heaviness, its slippery particles coating the skin of any-one who dared to linger outside for more than a few seconds.

This wasn't unusual; Washington was built on a swamp, after all. Even so, it was hard to endure. The sidewalks around the shopping center were empty. There was nobody browsing idly or wandering door to door. People pulled up in their air-conditioned cars, strode as quickly as possible across the sticky asphalt parking lot, and headed directly toward whichever air-conditioned store they needed to visit, shield-ing their eyes with one hand.

The teenage boys who worked loading groceries into cus-tomers' cars at the supermarket rolled up the sleeves of their official Giant Food T-shirts, showing off their nonexistent bi-ceps, and wore shorts and flip-flops. Employees at the dry cleaners, the sandwich shop, and the greeting card store dressed like they were going to the beach. Even those whose jobs required more formal attire found some way to beat the heat: The women who worked at the private professional of-fices alongside mine in the rear of the complex—accoun-tants, lawyers, dental hygienists—chose lightweight skirts and loose blouses and sandals, while their male counterparts donned baggy khakis and short-sleeved oxfords.

For an old man like Rabbi Zuckerman, who was probably over eighty and looked every day of it, the weather was par-ticularly tough. He didn't seem to have a summer wardrobe. True, he wore a blazer only in cooler weather, but otherwise his outfit stayed the same regardless of the temperature: a long-sleeved, white, button-down shirt, a pair of black or gray or navy blue slacks, and hard-soled black shoes. No matter how much he sweated, he didn't roll up his sleeves, or un-button more than one button. It simply wasn't his style, even if the heat was beating him.

So it was no surprise to me when Mrs. Goldfarb knocked on my office door again on Tuesday afternoon, and opened the door before I could answer. The rabbi was behind her this time, holding himself up against the wall, sweat dripping down his face.

"Benjamin," she said, "would you mind? You know, again?" She motioned toward the rabbi, then toward the couch.

"Sure, sure," I said, waving her in. What else could I say? She was already leading him inside.

Rabbi Zuckerman lay down on the couch, same position as the day before. Mrs. Goldfarb handed him a wet washcloth she'd been holding. "Put this on your forehead," she instructed. He did.

"It's this heat," she said to me. "Unbelievable, right? It's only June but it feels like the middle of August."

I nodded.

"Your office is so much cooler than the store," she said.

"We don't get direct sunlight back here," I told her.

"And your air-conditioning works better than ours," she added, looking up at the vents in my ceiling. "I should talk to our landlord."

I nodded again.

"I'll be back to check on you in a little while," she said to Rabbi Zuckerman. Then, just like the day before, she walked outside to light a cigarette—smokers apparently have no problem inhaling hot air on a hot day—and I followed her.

"Are you positive he's okay?" I asked again.

"It's just the heat, I'm sure," she answered. "I'll go call about the air conditioner right now. And then I'll come back in an hour or so for Rabbi Zuckerman."

I looked at her blankly.

"Okay, forty-five minutes," she said. "I don't mean to impose, but lying down really did help him yesterday. All he needs is some time to cool off."

"I'll see you in a little while," I said, tacitly accepting this arrangement.

"Thanks, Benjamin, you're doing a mitzvah," she said. And then she was gone.

I made the same accommodations as last time in the office, shutting off the overhead light, closing the blinds, silencing the ringer on the phone. But I didn't switch my design projects. I was working on the mock-up ads for Paradise, complete with nearly naked men I'd found online. It wasn't anything more shocking than someone might see on Showtime or Cinemax any night of the week, but it might have been enough to scandalize a rabbi. I didn't know, and I didn't much care. Doing a mitzvah was one thing, I decided, but I wasn't going to stop doing my job just because some old man needed a place to get out of the sun.

Rabbi Zuckerman was making more noise this time. His breathing was more labored and he'd moan occasionally. Each time he made a sound, I'd look up to see if something was the matter, but he seemed the same: Hot. Tired. Old. Water from the washcloth dripped down his temples into his hair, already matted with sweat. He didn't move.

After a couple of quick glances, though, I found myself simply staring at him, ignoring my computer screen and its carefully cropped porn.

Who is he? I thought. Does he have a family—children, grandchildren? Is he sick? Why does he keep coming to work? Why doesn't he ever talk? Does he speak English? Yes, of course, he must understand it—Mrs. Goldfarb speaks to him in English. But does he *speak* English? Or Yiddish? Or Hebrew? Or Russian? Or German? Or Polish? Does he speak anything at all? Has this bookstore owner devoted himself so totally to the printed word that he has forgotten how to talk? Or does he simply have nothing to say to me, a little *pisher* of a lapsed Jew who's only worth this rabbi's consideration because of my comfortable furniture?

Then I noticed one thing that was different from the previous day. Rabbi Zuckerman had kicked off his shoes next to the couch.

I wondered: Was he trying to be considerate? Or was he making himself at home?

"Great to meet you last night at Paradise," Mister Izod's e-mail began. "I must have been a total bore, going on and on about myself. The cosmopolitans made me do it! I only had one or two . . . or five! I don't remember. Now I'm sitting in my office, downing Tylenol and black coffee with the lights off. And looking at your business card. Benji Steiner: Graphic Design. Such a cool card—did you design it? I mean, you probably did, duh! Anyway, you hardly told me anything about you. Didn't even know you were a graphic designer until I looked at your card. You live somewhere in Maryland. Wheaton? Silver Spring? Somewhere out the red line on the Metro, right? I don't know where all those places are, really. I'll look for a map online. Anyway, I'd love to get together if you're into it. Friday night?"

The e-mail had an attachment, a photo titled "Pete and Punky" that showed Pete (once again wearing an Izod—was this his signature look?) holding his beloved Chihuahua, whom he'd named after Punky Brewster. He didn't know I was a graphic designer, while I already knew his stupid dog was named after some stupid television show? Talk about a lopsided conversation. Well, it was my fault as much as his, I figured.

I wrote back:

"Hey, Pete, good to hear from you (and Punky). Yes, I designed that card, and yes, I live in Wheaton, out the red line. It's a beautiful place. Blockbuster Video, drive-thru McDonald's, Jiffy Lube, a Dunkin' Donuts. We've even got a shopping mall, complete with a food court, a multiplex movie theater, and a JCPenney. If you play your cards right, I'll show you the wonders of suburbia sometime, sort of a not-so-wildlife safari. You'll wonder why anyone wants to live in the city. Friday night sounds like a good idea. A return to Paradise?"

On Wednesday, the rabbi arrived alone. He tapped at the door and turned the knob without waiting for a reply. He pointed to the couch and looked at me with a shrug. But no words.

I motioned to the couch with a nod and he came in. He shut off the light himself and closed the blinds.

And so on Wednesday we began a new, wordless routine, without Mrs. Goldfarb playing intermediary with her chatter and smoke. Rabbi Zuckerman lay down on my couch once more. A passerby peering through my window might have thought I was a shrink. But the rabbi never spoke. And he didn't pay me for my time.

He did, however, inspire me. I had been a bit stymied by the Paradise ad campaign, toying with an idea for a few hours before trashing it and starting over. But Wednesday afternoon, as I watched Rabbi Zuckerman dozing, an idea struck me: the Bible.

I had loved Bible stories as a child; I had an illustrated book that told tales from the Old Testament. When I was very little, my father would read them to me while I studied the pictures, line drawings filled in with bright watercolors. Later, when I was a little older and liked to stay up late, I'd wait until my parents went to sleep and then I'd close my bedroom door and turn on the light and read the book myself, memorizing the words.

There was, of course, a story about Adam and Eve in that book. I could still recall the illustration: Eve (standing behind a tree to cover up her nudity) held out a red apple to Adam (seated on the ground with his legs modestly crossed), while a snake dangled from the tree branch above. I remembered the caption: "The Garden of Eden was Paradise. But Adam and Eve did not obey God's rules."

Paradise.

Maybe I would have decided on a biblical theme for the ad campaign all on my own. But with the rabbi lying there across from my desk, it seemed that there was no other possibility.

"Hey, how's your new boyfriend?" Dan asked me that evening as he sat in our living room waiting for Michelle to finish getting dressed.

"Very funny," I said. "I suppose Michelle's told you all about him and how creepy he is?"

"Creepy?"

"Yeah, that he's on my couch every afternoon, but we've never even had a conversation?"

"That doesn't sound so bad, dude," he said with a sly grin, like a real guy. "Cut right to the chase."

I stopped for a moment.

"You're talking about the rabbi, right?" I asked.

"Rabbi?" said Dan. "You're dating a rabbi?"

"No, I am not dating a rabbi," I clarified. "What did Michelle tell you?"

Michelle came out of her bedroom and joined the conversation. "I told Dan that you met a guy the other night at that new bar," she said. "That guy. You know, what's his name?"

"Pete," I said.

"Right, Pete," she said.

"That's who I'm talking about," said Dan.

"Oh," I said. "Well, I wouldn't call him my new boyfriend. We just met. But we're getting together on Friday night."

"So what's he like?" Dan asked. "Is he hot?"

I loved that Dan wanted to know if my date was "hot." Straight guys get a bad rap a lot of the time, but sometimes they can be the perfect antidotes to everyone else. A straight girl might have asked what Pete did for a living, or what we talked about when we met—Michelle's first two questions. A gay guy might have asked where he lived (to see how much commuting would be involved in a relationship) or what he liked to do in bed. Dan didn't care about Pete's job, or his apartment, or his sexual preferences, or even what he looked like objectively. He wanted to know if Pete turned me on.

"Yeah, he's pretty hot," I said.

"Good for you, dude," said Dan. And then he gave me a thumbs-up.

Approval.

"But wait a minute," Dan said, "who did you *think* I was talking about? Who's this rabbi?"

I looked at Michelle: "You didn't tell him? I figured you'd have told everyone by now."

"Honestly, Benji," she said, "I didn't think the old guy would stick around this long."

"How old?" said Dan.

"I don't know," I said. "Eighty, eighty-five."

"Dude!" said twenty-something Dan, this time with definite disapproval. Such a versatile word—dude.

"It's not like that," I insisted.

"So what's the deal?" he asked.

"I'll tell you all about it," Michelle said before I could get a word out. "But let's get going, or we'll miss the movie."

"Right," said Dan, getting out of our easy chair and running a hand through his fine blond hair, pushing it out of his face. Standing side by side, both in T-shirts and shorts, they were a good match: Dan tall and lanky, his shoulders permanently hunched slightly forward, his large hands hanging loose at his side; Michelle petite and darker, her green eyes always alert, curly brown hair piled atop her head to keep her neck cool. The height difference made their casual kisses seem awkward, but Michelle was the perfect height for Dan to wrap his arm around her shoulder. Which he did, often. Michelle loved that. I could see it in her eyes.

"You going out tonight, Benji?" Dan asked.

"I haven't decided yet," I said, even though I'd already decided to stay home and get reacquainted with some old Bible stories; I'd dug my childhood picture book out of a box of my old stuff that my mother had given me when she commandeered my childhood closet for her "papers." But that's just not the kind of thing I could have easily explained without seriously damaging the coolness I'd started to build up in Dan's estimation.

"Whatever, dude, have fun," he said.

"Don't wait up," said Michelle as she opened the front door.

"I won't," I said, closing the door behind them. Then it was off to my bedroom with my picture book. Just like old times.

I knew, because my mother told me, that the book was a hand-me-down, a gift my grandparents originally gave to my sister when I was just a baby. But as far as I was concerned, the book was mine and always had been.

The book took me back to a time when I really loved Judaism. It was never about God for me; I'd never been a real believer as a kid, and I'd never had a spiritual crisis that made me change my mind since then. But that lack of belief didn't matter. I still loved Judaism and the way it was represented in this book. I relished the ancient melodramas, the neatly resolved plots, the simple life lessons. And I adored the drawings, images that blended the freeform style of 1970s cartoons with reverent depictions of historical heroes. As a child, this was what being Jewish meant: stories, characters, history, color.

My parents added on another layer of meaning—primarily involving food—that also appealed, with their semitraditional, modest observance of holidays and traditions. Latkes for Hanukkah, apples and honey for Rosh Hashanah, challah for the Sabbath. Being Jewish wasn't just who I was inside, it was something tangible, something I could taste. And it tasted sweet.

This, of course, was before years of Hebrew school classes and topical Saturday morning sermons at my family's Conservative synagogue drained away almost everything I liked about being Jewish and buried it under an airless layer of laws and restrictions and suffering. The chosen people's celebratory rites were grayed by cautionary tales of persecution and woe and impending collective trauma. By the time I was bar mitzvahed, my whole impression of Judaism had changed. I thought not of braided loaves of challah shiny with egg, but of death camp rations of black bread and brown soup. Not of Hanukkah's miracle of the Maccabees, but of Israel's War of Independence, the Six-Day War, the invasion of Lebanon. Anti-Semites lurked around every corner, and we would always be pariahs wherever we went. The only things keeping us together were God and our community, both of which made constant demands and neither of which was ever satisfied. Whatever you did, there were rules to govern you; whatever you thought, there was shame to paralyze you. Thou-shalt-not this, thou-shalt-not that. Listen to your mother and pray for the Almighty's forgiveness.

But opening my old picture book, I was reminded of a less complicated version of Judaism: Moses coming down from Mt. Sinai, while the children of Israel danced with abandon around the golden calf below. Jacob and his twelve sons— one of them dressed in a vibrant, almost psychedelic coat— tending sheep in the fields. Abraham preparing to sacrifice his son Isaac, a knife held firmly in his raised hand. Noah and the animals on a giant wooden ark, a rainbow on the horizon. And that picture of Adam and Eve in Paradise. Under the apple tree. Just as I remembered it.

The last picture in the book was from a different Bible story that I'd almost forgotten: Queen Esther stood in the middle of an elegant banquet, amid tables laden with golden pastries and green grapes. Her accusing finger pointed at Haman, the man who would kill all the Jews in Persia, cowering before her. Esther's face betrayed only steely confidence, her long dress a swirl of angry reds and purples.

I remembered a Purim from many years before.

I was seven years old and I was crying.

We were supposed to show up for Hebrew school in costumes. Ideally, they should have been relevant to the holiday, a sort of masquerade based on the Book of Esther. But kids who attended Congregation Beth Shalom of Rockville, Maryland, weren't so hung up on biblical authenticity. They were planning to come as Batman or the Little Mermaid or miniature Washington Redskins.

My mother laid out a clown costume for me, complete with baggy orange pants and yellow suspenders, and a red ball to stick on the end of my nose. I was not having it.

My sister, Rachel, was already eleven, and sixth graders didn't have to put on stupid costumes anymore. But they'd be performing the annual Purim play for the whole school, and she was playing the lead, so Rachel dressed up as Queen Esther, the heroine of the Purim story. My mother was allowing Rachel to wear makeup for the play and she helped her make gold slippers out of old ballet shoes and glitter. She was wearing her fanciest skirt, made of shimmery black material, and my mom loaned her a gold blouse, which my sister could almost fill out already.

Rachel looked like a grown woman. After reminding my sister not to get that blouse dirty, my mother stepped back and told her that she looked beautiful.

Nobody was paying attention to me. I stood pouting in the doorway of the bathroom, where they were fixing Rachel's hair. "I want to be Queen Esther, too," I insisted.

"You mean you want to be King Ahasuerus," Rachel spat at me without turning away from the mirror. "Boys can't be queens." She didn't look so beautiful anymore.

"No, I want to be Queen Esther," I repeated.

Rachel put down her hairbrush. "That is so queer."

I started to bawl.

My mother led me into my bedroom and tried to coax me into the clown costume, but I refused. She handed me the baggy pants and I threw them on the floor. She offered me the round red nose and I hit it out of her hands.

"Mom, make him get dressed," Rachel protested from the hallway. "He's going to make us late."

My father would have put his foot down: "Stop crying and get in the damn clown costume, or you can forget about watching television this week." But my father was playing tennis, and my mother had to get everyone ready in time to drive the Sunday morning carpool. She considered the situation for a moment. Then, caught between my tantrum and my sister's impatience, she caved in.

The costume was simple, piecing together bits of an old fairy princess costume that Rachel wore for Halloween years before: a lavender skirt, a pink top, a blond wig, a gold tiara. I skipped the clip-on wings. But I was drawn to the star-tipped wand; my mother told me that they didn't have magic wands in ancient Persia, and I conceded the point. She also wouldn't let me wear makeup, despite my repeated requests.

My sister refused to sit near me in the station wagon, so I climbed up front with my mom while Rachel got in back. We picked up two other kids from around the corner, a boy wearing a karate uniform and a girl dressed as a ballerina, who squeezed in next to Rachel. They were snickering, but nobody dared to say anything out loud while my mother was there.

Once we got dropped off at Beth Shalom, however, everything changed. The karate boy pushed me into a door and sneered, "Ladies first." The ballerina told me I looked funny.

"I'm Queen Esther," I responded. "She's a hero. She saved the Jews. You're just some dumb ballet dancer."

"Boys can't wear skirts," the ballerina snipped. Apparently, Esther's heroism meant nothing to her.

My sister, who was big enough to defend me from these taunts, had already gone inside to get ready for the play. I was alone.

When I walked into my classroom, I tried to muster a smile. Mrs. Goldfarb looked over with a pleased look—a look that quickly changed once she realized who was beneath this cheap wig and plastic crown.

"Benjamin?" she asked quietly. "Oh, dear."

I would soon forget what all my classmates wore for this masquerade, and I would never even notice Mrs. Goldfarb's clothes. But for them, for all of them, this image of me, a vision in lavender and pink polyester, would become indelibly etched in their memories. They were all paying attention. They would not soon forget this seven-year-old boy standing before them, bravely adjusting my wig even as the tears began to stream down my cheeks.

Thursday and Friday the rabbi came as usual, knocking on the door around three in the afternoon, when the heat was at its worst, and heading back to the store about an hour later. Mrs. Goldfarb had apparently recused herself permanently and left any further negotiations to the men.

Rabbi Zuckerman didn't disturb me at all anymore. He didn't make any demands or require any attention from me.

Plus, while I was working on the Paradise campaign, he became my silent muse, keeping me focused on the biblical themes. I surfed online for Jewish websites that might have more images connected to Bible stories. There were many, of course: some with long religious explanations that quickly grew tedious, some with childish rhymes to tell the simple tales. The pictures ranged from classical paintings to downloadable clip art. I spent hours poring over the Jewish sites while the rabbi lay on my couch. I never found anything as compelling as my own picture book.

I sat in my dimly lit, comfortably cool office, experimenting with fonts and colors, trying one picture and then another, until I was satisfied that I was onto something.

Using photos I'd found online—on gay sites, not the Jewish ones—I made three prototype advertisements, each bearing the same tag line at the bottom in a bold sans-serif typeface: **Paradise: Found.**

"Let There Be Light!" the first ad proclaimed. Two men with impeccable pecs stood on the left side of the page, seen from the waist up; they wore only dark sunglasses, staring up at the sun on the right side of the page. In between, the copy read: "The city's best nightlife—now available during the day. With the only Sunday afternoon beer blast in town, Washington's newest bar is the hottest spot in creation."

"Sin Is In" read the second ad, which featured a goateed man holding a red pitchfork and wearing nothing but two small red horns and a tail—shot from the side to hide anything too explicit. "Grab some tail at our red-hot weekly party with DJ Damien, every Friday night," read the text. "At Washington's newest bar, the only real sin is going anywhere else."

The last one drew directly on my childhood picture book. "Give in to Temptation" it said across the top, in tall red letters. The text read: "Get fresh fruits. With two-for-one appletinis every happy hour, Washington's newest bar is like heaven on earth." The image was reminiscent of the Adam and Eve drawing in my book, except in my illustration, doctored heavily with Photoshop, the snake was wrapped around a martini glass rather than a tree, the seated Adam was a gym-buffed stud, and Eve had been replaced by a second gym-buffed Adam, standing in front of the glass and holding a strategically placed Red Delicious apple.

I was printing out the mock-ups on Friday afternoon when the rabbi got up to leave my office. For a moment I considered showing them to him and explaining how he had inspired me. I quickly regained my senses, though, just in time to see him put his yarmulke back on his head, open my door, and walk outside into the heat.

* * *

I put the mock-ups and a cover letter in a manila envelope and brought them to the bar Friday evening. The bartender told me to slip them under the door of the office in the back.

Phil was sitting at the bar, fingers wrapped around a gin and tonic; I'd phoned him barely an hour earlier and he said he'd meet me at Paradise "for a quickie."

"Can't stay long," he said as I pulled up a stool. "Dinner plans."

"Wow, that's more than a whole week with the same guy," I said.

"No, this is someone new," he said, chuckling at himself. "I know. *Quelle surprise.*"

"I just don't know how you keep their names straight."

"If I forget, I just call them 'baby,'" he said.

"Seriously?"

"Geez, Benji, what kind of guy do you think I am?" he teased. "I write their names on the palm of my hand."

I took Phil's hand and checked his palm. Clean.

"And how about you?" he asked. "Meeting the guy from Monday night? Benji's latest blond?"

"His name is Pete," I said.

"And this time you don't have to work tomorrow. Maybe little Benji is gonna get lucky?"

"Luck," I deadpanned, "has nothing to do with it."

I told him about the ad campaign I'd proposed for Paradise.

"You went biblical?" he asked. "Seems like a strange way to sell a gay bar."

"I don't know," I said. "Guys wearing fig leaves seemed like a pretty good place to start."

"Just quit before you get to crucifixion. Too kinky."

"That's your Bible," I said. "Not mine."

"Right, like you have a Bible."

"Just because I don't believe it, that doesn't mean it's not mine."

"I suppose," he said.

Phil left after he finished his drink and Pete arrived a few minutes later, wearing—thank goodness—a shirt without an alligator. I didn't want to stick around long, because at that point Paradise reminded me of work. So after one quick cocktail, we ducked out and walked over to Seventeenth Street, to a coffeehouse.

I asked him about his week and he recounted a couple of funny stories about one of the attorneys in his office, a closet case with bad breath. Then Pete, true to his word, started asking me about myself.

I told him about growing up in the suburbs of D.C. and how I had decided to stay in the area while my sister had chosen to move all the way across the country, to Seattle. I told him about how I double-majored in English and art at the University of Maryland, despite my parents' insistence that neither of these majors would ever earn me a dime. I told him about the string of jobs I'd endured after college—designing advertisements for a local magazine, crafting pamphlets for a nonprofit AIDS service organization, teaching arts and crafts at the YMCA, working in a printing shop in a mall—and how I'd taken a gamble and opened my own office the previous winter with just two steady clients: a suburban gardening club that needed someone to lay out its monthly newsletter and a downtown rock venue that hired me to design posters and newspaper ads, barely enough to pay rent on my office.

And I told him about the rabbi.

"Freaky," was his first reaction.

"Which part?"

"The whole thing," he said. "Is he one of those whatever-they're-calleds, with the black hats and the curls?"

"Hasidim? No. He's just a rabbi."

"Still."

"I know, it's pretty weird. But I don't really mind it, to be honest."

"You're Jewish, right? Steiner?"

"Yeah."

"We didn't have many Jews in Greensboro," he said. "You're the first Jewish guy I've ever gone out with."

"Want to know something? I've never dated a Jewish guy."

"You're kidding me," he said. "Why not?"

"Never really thought about it," I said. "I guess I've always had a thing for blonds."

"Lucky for me," said Pete, with a smirk.

We sat for a while longer while he asked me about the other blond guys I'd dated. He was a good listener.

We left the coffeehouse and headed to a little disco on P Street. He was a good dancer.

We took a break from dancing and kissed next to the coat check. He was a good kisser.

So far, I thought, so good.

Saturday, I went to visit my parents, who lived about twenty minutes from me, in Rockville. I typically saw them maybe once every other week. I'd go over for dinner, or they'd take Michelle and me to a show downtown, or some family friend would have some kind of affair—bris, bar mitzvah, wedding, funeral—that we'd go to together. We all got along, particularly when our time together was limited to a couple of hours.

This time, though, I wasn't looking forward to the visit. My folks were having their old friends the Mehlmans over for brunch, including the Mehlmans' son Andy, visiting from San Diego. Andy and I never had much in common; he was a year older, something of a jock in high school, smart but too cool to get good grades, the kind of guy who used to tease guys like me. But we had known each other through our parents since we were toddlers, and they all still assumed we'd prefer having each other's company to having nobody our own age at the table. That assumption wasn't true for me, and I suspected it wasn't for Andy, but nevertheless. Honor thy parents. I had to go.

My mother asked me to pick up a gallon of orange juice on my way over, so I stopped by the supermarket next to my office. As I was putting the juice in my car, Saturday morning services were letting out at B'nai Tikvah, the little Orthodox synagogue just across the main parking lot. The women came out first, maybe forty of them in long skirts and long-sleeved blouses, with small children trailing behind. The men followed, a larger group in dark suits and white shirts, old men and teenage boys together; black yarmulkes topped almost every head, glasses graced almost every face. Rabbi Zuckerman was among them, one of the older men who favored hats, but he lagged behind the rest. And while the other men made conversation punctuated with nods and gesticulations, the rabbi seemed to focus all his energy on the simple act of walking in the midday heat.

I stood next to my car, unseen, and watched him. With great effort, he made it to the corner crosswalk. Already, though, he was left alone; the others had made it across and were heading down the opposite sidewalks in every direction. He wiped his brow as he waited for the light to change, then slowly crossed the street with the walk signal. He continued straight ahead, up the hill into a residential development, struggling with the side street's gentle rise as if he were climbing a mountain.

After he vanished from view, I got into my car and drove to Rockville, turning up the stereo so I could hear Coldplay over the blast of the air conditioner.

Andy was the center of attention at brunch, since he had come the farthest, so he got to talk about his job and his house and his Hawaiian vacation and his sports car. The dads asked him some questions about the Padres and the Chargers. I didn't have any questions. I was more interested in the bagels and lox.

But when Mrs. Mehlman finally interrupted and asked what I'd been doing lately, I told everyone about Rabbi Zuckerman sleeping on my couch all week, and it seemed to entertain them more than anything Andy had to talk about. I played it up to keep the conversation from shifting back to professional sports or something equally mundane. And the questions kept coming.

"On your *couch?*"

"Was he *asleep?*"

"He came *back?*"

"Didn't anyone call a *doctor?*"

And then my mother's question: "What kind of a rabbi is he?"

"What do you mean?" I asked.

"Does he have a congregation?" she asked.

"No, he owns the Jewish bookstore."

"I thought you had to have a congregation to be a rabbi." That was Andy's contribution.

"Apparently not," I said.

"Well, is he Conservative? Reform?"

"I think he's Orthodox. He wears a yarmulke all the time. And he goes to B'nai Tikvah. That's Orthodox, right?"

"Yes, it is," my father said.

"He's not trying to convert you, is he?" my mother asked.

"Convert me to what?" I asked. "I'm already Jewish."

"Not to him, you're not," she said. "As far as the Orthodox are concerned, we might as well be Baptists. Or devil worshippers."

"Judy, don't be ridiculous," my father added gently.

"Mom, we've never even spoken."

"Good, just keep it that way," my mother said. "Those Orthodox are just like a cult. You know that Edie Hirsch's son Adam became Orthodox and now he won't even eat in his parents' house and he won't even let them babysit for their own grandchildren overnight because he's afraid they'll fill the kids' heads with other ideas—ideas that he grew up with himself before he got brainwashed! They're crazy, I'm telling you. Just stay away from them."

"He's not going to brainwash me," I said. "He can barely stand up."

"Well, just keep an eye on him. I don't want you coming home with *payes* and those tzitzis hanging out. I knew it was a bad idea to open your office in Glenbrook. Too many black hats."

I didn't respond.

My father, never a fan of drama, tried to ratchet things down: "Judy, B'nai Tikvah isn't for black hats. It's Modern Orthodox."

"What's that mean?" asked Andy.

"It means they observe all the laws of Judaism, and men and women sit separately in synagogue, but they live in the modern world," my father explained. "They work in all kinds of jobs—lawyers, teachers, businessmen—and they go to Redskins games and movies, and they wear normal clothes and they even shave. They're just observant, that's all. They're not like Hasidim, with furry hats and black coats and long beards."

"So they don't wear funny hats, big deal," my mother said. "They're still religious nuts."

My father replied: "First you're upset that he doesn't go to synagogue anymore and he isn't observant enough. And now you're worried that he'll become too observant?"

Yes, if there was anything worse than her children neglecting the traditions she held dear, it was the notion that her children might berate her for her own random assortment of religious observances and nonobservances: keeping kosher

at home but eating *treyf* outside the house; going to synagogue on Saturday mornings but shopping at the mall on Saturday afternoons; having a seder every year but ignoring
Passover for the other seven days.

"Nothing's changed, Mom," I said. "I'm not becoming Orthodox, or Conservative, or Reform. Or Satanist. So don't
worry about it."

By this point, I'd have been thrilled to have the conversation shift to baseball or football or anything else. And sure
enough, Andy came through with a brilliant California-
themed segue—"I heard a joke the other day: A rabbi and a
priest and a Buddhist monk are in a rowboat with Arnold
Schwarzenegger . . ."—and my mother's tirade was over, for
the time being.

After we were done eating, the Mehlmans said their good-
byes. And then, as I helped my mother clear the table, she
started in again.

"I just don't understand it. You never want to come to synagogue with us, your own parents. You tell us it's just not for
you. Fine. I don't like it, but fine. But now you're hanging
out with some Orthodox rabbi from Glenbrook?"

"We're not 'hanging out.'"

"Well, whatever you want to call it."

"He needed a place to lie down. That's all."

She gave me one of her looks that said, "I know better, believe me." There was no comeback for a look like that.

I went upstairs to my old bedroom, which had recently become my mother's "office," meaning she kept a computer on
my desk and a fax machine on my dresser, which she used
for "making arrangements" like buying airplane tickets and
reserving hotels. The things I used to keep on my desk were
now stuffed inside. I opened the bottom drawer and found
some old CDs from high school: Nirvana, Nine Inch Nails,
Portishead. Depressing music for angst-ridden nineties
teens. I grabbed a few for nostalgia's sake.

My father walked in behind me. "Don't take your mother too seriously," he said, his way of taking my side privately without criticizing her publicly—his usual course of action.

"I don't," I said.

He took out his wallet. "Do you need some money?"

I did. Business was a bit slow. But I didn't want to take it.

"I'm fine, Dad."

He fished out a twenty.

"Here, take it," he said, holding out the bill. "For gas. We're always making you drive out here."

The drive to my parents' house required about a buck's worth of gas. But I took the money.

"Thanks," I said, stuffing it in my front pocket.

"Listen," he said, changing the subject, "what are you doing for the Fourth of July? We were thinking of going somewhere for the day. Annapolis, or Baltimore. If you and Michelle aren't doing anything . . ."

"Thanks, but we both have plans."

"Oh," he said. "That's nice. She still seeing Dan?"

"Yeah."

"And who's your date?" he asked tentatively. I'd been out to them since my sophomore year of college, and they'd met a handful of guys I'd gone out with and heard about several more, particularly after things had gone sour. But even after all these years, despite being relatively comfortable having a gay son, my folks were still reluctant to ask me directly about who I might be dating—although at least my father took the bait sometimes if I brought it up first. I think he was primarily worried about prying into my private life, something Rachel had often berated him about when she was dating, rather than uncomfortable hearing me talk about other men. Not that I'd ever asked.

"His name's Pete," I said.

"Is it serious?" he asked.

"I'll let you know."

* * *

The manager of Paradise called Monday morning with good news: I got the job. They signed me up for a yearlong deal, creating one new ad for each month. They would run in local gay papers and alternative weeklies and would be slightly modified as posters to be hung around Dupont Circle in windows, on bulletin boards, and on lightposts. He wanted to kick off the campaign with the devil poster and move on from there; we'd meet occasionally to go over new ideas. The manager already had a photographer lined up. All we needed to do now was land the right models.

"This is the fun part," I said. "Finding guys who look good with their clothes off."

"Hardly sounds like work," said the manager.

I was playing it cool, but the job was important to me. I needed the money. Next time, I thought to myself, I won't need to take "gas money" from my dad.

Monday afternoon, the rabbi came at the usual time, without a word. But once he got settled, I left my office and walked around to the front of the shopping center to the Jewish bookstore.

"Hello, Benjamin," Mrs. Goldfarb called from behind the counter. "I know why you're here. But this is the last time. Look, they're working on the air conditioner right now."

She pointed to a man on a ladder in the back of the store.

"We should be just fine by tomorrow," she said. "The store will be cooler, and Rabbi Zuckerman won't need to lie down, and everything will be back to normal. You can have your couch back."

Strangely enough, I was disappointed.

"Actually, that's not why I'm here," I said. "The rabbi isn't even bugging me."

"Well, that makes one of us!" she blurted before catching herself. "Oh, I'm sorry, I shouldn't have said that."

"What's the problem?"

"He's just a difficult man to work with sometimes," she said diplomatically. "But it's perfectly understandable. If I were in his position . . ." She drifted off without finishing the sentence, assuming I'd know what she meant. I didn't. But I didn't ask.

I told Mrs. Goldfarb that I'd seen the rabbi walking uphill on Saturday afternoon, in the heat. I asked if she knew where he lived.

"Just a few blocks from here," she said, "right in the development across the street."

"He walks to work every day?" I asked.

"He sure does," she replied. "Every day. Back and forth."

"It's straight up the hill. Why doesn't he drive?"

"They took away his license after he crashed into a telephone pole last winter," she said. "We should all be thankful—that little old man in that huge old Pontiac, he was a menace on the road. Scraped my car once, in the parking lot. In broad daylight!"

"Couldn't someone give him a ride home?"

At this point she snorted out loud. "Someone, maybe. But not me. I've offered, believe me, I've offered many times. But I tell you, the man is stubborn. Once I was pulling out of the parking lot when I saw him standing at the entrance to the shopping center, leaning against the Don't Walk sign, trying to catch his breath. 'Rabbi, please just get in,' I said to him. He leaned over and looked in my car—which is very neat, by the way, no clutter or cat hair or anything—and said no."

"Why would he say no?"

"He's an old-fashioned man," she said.

Mrs. Goldfarb presented her supporting evidence: The rabbi grumbled whenever she wore pants to work. He had complained when she suggested selling a line of yarmulkes and prayer shawls specially designed for women. ("I finally won that argument," she said with pride, "and these are very big sellers for us, thank you very much.") He had balked at her idea of creating a humor section for the books, claiming—so Mrs. Goldfarb recounted—that "there's nothing funny about being Jewish."

"So why is it so hard for you to believe," she said, "that maybe he doesn't like women drivers?"

"Come on," I said.

"Rabbi Zuckerman has some very strange ideas stuck in his head," she said. "This one is no stranger than the rest."

"Do you think he'd let me drive him home?" I asked.

"Well, you're not a woman. . . ."

"Is that a yes?"

"I have no idea, Benjamin, but if you really want to, you can ask him yourself," said Mrs. Goldfarb. "You know where to find him."

The rabbi and I hadn't exchanged a single word that week—or ever—but I broke the silence in my office that afternoon. When he sat up after his spell on the couch and put his shoes back on, I asked him: "Rabbi Zuckerman, it's still very hot when it's time for you to go home. Would you like me to give you a ride?"

He looked up at me, and stood up, surprised, head cocked.

"Yes, Mr. Steiner, I would," he said in a gravelly voice, bowing slightly toward me.

So he does speak English, I thought. Not even an accent.

"My car is right outside, the blue Corolla. Just come knock when you're ready to go."

He nodded and opened my office door. Back to the silent routine.

"Rabbi?" I asked him. "How did you know my name?" Mrs. Goldfarb had never used it and we had never been introduced.

He pointed at the nameplate on my door. Then he walked out.

His knock came around six o'clock. I grabbed my back-pack, shut down my computer, and got up to leave.

"I'm parked over here," I said on the sidewalk, pointing to my little sedan. The rabbi walked slowly, a few steps behind me. If he noticed my anti-Bush bumper sticker—a simple black "W" with a red circle and a slash over it—I couldn't see his reaction.

I opened the passenger door and waited to see if he needed my help getting in; he didn't. Then I got in the driver's side, tossed my bag in the back, and started the car.

The stereo was blaring, the same Nine Inch Nails album I'd been listening to that morning, at a volume my parents would call "ear-splitting": *My whole existence is flawed. You get me closer to God.*

Rabbi Zuckerman sat up straight—from the sheer loud-ness of the unexpected assault, not, I assumed, from the mention of God. I punched the off button. I couldn't imag-ine what the rabbi would do if we got to the part where Trent Reznor sings, *"I want to fuck you like an animal."* He'd proba-bly jump out of the car, then and there.

I chuckled sheepishly and apologized. He didn't say any-thing, just adjusted the air conditioner vent and looked straight ahead. I backed out of my parking space and headed for the exit.

"How far up the hill are you?" I asked.

"Four blocks, on the right," he said. "I'll show you."

The drive was quick and quiet. His house was a small brick cottage with three concrete steps to the front door. A maple tree took up most of his modest front yard. No flow-ers, just grass and a couple of small bushes on either side of the doorway. I pulled into his short, empty driveway.

He unbuckled his seat belt.

"Thank you, Mr. Steiner," he said.

"No problem, Rabbi Zuckerman, but please call me Benji."

* * *

"Fine. Thank you, Benji, for the ride."

It was the longest sentence he'd uttered to me. I decided to push further.

"You know, Mrs. Goldfarb told me that she offered you a ride, but you turned her down because you don't trust women drivers."

"Linda Goldfarb knows far less than she thinks she does," he said.

"What do you mean?" I asked.

"I don't care about women drivers," he said. "I won't ride in her car because it stinks of perfume and cigarettes. It's hard enough to work in the same store with her sometimes."

I looked at him and he cracked a smile. The first time I'd ever seen that.

"But let her think what she wants," he said.

I laughed, and he laughed, too.

He opened the door to get out, assuring me again (by waving me off before I could even ask) that he didn't need any help.

"Next time, Benji," he said before he closed the door and headed up his walkway, "not such loud music, okay?"

CHAPTER 3

With the bookstore's air conditioner fixed, the rabbi's daily breaks in my office ended.

No matter. We had developed a new routine. He didn't stop by during the afternoon anymore, but I continued driving him home at the end of the day, a few blocks up the hill. Most often, we didn't exchange more than simple pleasantries: "How was your day?" "Did you have a nice weekend?" "How are you feeling?" Nonetheless, it wasn't a major imposition for me and he seemed grateful for the gesture.

I ran into Mrs. Goldfarb one day at lunchtime in the shopping center's sandwich shop.

"I hear you're Rabbi Zuckerman's chauffeur now," she said. I couldn't tell if she was being sarcastic or just teasing me.

"I drive him home," I said. "That's all."

"So I guess he just doesn't like *me*," she said.

"No," I said, "you were right about him. He doesn't trust women drivers."

"I *knew* it," said Mrs. Goldfarb, with a satisfied expression.

Let her think what she wants.

Pete, I realized on the Fourth of July, was not the guy for me. There were little things that tipped me off: He was half an hour late meeting me at the Dupont Circle Metro station, and didn't think to call my cell, or to apologize when he finally arrived. He was wearing a Clay Aiken concert T-shirt—without apparent irony. He had already eaten, even though we were supposed to have lunch together; I was stuck scarfing down a Subway sub on a park bench.

Nonetheless, all of that could have been forgiven. Even Clay Aiken.

The real problem started when we went downtown, walking along the Mall. The main lawn around the monuments was thick with families on picnic blankets and teenagers throwing Frisbees. Lafayette Square, across from the White House, was crowded, too—with protesters. A demonstration against the Iraq War was going strong. People with megaphones led chants like "Two-four-six-eight, end the war, it's not too late" and "Hey-hey-ho-ho, Bush and Cheney have got to go!" Many people waved small American flags, while others held signs saying "No Penalty For Early Withdrawal" and "Bush's Mission Accomplished: 3,000 Troops Dead."

"Want to stick around?" Pete asked. I did, assuming that we were on the same page politically, beyond both hating Bush. But while we were both against the war, I soon found out that we were coming from different perspectives.

"End the Zionist Occupations: U.S. Out of Iraq, Israel Out of Palestine" read a sign in the middle of the park. The "o" in Zionist had a small red swastika inside.

I pointed and said, almost involuntarily, in an exasperated voice, "Can't we have one antiwar protest without the crazies ruining it?"

"What's so crazy about that?" Pete asked.

That's where it started. I was no hardliner—I supported Palestinian statehood and opposed the settlements in the West Bank, both stances that made my parents uneasy—but when I saw people making bogus connections like the one on that sign, I smelled something rotten.

"How exactly is our occupation of Iraq 'Zionist'?" I asked.

"Well, look who started the war."

I started the list, counting off names on my fingers: "Bush. Cheney. Colin Powell. Donald Rumsfeld. Condoleezza Rice."

"Oh, come on," Pete countered. "Jewish neocons were pushing for this war from the beginning, and they pulled all the strings to get what they wanted, like they always do. Seems pretty obvious that we're only there to protect Israel."

"You have an interesting idea about how much power Jews have in this country, especially considering how few there are in this administration," I said. "Do you realize that there's no group in America that's more consistently *opposed* to this war than the Jews?"

It devolved from there. He repeated some conspiracy-theory baloney about Jews being warned to stay out of the Twin Towers on September 11. ("I'm not saying I believe it, necessarily," he said. "I'm just saying it's something to think about.") He segued into an explanation about how suicide bombers blowing up kids in a Jerusalem pizza parlor could be justified. ("You know, out of sheer desperation.") It only took about five more minutes before he got around to comparing Israel to the Third Reich: "What they're doing to the Palestinians really isn't so different . . ."

I was done.

"I'm taking the Metro home," I told him.

"Geez, Benji, don't be so oversensitive," he said. "Can't we even have a simple political disagreement? Isn't this why people move to D.C.?"

"I don't know," I said. "I've always lived here."

And I walked away. The trains heading out of the city were empty; most people were headed into town for the festivities. I made it home in time to microwave a frozen pizza and watch the fireworks on television.

Dan dropped off Michelle before midnight. She could see that I was brooding.

"All right, what's wrong with this one?" she asked.

"How do you know something's wrong?"

"Well, he ain't here, is he?"

"True."

"So what is it *this* time?" she asked. "Last time the guy had a dog you didn't like. Before that was the one who played video games too much. Then there was that guy who did drag on the weekends—what was his name? Simon? I liked him. But I guess you were freaked out by all the makeup."

"And the chest stubble."

"Major ick," said Michelle, wincing.

"Exactly."

"And what is Pete's problem?"

Politics were never a big deal to Michelle, but she understood; she was Jewish, too. She also remembered the campus debates about Zionism when we were undergraduates. When the second Intifada broke out in 2000, pro-Israel and pro-Palestinian student groups organized competing teach-ins, as well as angry protests and counterprotests on campus. Any time I dared to defend the middle ground—territorial compromise and peace based on a two-state solution—I found myself attacked from both sides. The progressive folks I'd befriended in the campus gay group said I was a "Zionist racist" for believing in a Jewish state at all; it was one subject that made me feel alienated from that otherwise welcoming crowd. Not that I felt any sympathy coming from the Jewish groups on campus, either. The outspoken activists who staffed the Stand With Israel table in the student center labeled me a "Nazi collaborator" for suggesting that the Palestinians deserved a state of their own.

Michelle, who wasn't as personally invested in the subject, knew how difficult that had been for me. So when I told her about Pete, just as she'd done several years earlier at Maryland, she suggested I simply stay out of this kind of conflict.

"You should have avoided talking about politics," she said, "until you knew him better."

"Yeah, right. He would have noticed that I kept ducking out of dates to attend meetings of worldwide Jewry where we make our plans to rule the world. I mean, those meetings take *hours*."

She sucked her teeth and gave me a look that said, "Oh, you're *so* droll."

"I don't see your boyfriend here, either," I said. "What gives?"

"Well, your little plan worked beautifully," she started. "We spent the afternoon with two of his friends. We went paddle-boating by the Jefferson Memorial, we played Frisbee, we walked by the sculpture garden. And then his friends left, and Dan and I had a picnic on the Mall and watched the fireworks, and it was great."

"Uh-huh. So I don't see the problem."

"There was no problem until we were driving home. I was telling him what a great day it had been. You know, trying some positive reinforcement. That's important when you're training a new male."

I pursed my lips and gave her a look that said, "Don't start on this again."

"And then he's like, 'See, you were all upset over nothing.' And I'm like, 'Excuse me?' And he's all, 'You said you didn't want to spend time with my friends, but now you see they're cool. So you were all worked up over nothing.' And I lost my shit. I told him that he'd missed the whole point, that I never said I didn't want to spend time with his friends, that all I said was that I wanted some time alone with the guy who is *supposed* to be my boyfriend. And that if he didn't understand that spending time with his *girlfriend* wasn't *nothing*, then maybe he wasn't ready for a girlfriend."

Michelle was my best friend and I backed her up, even as

I felt sorry for Dan, who had unknowingly stepped into a minefield—stupidly but without malice.

"Did you guys break up?"

She looked confused.

"No, Benji, it's not that big a deal. We're getting together this weekend."

"I don't get it."

"I cried, I made him feel like shit, and he's got one day to come up with some really great apology. Maybe flowers. Or tickets to something. But he'll come through. He's not an asshole. He just needs to learn."

"Learn what?"

"That he ain't gonna be getting any from *this* girlfriend until I forgive him."

She pursed her lips and punctuated her remark with a diva snap. We both cracked up.

Then we both went to our rooms. Alone.

Before I went to bed, I logged on and checked out Man-Mate, a website for gay personal ads. I wasn't a member, so I couldn't send or receive messages, but I could read people's profiles and look at their pictures. To see who was out there.

This kind of thing always struck me as a place for people too afraid to show their faces (or use their real speaking voices) in public. That's why I'd never signed up. Plus, the design was ridiculous: each photo in a star-shaped frame, set against a tacky rainbow-striped background.

It was a meeting place of last resort. But sometimes a last resort is better than nothing. This was one of those nights.

I could cross almost everyone off my list right away: too old, unattractive, smokes cigarettes. Or else I could cross myself off their lists, if they were looking specifically for something I wasn't: Asian, into leather, "discreet" (read: closeted). Guys from Virginia were excluded—it was hard enough to get someone from the District to consider coming to Maryland. A couple of guys looked familiar, people I'd seen at the bars; if they weren't interested in person, I thought, they won't be interested online.

The top of the page flashed: "Over three hundred men in your area—online now!" But within minutes, I'd narrowed my list of possibilities to a handful.

If I find someone promising, I told myself, *I'll pay the damn fee right now and send him a note while he's still online.* I didn't want the Fourth of July to be a total loss.

The first guy was handsome. Square jawline. Crew cut. His profile said he was a "military type." I didn't know if that meant he wore a uniform for work or merely for pleasure, but either way, we weren't a match. I didn't need someone barking orders at me. I had my mother for that.

The next one was younger, still in college, with shaggy blond hair. Cute. But his main interests were "Frisbee, beer, and BBQ!" I had nothing against any of those things, but would never have described them as "interests." Much less my "main" interests.

Before I could even open the next profile—from a guy with a parted-hair, button-collar sort of preppy look—a box popped up on my screen. "You have used up your daily minutes as a trial member. But all you have to do to keep looking for Mister Right is click here, and join ManMate!"

I thought about it for just a few seconds before closing the browser and turning off my computer. It wasn't going to happen. I wasn't desperate enough. The Fourth of July was a dud. No fireworks at all.

A thunderstorm erupted unexpectedly late the next afternoon, the kind of summer storm that flares up with sudden ferocity but then moves on with determined speed. In most cities, these storms are welcome because they leave cooler, drier air in their wake. Not Washington: The heat that oppressed everyone before the storm returns immediately after the last drops fall; the humidity gets even worse.

When Rabbi Zuckerman knocked on my door, he was already wet after the short walk from his store, holding a newspaper over his head. "I didn't bring my umbrella today," he said.

I grabbed mine and escorted him to the car. The rain was coming in sheets, and my windshield wipers couldn't keep up. It was hard to see. Fortunately, we didn't have far to go.

When we pulled into his driveway, I turned off the car and got out so I could walk him to his front door.

"Thank you so much, Benji," he said over the noise of the rain as he fumbled for his key. "Why don't you come in for a moment?"

"I really should—"

"Just for a few minutes," he interrupted. "This storm won't last long. You might as well wait until it passes."

I glanced up at the sky, then went inside.

Heavy off-white drapes were pulled over most of the windows and mustard-colored shag carpets lined the floors. The house was damp and suffocatingly warm, the air heavy with the scent of books and mildew. Bookshelves lined nearly every wall, in the living room on the right and the dining room on the left. Looking straight ahead up the carpeted steps, I could see more shelves in the upstairs hallway.

"Please, sit down, dry off for a moment," said the rabbi, pointing to a lumpy wingback chair in the living room. "I'll go get you a glass of water." He walked toward the kitchen, in the back of the house, behind the staircase.

I didn't want to get his chair wet, but even more, I wanted to snoop. So I remained standing, checking out his living room.

The furniture was old and well-worn: a three-seat sofa covered in golden brown velvet with a pair of needlepoint accent pillows, the wingback chair with its threadbare tweed upholstery, a glass oval coffee table with an empty cut-glass candy dish on top. I could tell that the rabbi always sat in the same spot, at one end of the sofa, within reach of the end table and the reading lamp's pull chain; the seat cushion had a permanent indentation in that spot. There was no mess in the room—no stacks of old newspapers, no unopened junk mail, no dirty coffee mug left behind—but there was also a sense that the room hadn't been cleaned properly in some time. Dusting, vacuuming, airing out the drapes. We could just as easily have been returning to the rabbi's summer house after a long season away, finding the place frozen in suspended animation exactly as he'd left it six months earlier. But he'd been gone only since the morning.

On the mantel over the fireplace, alongside an empty vase and a silver menorah, sat a couple of framed photos. One was an old black-and-white picture of a man and a woman, a professional eight-by-ten portrait in a tarnished metal frame that had small roses in the corners. The other was a more recent color snapshot, in a tacky orange ceramic frame that said "Greetings from Florida" and had a small green alligator in the bottom corner, opening his grinning mouth—souvenir alligators always grin—at the elderly couple in the photograph.

I had the Florida picture in my hand when the rabbi came in with a glass of water. He had a can of mixed nuts in his other hand. He handed me the water and emptied the nuts into the candy dish.

"That's my wife, Sophie, may she rest in peace," he said. "She passed away last fall. That's the last picture I have of the two of us together."

I hadn't even recognized Rabbi Zuckerman. He looked at least a decade younger and he didn't have his short gray beard; he must have grown it after she died.

"I'm sorry," I said, putting the picture back on the mantel. Sorry that his wife was dead, and sorry to be snooping in an old man's house.

"That's us, too," he said, pointing to the black-and-white photo. "We had that taken on our tenth anniversary, right after we moved into this house. That was 1962."

The man in the old photo certainly resembled the man in the newer photo, even if some forty-five years separated them. Both looked proud, confident, with a flash of vigor in their smiles. But the man standing before me, wet and small and scarcely more alive than his moribund furnishings, seemed another person entirely.

He picked up the candy dish and extended it in my direction. I demurred. He frowned and sat down in his usual spot by the reading lamp.

"Cancer," he said with a sigh. "It was terribly fast."

He was quiet, and I didn't know how to fill the space, so I tried to change the subject.

"What are all these books?" I asked.

He didn't answer, and a silence blossomed in the room. Had I spoiled his moment? Perhaps he'd been waiting to talk to someone, anyone, about his wife, and he finally saw his chance in me. It didn't look like he had many visitors. Maybe he'd been waiting for the opportunity to invite me in and talk about her. But maybe now he was thinking that I wasn't the one, that I heard a mention of death and quickly changed the subject, preferring the mundane to the profound, the silly to the important. Too young, too shallow, not a serious man. Have a cashew and thanks for the ride.

"I think I should go lie down," he said, rising from the sofa. "The storm sounds like it's easing up. You should be okay now."

I took my cue, walking toward the front door and picking up my umbrella from the floor.

"I'm sorry about your wife," I said.

"I'll see you tomorrow," he said, waving me off while he started up his stairs.

*   *   *

My parents had a family snapshot on their mantel, in a bright, plastic frame much like the one in Rabbi Zuckerman's house. It was a memento of our first vacation in Florida, a trip to Disney.

I met Mickey Mouse on that trip. He was surprisingly tall.

He towered over me, a white-gloved hand extended in my direction, his face permanently molded into an open-mouthed smile, black ears blocking out the sun. He scared me. I hid behind my mom. Mickey turned to my sister, Rachel. She was twelve and thought she was too cool for this kind of thing. Physically unable to stop smiling, Mickey waved his white-gloved hand at Rachel; she rolled her eyes and offered a single pathetic wave in return, muttering, "Yeah, hi," as if she saw Mickey Mouse on the school bus every morning and couldn't wait to be rid of him.

But we were not rid of Mickey for long. He popped up around every corner at Walt Disney World—Mickey or one of his friends, all of whom were unexpectedly large and scary, their friendly expressions notwithstanding.

"I want to ride Space Mountain," I told my dad.

"We just ate lunch, Benjamin," he said. "Maybe later."

"I want to go now," I insisted.

He turned to my sister. "Rachel, do you want to take your brother on the roller coaster?"

She did not. She didn't want to be there, with any relatives or cartoon characters or fabulous rides, at all.

"No way," she said.

My father shrugged as if to say, "I tried."

"Sid, you two go," my mother told my father. "Rachel and I are going to look in the shops."

Shopping. The one interest my mother and sister shared.

We were off, my dad and I, to Space Mountain. Just us guys, in silence. My mom and I argued a lot but we were never at a loss for words; it was different with my dad. We weren't uncomfortable together, but we didn't usually talk much, so once we were alone, he appeared as unsure as I was about what to say without my mother to keep the conversation going. We were quiet, me pulling him by the hand through the crowd.

It was a relief, this quiet. Rachel hadn't had anything pleasant to say for months; Mom said it was just part of being twelve and she'd grow out of it. Mostly she ignored Dad and me; she sniped at Mom constantly.

But Mom wasn't fighting back this week. She was sullen and atypically silent. This Florida trip had been planned around Grandpa Jack's unveiling. When he died the previous summer of a heart attack, Mom went to Florida alone, while Dad took care of Rachel and me; the news of his death was shocking enough and they didn't think we could handle the funeral. This year, my parents planned a week in Florida for the whole family right before school started: a few days with Grandma in her Delray Beach condo, during which time we had the ceremony unveiling Grandpa's tombstone at the Magen David Memorial Grounds, followed by a few days in Orlando visiting the Magic Kingdom and Epcot Center. It was an odd combination—a cemetery and a theme park—but I wasn't bothered. I was at Disney for the first time, headed for my first roller coaster, and nothing else mattered.

"Do you miss Grandpa Jack?" my father asked me while we stood on line, under the sign that said "Sixty-minute Wait from This Point."

I did. I missed the times he took me to the playground when he visited, and the corny jokes he saved up to tell me, and the orange Tic Tacs he always had stashed in his pants pocket. He never treated me like I was Rachel's little brother, the way my parents and teachers sometimes did; he treated me like I was my own person. But I didn't really want to talk about that with my dad. I thought I might cry, and he didn't like it when I cried.

"Yeah," I said, looking down at my feet. "I guess."

"You know, Grandma is still going to come visit us, and maybe we can come down here again to see her," he said. "Go to the beach next time, or maybe Sea World."

"Okay," I said, inching forward toward the people in front of us.

"*You were lucky to know Grandpa Jack,*" *he said.* "*You never knew your other grandfather, my father. But that's not entirely a bad thing. He was a real SOB. Not like Jack.*"

"*Uh-huh,*" *I said. I'd heard stories, mostly from my mother.*

"*I never knew either of my grandfathers,*" *he continued.* "*My mom's parents stayed behind in Russia, and my dad's dad died before I was born.*"

"*Mm-hmm,*" *I mumbled.* "*How much longer till it's our turn?*"

My father shook his head for a second. "*I don't know, Benjamin, it could be another hour. Do you want to come back later?*"

"*No, I'll wait.*"

The rest of the time on line, my father didn't say much. I kept checking the new watch that Grandma Gertie gave me—a digital watch with a bright orange plastic strap that said "Florida" and had a green cartoon alligator on it. The wait didn't take a full hour.

When it was time to board the roller coaster, I got a seat at the front, sitting close to the bullet-shaped car's tapered nose. My father sat directly behind me.

"*The front is pretty scary,*" *he said into my ear.* "*Are you sure you want to sit there?*"

I nodded.

"*Hold on tight,*" *he said.* "*I'm right behind you.*" *And we shot off into the dark.*

The ride was fast but smooth, hurtling through blackness punctuated only by the occasional flashing colored light and the glowing white streaks painted on the sides of other cars, snaking up and down all around us. Screams echoed around the inside of the mountain as we climbed and plummeted, swerved and dipped. My father was right: The front seat was a scary place to be. I tried to turn around to see if he was scared, too, but he shouted, "Face the front, Benjamin, I'm right behind you." I reached one hand behind my head, hoping he'd grab it, but he didn't. "Hold on to the bars," he instructed. "It's safer."

I gripped the metal bars on each side of the car so tightly that my fingers went numb. I knew the next fall could be coming any sec-

ond—no way to prepare, yet no way to pretend it wasn't coming. I tensed my body and held my breath, darkness all around me, wishing my new watch had a stopwatch so I could count the seconds until this ride ended and I could breathe again.

"That was awesome," a kid behind me told his friend as we stepped out onto the platform. "Let's go on again."

I looked at my father. He was a bit unsteady on his feet, looking pale, sweating. He looked like he could barf.

"I need to sit down for a minute," he said to me, heading for a bench by the exit. "Don't go where I can't see you."

I turned around and saw Mickey Mouse standing by the doors, Japanese tourists taking his photo. When they dispersed, he spotted me, perhaps remembering me from an earlier hour. He spread his arms, both his hands open. I looked back at my father, mopping his forehead with a handkerchief; he wasn't watching. I turned around and ran toward Mickey, putting my numb hands in his white-gloved paws for a moment. He squeezed my hands; I felt it. Then I threw my arms around Mickey and pushed my head against his stomach, hugging him tight. And he put his hands on my shoulders and hugged me back.

The following day the rabbi didn't come to work. I didn't realize it until the end of the day, when Mrs. Goldfarb knocked on my door as she passed on her way to her car.

"You've got the car to yourself today, Benjamin," she said. "Rabbi Zuckerman stayed home."

"Is he sick?" I asked. I wondered if he'd caught a cold from the previous day's downpour. Had I covered him enough with my umbrella?

"He didn't sound too bad when he called this morning, maybe just a little under the weather," she said. "I wouldn't worry. It's probably better for him to take a day off now and then anyway, at his age. I can run the store just fine without him."

She left.

Mrs. Goldfarb might not have been concerned about him, but I was. I drove up to his house alone and parked in the driveway. I walked up to the door and rang the bell.

He opened the front door, dressed not in a bathrobe or pajamas, but in the exact same clothes he usually wore to work. Including the hard shoes.

"Benji? What are you doing here?" he asked through the screen door.

"Mrs. Goldfarb told me you were home sick and I wanted to stop by and make sure you were all right."

He opened the screen door and ushered me in. "You were worried about me?" he asked, perhaps hopeful, perhaps incredulous.

"I thought maybe you might need something from the store, some medicine or some food, if you're sick," I said. Then, simply: "Yes, I was worried about you."

He offered me the wingback chair again and the same dish of old nuts. I accepted this time. "I'll get you a glass of water," he said, excusing himself to go to the kitchen for what must have been his automatic response to houseguests.

He returned with two glasses and sat on the sofa across from me.

"So are you sick?" I asked.

"Yes and no," he said.

I looked at him quizzically.

"My body is fine, old and feeble, but fine," he said, looking down at his glass. "It's my heart that is sick. I've just been thinking about my Sophie."

Sure, I thought, ever since yesterday's awkward visit. But here was my second chance.

"What was she like?" I asked.

He brushed me off. "You don't want to hear about her."

"Yes," I said. "I do."

He lifted his head to look into my eyes. I nodded, and he began.

"I met her in 1951, when I was teaching at a yeshiva in Brooklyn. She was such a beauty—long brown hair and the most delicate hands, but eyes so sad and far away," he said. "But after all they had seen . . ."

Sophie had arrived in America only a few years before, the sole member of her extended family to survive the Holocaust. After all the indignities and offenses she had witnessed during the war, she had to suffer still more in peacetime: She couldn't go home to her village in Poland and instead had to enjoy her so-called freedom in a displaced persons camp in Germany. It was there, in the camp, that she befriended an American soldier, a medic, a Jew who spoke to her in Yiddish. Although she was a beautiful young woman, almost twenty at the time, and the soldier was only seven or eight years older and as handsome as all kind, healthy American soldiers must have seemed, their connection was not romantic.

"They were like brother and sister," Rabbi Zuckerman explained. "They would talk in Yiddish, but he also began to teach her English words. She would stay near him during the day, watching him work, and keeping up to date on the news of the world. New people arrived at the camp, and others left for Palestine or America, but Sophie had nowhere to go."

When it was time for the soldier to end his tour of duty and return stateside, he made arrangements with a Jewish aid agency to bring Sophie to America. The soldier's family took her in as one of their own, essentially adopting her and giving her a whole new set of brothers and sisters and parents, and the soldier set her up to train as a nurse's aide.

"She was working in the clinic at the girls' school across the street from my yeshiva, when I first saw her," the rabbi recalled. "I had spent years at that yeshiva, teaching boys prayers and Torah lessons, and studying with the other rabbis in the evenings. But once I saw Sophie, I couldn't think about anything else. She was my *bashert*."

"Your what?" I asked.

"My *bashert*," he repeated. "The one I was destined to meet, to share my life with."

"You really believe that?" This came out sounding sharper than I'd intended, and the rabbi cocked his head at me, stung.

"I do," he said. "You'll see. You'll meet the right girl one day."

"I doubt it," I said, leaving it at that.

"We are all destined to have someone special come into our lives, Benji," he said gently but with conviction, like a teacher explaining something utterly simple to a particularly dim student. "Even you."

CHAPTER 4

The rabbi's words stayed with me for days. Was there really someone I was destined to meet?

Obviously, I hadn't met my *bashert* yet. Or maybe I had met him, but didn't even know it. Maybe I'd already dated him but had cast him aside for some ridiculous reason: he bit his fingernails, he wore the wrong shoes, he didn't like *The Kids in the Hall*. Maybe I'd blown my only chance.

Would I know my *bashert* if I saw him? Would I recognize him?

I sat at my desk on Saturday morning, scanning the photos of a dozen different models the photographer had suggested to be the devil in the Paradise ad. I wasn't thrilled to be at my office on a weekend, but the bar manager seemed serious about deadlines, and I wanted to impress him—I needed the job. Besides, looking at photos of hot guys wasn't such a bad way to spend a Saturday morning.

As I flipped through the pictures, I searched for my *bashert*. Was this him—the curly-haired boy with the dimpled chin and perfect eyebrows? Or this one, a daddy type with a trim goatee and a shaved head? Or the blond one with the blue eyes? I'd always had a thing for blonds; was this because my *bashert* was blond, or because he was anything but blond—

the universe's churlish way of throwing me off my future husband's track?

The blonds I'd dated weren't exactly a parade of winners.

There was Rick, my boyfriend senior year at Maryland. A psych major. Seemed like a catch: funny as hell, well-read, the body of an athlete without any of the actual annoying athletics. We dated most of spring semester before I realized that Rick was studying psychology for a reason—because he was crazy.

Brad lasted half a summer after graduation. He was gaga over me, bringing me flowers and cooking me dinner and giving me massages every night. Too bad I didn't find him sexually attractive. I mean, I tried, I really tried. But at some point you have to open your eyes. Literally.

Gordy was a dog groomer. Sexual attraction was definitely not a problem with him. Men would stop in their tracks and peer over their sunglasses to get a gander at Gordy. "I don't even notice those other guys," he'd say. "You're the only one for me." I believed that for a solid six weeks, until he gave me a case of something itchy that he assured me were fleas, but turned out to be crabs.

A bunch of blonds. And me, still single, without anyone whose photo belonged in a tacky frame over my fireplace.

Should I have taken the hint? Or kept trying until I found the right blond?

I went over the photos for Paradise again, imagining how each model might look in the ad, trying to see which one could most convincingly represent pure evil. Surprise, surprise: The blond guy—with his coolly mischievous eyes and broad shoulders—turned me on. I took a Magic Marker and drew horns and a tail on his eight-by-ten glossy. It was a good look on him.

Better the devil you know, I thought. I called the photographer and told him the blond was my favorite.

"He's hot, right?" the photographer said.

"Hot as hell," I said.

* * *

As I pulled my car around to head home, services at B'nai Tikvah were letting out across the parking lot.

Black yarmulke. Black yarmulke. Black yarmulke.

I stopped at the end of a row to see if Rabbi Zuckerman would appear in the doorway. He did, again, lagging behind the other men. As I looked at him, he looked up and met my eyes through the windshield. And then, a second later, his knees gave out and he crumpled to the ground.

One young congregant saw it happen; he turned and ran back to assist Rabbi Zuckerman, calling several other young men to come with him. I pulled into the nearest parking space and raced to the rabbi.

The men had pulled the rabbi to his feet by the time I approached. He was leaning against the wall of the synagogue, his hands trembling, his face pale even for him. One of the young men was using the rabbi's hat to fan him.

"Rabbi, are you okay?" I asked.

All the black yarmulkes turned and stared. They said nothing; they wouldn't have known where to begin to engage me in conversation. I was wearing camouflage shorts and a powder blue T-shirt that said "Rehoboth Beach." No suit, no hat, no yarmulke. I might as well have been naked.

"I'm fine, Benji," said the rabbi. "Just a little light-headed."

If anything could have surprised the congregants more than me rushing to the rabbi's side, it was finding out that the rabbi knew me by name. Their confusion was evident in their expressions.

"I work right behind his bookstore," I said to them.

No response, except for fewer raised eyebrows.

"Benjamin Steiner," the rabbi said to them, gesturing toward me with one shaky hand, to introduce me. And to indicate by mentioning my name that I, too, was a Jew. Not quite one of them, but not quite not, either.

After a minute or two, the rabbi's color had started to

return and his breathing was steady, but he still didn't look ready to tackle the hill to his house.

"I think I just need to get off my feet for a moment," he said.

One of the congregants opened the door to B'nai Tikvah, while another took the rabbi's elbow to lead him back inside the synagogue. A wall of backs turned to me.

"You could lie down on my couch," I offered to the backs of their heads.

The rabbi stopped. Turned. Nodded at me once.

Had he chosen me over his fellow worshippers? Or merely my cushioned futon over B'nai Tikvah's wooden benches? The man at the rabbi's side stepped back and I took the rabbi's arm, walking him slowly toward my office. The congregants stood for a moment, waiting.

"Thank you very much," the rabbi said to them without looking back. *"Gut Shabbes."* And they dispersed.

Leaning on me for support as we walked across the parking lot, past his closed bookstore, the rabbi had no words for me until we reached my office. Then he spoke.

"You were at work this morning?" he asked while I unlocked the door. "On Saturday?"

I nodded. He shook his head. I opened the door.

"No lights," he said, holding up his hand to stop me as I reached for the switch. "It's Shabbat."

We weren't stuck in the dark; I simply opened the blinds and let in the daylight. But I quickly realized that "no lights" had other implications: Observing the Sabbath meant no computer, no phone, no writing. No work. What was I supposed to do while he was there lying down?

We could talk. That, at least, was allowed.

He kicked off his shoes, put his hat on my desk, and draped his suit jacket over the doorknob. His white shirt was missing a button and his collar was stained from sweat.

Then he lay down on my couch. He hadn't been there for weeks.

"So what happened?" I asked him finally.

"What happened?" he repeated. "I fell."

"I know you fell. But why?"

He shrugged.

"Are you sick?"

He shook his head.

"It can't be the heat this time," I said. It was a gorgeous eighty-degree day, the kind Washingtonians long for all summer.

Another shrug. This wasn't going to be a heartfelt dialogue, I could tell. It was more like pulling teeth.

I asked the rabbi if he wanted a glass of water. He said no.

I asked the rabbi if he'd eaten anything. He said no. He'd forgotten.

I told the rabbi I'd get him something from the sandwich shop. He said no. It was forbidden to use money on Shabbat. Besides, everything in that shop, he said, was *treyf*.

"They have veggie subs," I said. "Mrs. Goldfarb says those are kosher."

"She is wrong," he said.

I'd forgotten about the thousand degrees of kosher. For some Jews, the ingredients had to be kosher; for others, the pots and pans and dishes had to be, too. Some were concerned only about the food, while others demanded certification of the entire restaurant from a central authority. No matter where you fell, one person would think your rules were unnecessarily strict, while another would consider them too lax.

I'd been eating bacon cheeseburgers so long, I'd forgotten about how, when I was growing up, my family had our own mishmash of rules, not unusual for a Conservative Jewish household. We checked packaged goods for a "K" certifying they were kosher, bought meat at a kosher butcher, and never had pork in the house. But Chinese food containing shrimp was granted a special exemption as long as it was eaten directly from cardboard carryout containers with plastic forks. And while my mother would never mix meat and dairy on the same plate, she'd serve kosher ice cream for dessert after a kosher chicken dinner. When I mentioned all this to my sixth-grade Hebrew school teacher, she told me that there was no such thing as "sort-of" kosher, so my mother might as well have served us pork chops and pepperoni pizza. What would the rabbi have said about that? What would he say if he knew I'd eaten sausage just hours before, as part of a pork-laden breakfast sandwich I bought at the drive-through at the very Temple of *Treyf,* McDonald's? I didn't want to know.

"You have to eat something," I said. "That's why you're feeling weak."

"I'm not hungry," he said.

"What's wrong?"

He wouldn't look at me.

"Why aren't you eating?" I asked.

"My Sophie used to cook for me." He sighed.

I wondered: This is an explanation? I looked at him and realized that it was.

He took off his glasses, rubbed his eyes, and rolled away from me on the futon, his back to me. Were there tears in his eyes? I could not see.

He rested, perhaps ten minutes, long enough to stop that conversation from going any further. Then he rolled back over, opened his eyes, and said, "It is time to go home."

"I'll get the car and drive you," I said.

"It is Shabbat," he said. Driving—even riding in a car— was forbidden.

"You're not strong enough to walk up that hill," I said. "I think God will understand."

"It is Shabbat," he repeated. Translation: God will most certainly not understand.

So I helped the rabbi put on his suit jacket, handed him his hat, took him by the elbow, and walked him out the door.

Past my Corolla, which had a folder filled with semiporno-graphic photos on the passenger seat, and clear across the parking lot. I walked him up the hill, slowly, stopping peri-odically so he could lean against a street sign and catch his breath. It took almost fifteen minutes to walk the four blocks to his house.

When we got to his door, we both went inside, and I made him a sandwich.

Sitting next to the wall at his small kitchen table, under a plastic wall clock that had Hebrew letters instead of num-bers, Rabbi Zuckerman ate slowly. Perhaps he wanted some company and figured I'd stay as long as he was eating. Or perhaps the sandwich I'd prepared left him unimpressed—prepackaged salami was the best thing I could find in his re-frigerator.

At least the rye bread looked good. From a bakery.

"My father was a baker," the rabbi told me between bites. "To this day, I only buy fresh bread. Never from a super-market."

I asked about his father, and he told me how his parents had come to the States after the First World War, with a young son and an infant daughter who had been born in Poland. They settled in Jersey City, where his father opened a bakery. And then, a few years later, came Jacob, the baby who would one day become a rabbi, the only member of his family born in America.

"My brother and sister didn't remember anything about Europe—they came as tiny children," he explained. "In the house, we spoke Yiddish with our parents, but we all spoke perfect English, too. Still, I used to tease them and tell them I couldn't understand their accent. I called them 'my brother and sister from Poland.'"

Seated across from me at his kitchen table, he was looking past me, out the window and into space, pausing for a moment to remember. "They are both gone," he said. "My brother for many years already. My sister just a year before my Sophie."

I didn't want the sad memories to lead him back to silence, just when he was starting to open up. I got up and fetched a glass of water, hoping I might get him back on track.

"You should drink something," I said, putting the glass in front of him. It worked; he snapped out of his trance and looked up at me. Grabbing the opportunity, I tried to get him back to the happier memories: "What was the name of your father's bakery?"

"Zuckerman's Bakery," he said. "Our stores did not have such clever names back then."

The rabbi's bookstore was called Glenbrook Books and Judaica. I thought: This is clever? Why not People of the Book? From Right to Left: Jewish Books from Aleph to Tav?

"You didn't want to follow in your father's footsteps?" I asked.

"When I was young, yes. But after high school, when I thought I would start work in the bakery, my parents sent me to study in a yeshiva in Brooklyn. And there I studied instead to become a rabbi."

He never had a congregation, he explained. He taught at a boys' school in Brooklyn while he continued his own studies. And then he met Sophie. They were soon married. She left the home where she'd lived with the soldier's family—her adopted American family—and moved into the rabbi's basement apartment in Brooklyn, and they continued to work at their respective jobs: He taught at the yeshiva while she worked as a nurse at the girls' school across the street.

One of the soldier's brothers was transferred to Washington for work in the early sixties, and it was he who suggested that there was a business opportunity there for the rabbi and Sophie. The Jewish community in the Maryland suburbs was booming, he said, but there were few businesses to serve them. A quick look in the Yellow Pages found no Jewish bookstores at all between Washington and Baltimore.

"It was a big move," the rabbi said, "and a big risk. Not just professionally—there is a risk in any business—but personally. We didn't know anything about living in the suburbs. I didn't know how to drive a car or mow a lawn. I had never lived so far from my family. And for Sophie, she had already lost one family and was quite frightened to lose another."

But they moved, and they learned about cars and grass and fireplaces, and how to run a business.

"You know, Benji, marriage is sacred. But this does not mean that every marriage is perfect. This was a difficult test for us. When we finally made this decision, to leave our families behind and start a new life here, we only had each other to depend on. But we did it together. And this is how I knew, looking back, that Sophie was the woman I was meant to marry."

I held up a finger to get him to pause while I got the black-and-white photograph from the mantel and laid it on the kitchen table.

"Yes, we had just moved here," he said, running a finger around the edge of the picture. "Look at our faces. Big, hopeful smiles. But inside we were scared. We didn't know what we were doing."

The suburban Jewish community grew, he explained, especially in the late sixties, when Jews fled Washington after the riots. The business thrived, expanded, diversified beyond books to include jewelry, posters, yarmulkes, and ritual objects from wineglasses to prayer shawls.

As the rabbi spoke about his wife, sweet memories framed in melancholy, his spirit lifted slightly. He spoke in paragraphs, gesturing with one hand while the other held the sandwich he kept forgetting to eat.

"Every day, Sophie was with me," he said. "We ran the

store together. She would work in the mornings, and then come home in the afternoon to cook dinner and take care of the house. I couldn't make it through one day without her."

"You were the only ones in the store?" I asked.

"For the first several years, yes," he said. "We couldn't afford any help. But we were fine on our own. Just the two of us."

"And you and Sophie never had kids?" I asked.

He paused, and his expression fell. "No."

"How come?" I asked.

Wrong question. As soon as I saw his face, I knew I shouldn't have asked.

He stopped and put his salami sandwich back on the plate.

"We could not," he said, his eyes growing suddenly heavy again.

He pushed his plate away from him and stood up from the table.

"They did horrible things to her," he said.

And he left me in his kitchen, alone, listening to the sound of his clock ticking.

Walking back down the hill to retrieve my car, I saw first-hand what the Sabbath looked like in Glenbrook. It was quiet.

Glenbrook wasn't a ghetto, exactly—there were certainly non-Orthodox Jews, and even non-Jews, living there. In truth, the Orthodox probably made up only half of the residents of this otherwise unremarkable suburban neighborhood. And since they were Modern Orthodox—dressing in "normal," if abnormally modest, clothing—the area might not even draw a second look from a casual passerby. People who lived nearby drove through Glenbrook every day: past its rows of medium-size brick-front houses graced with oaks and maples in the yards, past its standard-issue sixties shopping center with a supermarket and a video store and a dry cleaner, past its utterly ordinary crosswalks and traffic lights and sidewalks and playgrounds. Most of them never realized that Glenbrook was an Orthodox enclave.

But if they looked closely, they'd notice the mezuzahs on every other door. They'd notice that the local pizza parlor was a kosher pizza parlor, that the local Dunkin' Donuts was a kosher Dunkin' Donuts, that most of the stores in the shopping center closed early on Friday night. If they were driving through around noon on a Saturday, they'd see the stream of families walking home from one of the neighborhood's three Orthodox synagogues; if they were driving through an hour later, they'd notice how few cars there were on the side streets. It's not that the Orthodox set the rules for the entire neighborhood. But they did set the tone.

Few towns in Maryland were officially incorporated, so their exact boundaries were always subject to debate. For an area like Glenbrook—which was really a neighborhood rather than a town—its very existence was sometimes erased. The Asian families in Glenbrook liked to say they lived in Wheaton, which was home to large numbers of first- and second-generation immigrants from Korea and China, and had a more obvious Asian flavor in its restaurants and shops. Working-class families, black and white, said they lived in Silver Spring, the older and more urban area where many of them had moved from, leaving crowded apartment buildings in search of detached homes with private driveways. Jewish residents of Glenbrook—those of the non-Orthodox variety— said they lived in Rockville, which was a way of saying they *aspired* to live in Rockville, since it was already home to their temples and their shopping malls and their Jewish Community Center; on maps, Rockville was right next to Potomac, a sylvan suburb of stone mansions with Lexuses and Land Rovers in the garages and enough acreage for a horse out back, where these same people hoped one day to claim to live if they were ever lucky enough to actually live in Rockville proper.

The Orthodox had no such problems. They lived in Glenbrook. It didn't matter if Glenbrook didn't appear on maps, that it was basically a no-man's-land between several other vaguely defined neighborhoods with equally ambiguous boundaries. Their aspirations were not to have bigger homes or closer department stores or easier access to public transportation. They wanted to live in an Orthodox area, where they could live among other Orthodox Jews in an Orthodox community, within walking distance of their Orthodox synagogues. The Orthodox didn't pretend they lived somewhere else; in their world, the name Glenbrook had great cachet.

Walking down the hill, I wondered if Rabbi Zuckerman ever left Glenbrook. He lived, worked, and prayed there. Where else would he go? He couldn't get far without a car.

I knew there had been a time when he traveled out of the neighborhood, or across the country—he had his souvenir frame to prove it. But for now, his entire universe was right here. Peaceful, stable, safe.

My apartment wasn't far away, just a couple of miles from the shopping center, but I went into Washington a lot, to watch Brazilian films or eat Ethiopian food or admire French paintings. As a gay man, I needed the city; no matter how many gay people lived in the suburbs, and there were more than a few, all the gay bars and restaurants and bookstores were in the District. So that's where I spent a lot of my time. I didn't hate the suburbs; I grew up in the suburbs and I appreciated things like having a car, living in a safe neighborhood, and saving on rent. But I needed the city, too, as an escape from the dullness that the suburbs invariably bred.

Not Rabbi Zuckerman. It took just a few minutes for me to walk the four blocks from his house back down to the parking lot where my car waited. In that brief time, I realized, I'd walked clear across his shrunken world.

"I know that I lost some aunts and uncles, but I never really knew much about them," Michelle said. "They were my grandparents' brothers and sisters."

In the years I'd known Michelle, we'd had numerous Jewish bonding moments, comparing notes on Hebrew school, holiday traditions, summer camps, family trips to Israel. But we had never talked about the Holocaust, at least not in personal terms.

Now, after I came home with stories of Sophie on my mind, we sat together on the floor around our coffee table, splitting a pepperoni pizza with Dan, sharing what little we knew of our own families' recent history,

"I think my family's pretty much the same," I said, slicing up the pie with a pizza cutter. I knew that some of my distant relatives had died during the war. My father had aunts and uncles and cousins in the Soviet Union who couldn't get out in time; my mother's family had all immigrated to the States long before Hitler came to power.

"It's weird that you guys don't even know this stuff about your own families," said Dan, taking a slice and shaking on extra Parmesan cheese.

"Well, it's not like it just happened," said Michelle. "We weren't even born yet. Our *parents* weren't even born yet. It was a long time ago."

"It wasn't that long ago," said Dan. Both of his grandparents on his mother's side were survivors, so he was well aware of his own connection to the Holocaust. "It's not like they ever talked a lot about it. They didn't want to freak us out when we were little, I guess. But I knew. It wasn't a secret. They still had tattoos on their arms."

"Wow," said Michelle. "How old were you when they first told you?"

"I can't remember. Maybe six or seven."

"I don't think I really learned about it until later," Michelle said. "We read *Anne Frank* in eighth-grade English class and my parents took me to see *Schindler's List*. But that was in junior high."

"Come on, Michelle," I said. "You must have heard about

it in Sunday school. Or do Reform Jews ignore the Holocaust, too?"

She smiled at me. It was a running gag with us: She'd
grown up Reform outside Philadelphia, while I'd grown up
Conservative outside Washington. Neither of us went to synagogue anymore or really observed the holidays on our own,
but we still teased each other about our upbringings—I'd
talk about how she was "*technically* Jewish" while she'd goad
me by calling me "Ben-Jew-man Steiner."

"Yeah, you're right, I'm sure we talked about it in Sunday
school," she said. "Right after we learned about the Five
Commandments."

Dan stopped midchew and looked confused.

"We sure talked about it in Hebrew school," I interjected,
without explaining the joke to Dan. I told them how Mr.
Bleyer, our principal, would hold a school assembly every
year on Holocaust Remembrance Day. "He brought in his
striped uniform from one of the camps, and he talked about
working outside in the middle of winter with no shoes on,
and watching people get beaten to death."

"Dude, sounds pretty intense," said Dan.

"I suppose it was," I said. "My parents talked to me a lot
about it, and they gave me a book of poetry by the children
at Theresienstadt. They took the Holocaust very personally—not because they had any close relatives who were
killed, but because it was such a big part of being Jewish for
them."

Still, I'd had to find out on my own that gay men were vic-
tims of the Nazis, too. "My parents never told me that part,"
I said.

"They probably didn't know," said Michelle.

"That I was gay?"

"About that part of the Holocaust."

*   *   *

The first time I rode the subway without my parents was on a He-brew school field trip to see the new Holocaust Museum on the Na-tional Mall.

My parents told me that I couldn't possibly understand what it meant to have such a prominent Jewish presence on the Mall, an ac-knowledgment that Jews were wholly Americans. The Jewish story had become, at last, part of the American story. I understood all that, I told them, but I didn't understand what the Holocaust, which happened in Europe, had to do with American history—why the museum belonged near the Lincoln Memorial, the Jefferson Memor-ial, the Washington Monument.

"The Mall is symbolic," my father explained. "Being on the Mall is a sign that you are truly part of America."

I didn't quite buy the argument—why, then, a Holocaust museum instead of a museum of American Jewry?—but my parents insisted (without seeing it themselves) that it would all make sense when I saw it in person. So off I went, on an outing with my Hebrew school class to take a special tour of the museum, an invitation-only sneak peek the day before it officially opened in April 1993. Mr. Bleyer was a survivor of Buchenwald and a member of the museum's ad-visory committee, and he had pulled a few strings to get tickets for Congregation Beth Shalom's seventh-grade class, the last year before kids get bar and bat mitzvahed and drop out of Hebrew school. We would see just what kinds of horrible things the Nazis had done.

We were eighteen students, plus two teachers and Mr. Bleyer him-self. We picked up the Metro at Grosvenor, one of the elevated subur-ban stations on the red line, not far from the synagogue.

I had been on the subway plenty of times—visits to the zoo, the Smithsonian, Union Station—but I had never seen it so crowded on a Sunday morning. And the crowd was unusually lively, chat-ting excitedly on the platform, waiting for the train downtown.

Mr. Bleyer herded us in a small group at one end of the station so he could keep track of us more easily.

"What's going on?" I asked my teacher, pointing to the crowd.

"I don't know," she responded. "The Cherry Blossom Festival is over. Must be some kind of parade."

The lights blinked on the edge of the platform, signaling an approaching train. Mr. Bleyer gathered us up in a close group so we could all enter through a single door and rush to claim seats. We were quick, throwing our bodies onto the orange and red cushioned seats and pushing one another out of the way to secure spots by the windows. The grown-ups stood next to us in the aisle. Our class staked out a small piece of territory in the rear car, a space big enough for us to tune out the rest of the passengers.

Almost.

The train was filled to capacity by the time we reached Bethesda. People were crammed shoulder to shoulder in the middle of the car, leaning against the metal doors. But this wasn't a grouchy rush-hour scene; people were in high spirits, talking loudly and laughing boisterously, cracking jokes with friends and greeting strangers with outstretched hands, cooing at babies cowering in strollers and kissing each other on the lips—men and women alike. "Are we going in the right direction?" someone asked. "Honey, we're all going to the same place," came the answer.

Many passengers carried placards. I strained to get a look. I saw "equal" signs, pink triangles, small rainbow flags. But I couldn't read the words. One man standing a few feet away had a sign tucked under his arm at his side; I cocked my head to try to make out the words. He looked down and noticed me. He held the sign up for me: a pink triangle with the slogan "Silence = Death." I nodded, but didn't understand what it meant.

The teachers looked uneasy, their eyes watchful of the crowd. The other boys were punching one another and whispering dirty jokes. The girls were the only ones chatting with the other passengers, in typically ballsy fashion.

"I totally love your earrings," Shira Epstein said to a woman standing nearby.

"Thanks, I made them myself," the woman replied. And the ice was broken.

"*So, um, where's everyone going?*" *Shira asked next.*

"*Today's the March on Washington,*" *the woman answered, as the woman next to her turned to see who was asking.*

Shira looked back blankly.

"*The March on Washington for Lesbian and Gay Rights,*" *the woman's friend clarified.*

"*Oh,*" *said Shira.* "*Cool.*" *She flashed a smile, which was returned in kind. The girl next to Shira giggled, but Shira elbowed her and mumbled,* "*Shut up.*"

A gay march. First I'd heard of it. And the first time I'd ever seen so many gay people in person. I started scanning the men to see what they looked like.

My eyes grazed over a cluster of middle-aged men with moustaches and bald heads, half a dozen young black guys in khaki shorts and white tennis shoes, one man in a military uniform, a couple carrying a pair of dachshunds with matching rainbow collars. Then my eyes came to rest on one guy, perhaps twenty, wearing a Cornell T-shirt. His dark hair was short and curly, his face freshly shaven, bushy eyebrows capping the retro sixties glasses balanced on his prominent nose.

He looked happy. He was among friends, seemed at home in his own skin. Another man a few feet away turned around and caught his eye. "*Buck!*" *he called, and the Cornell guy turned to face him. So, his name was Buck. His eyes lit up, his arms reached out, and the two men kissed. On the lips. Not briefly. I was staring. So were my classmates. Even the boys stopped punching one another.*

My teacher muttered to herself, "*Oh, really, this is too much.*"

Mr. Bleyer looked over and cleared his throat loudly: "*Ahem!*"

The kisser opened his eyes, pulled away from Buck, and said, "*We've got an audience.*"

Buck looked over at our group, smiled weakly, then whispered loud enough for us to hear: "*So let them watch if they want.*"

I turned away, pretending to stare out the window, but he caught my eye in the reflection. Revelation was instant, unspoken, traveling on invisible radio waves.

Buck turned back to the kisser and said, "Some of them should be taking notes."

Some of us were.

We transferred at Metro Center to the orange line, grabbing buddies to stay together. We arrived at the museum to find a completely different crowd waiting: suits instead of T-shirts, solemnly quiet, no signs.

Mr. Bleyer had our tickets ready, and as we walked into the museum, each of us was handed a card representing an actual victim of the Holocaust. We would follow our real-life victim through the events that unfolded for him or her, as the timeline of the Holocaust progressed in the exhibit. I got Ruth, a Jewish woman from Vienna. My classmates followed a Catholic priest from Krakow, a Jewish banker from Paris, a Gypsy grandfather from Czechoslovakia. Two cards drew the most attention: one, a Jewish teenager from Prague, who could have been any of us; the other, an artist from Berlin, who was sent to Dachau for being homosexual. The latter was dealt to Barry Schwartz, a quiet, nerdy boy I'd known since kindergarten who had recently grown obsessed with Dungeons and Dragons.

"Oooh, Barry drew the fag card!" shouted one of the boys.

"Hey, Barry, is that your new boyfriend?" shouted another.

Then came the boys blowing kisses. The girls giggling. The teachers ignoring the whole scene. And me, standing in silence.

After pizza, Michelle and Dan headed to a movie; they had plans to spend the night at Dan's apartment. He lived alone, so they had more privacy there than they did at our place. The fact that they *wanted* more privacy meant that things between them were good.

"What was that stuff about the Five Commandments?" Dan asked while he waited for Michelle to get an overnight bag together.

"It's just a running joke between us," I said. "I tease her because she grew up Reform."

"So did I," he said. "What about you?"

"Conservative."

"Keep kosher?"

"I did," I said. "Growing up."

"Not anymore, huh? You scarfed down that pepperoni pizza."

"Being Jewish is important to me," I said, "but not important enough to pass up a good pizza. I mean, I'm gay. A little pork is the least of my sins."

He laughed, but just for a second.

"Seriously, how important is it to you?" he asked.

"I don't know," I said. "It was important when I was a kid. And then when I left home, it didn't seem so important anymore. I had other things to think about in college, you know?"

"Like what?"

"Coming out."

"Right," he said. "But how about now? I've never heard you talk about this stuff before, but now you've got this rabbi in your office, and you're talking about the Holocaust. Sounds like something's going on. So what does it all mean to you now, as a gay grown-up?"

I mulled it over for a minute. "I guess I'm trying to figure that out."

We stood silently until Michelle interrupted us with a call from her bedroom: "Be right out!"

Dan checked his watch.

"What are you seeing tonight?" I asked.

"Some chick flick," he said. "Whatever. It doesn't matter."

Compromise without complaint. Things between them did sound good.

Michelle came out of her bedroom with a knapsack over her shoulder.

"What are you doing tonight, Benji?" she asked.

"I don't know."

She looked at Dan and gave him a knowing look. "He's got the apartment to himself. Probably gonna go to Dupont Circle and pick up three different guys and have some wild orgy here in the apartment."

He slung his arm over Michelle's shoulder.

"Gay guys have it made," he said, half-serious. "I wish I could pick up three different girls."

Michelle punched him in the ribs, playfully.

"Kidding! *Ouch*—geez, I was only kidding! Good luck, dude," he said, grabbing Michelle's fists in his much larger hands. He bent down to kiss Michelle. And they were out the door.

I wished my real life were as much fun as the life they thought I had.

Standing in the living room, without any plans, I felt a twinge of jealousy in the back of my mind. It's not that I envied Michelle for having Dan; he was cute and undeniably sweet, but I'd never been one to chase straight men. It was Michelle, who'd been a more constant companion than any guy I'd dated, that I was worried about losing. We'd been inseparable since we first met during orientation week at college, fast friends who crammed for tests together, went to movies together, stayed up late together bitching about our roommates. I'd feared losing her once before, when she'd made a pass at me outside the freshman dance over Homecoming weekend; "It's not you, it's me," I sputtered—and when that hackneyed excuse didn't seem to quell her embarrassment, I quickly added in a whisper, "I'm gay." A lonely week of silence followed, before she popped by my dorm room unannounced, ready to simply resume our friendship where we'd left off with a solemn promise that we'd always be honest with each other from that point forward. "It'll be like that new show *Will & Grace*," she said, half-joking. We'd been best friends ever since.

But now I had that feeling again, that it might not last.

Even *Will & Grace* had ended eventually. She'd move on. And I'd be left behind. Alone.

It was Saturday night. I didn't have a date. Nobody to see a movie with, nobody to spend the night with. Not even anyone to stay home and watch *Saturday Night Live* with. Pathetic.

I called Phil, and he agreed to meet me; I knew he'd cheer me up with tales of his latest boyfriend-for-a-day. I showered, got dressed, and got in the car, heading for Dupont Circle.

"What happened to the guy from Paradise?" he asked as we stood in a video bar on P Street.

I shook my head. "Political differences," I said.

"Gay Republican, huh?"

I didn't feel like going into the details, so I just said, "Something like that."

"Anyone new?"

"Not really," I said. "But I have been spending a lot of time with someone. . . ."

I told him about the rabbi. He was a bit confused.

"Sorry, Benji, I just can't imagine what you two have to talk about," he said. "I mean, if one of the priests from Saint Veronica's popped into my office, I think I'd have a heart attack."

"Yeah, your confession could take all day."

"Forgive me, Father, it's been about fifteen years since my last confession, and a *lot* has happened."

"It's not like that with the rabbi," I said. "It's not like he's there on official rabbi business."

"Still," he said. "If that's the only man in your life right now, you definitely need to get out more."

Fortunately, the fact that Phil and I were together drew men to us like magic. It's got to be some kind of hard-wired biological phenomenon: Guys who would ordinarily ignore you in a bar suddenly find you attractive when they see that someone else is talking to you. Maybe it's the idea that you're already with someone, unattainable, that makes the pursuit suddenly seem like a thrilling challenge—or, for the masochists, a hopeless misadventure. Or maybe it's men's competitive nature, trying to beat out all other suitors once they realize there are others vying for the same person. Whatever the reason, it was working. For both of us.

Phil walked over to the bar, where he was quickly grabbed by an admirer, and as soon as I was alone, a guy moved in on me, too. Christopher was his name. A staffer for a midwestern congressman. Around thirty. Great arms, terrific laugh, breath that smelled like cinnamon. And he was a redhead.

For a change.

CHAPTER 5

Once I'd seen the rabbi collapse in the parking lot, I knew he wasn't in any condition to be walking up or down that hill anymore. The next Monday, I stopped by the store to make sure he was all right and offered to drive him to a doctor.

"No doctors," he barked. "I'm fine."

"You collapsed in the parking lot."

"It was the heat," he said through gritted teeth. "I'm fine."

He folded his arms. I wasn't going to win this one.

"Well, you certainly shouldn't be walking up and down these hills," I said. "Starting tomorrow, I'll come pick you up before work and take you to the store."

He mulled this for a few seconds, searching for a reason to object, but apparently not finding any. He accepted this arrangement with a single nod and shooed me out the door.

And so it began, me pulling into his driveway each morning and depositing him at his house each evening. Sometimes I waited for him after work while he did his shopping—at the kosher butcher, the kosher bakery, the supermarket—and then put his bags in my trunk.

Our interactions were frequent, but typically brief. Occasionally, though, he would touch on a subject in the car that would result in a longer conversation inside his house.

"You want to see where I build the sukkah every year? Come, I'll show you."

"I'll never finish that whole challah myself. Come in, I'll wrap up half for you."

"The sink in the kitchen is dripping again. You could maybe come inside and take a look?"

We were becoming friends. Or something. Something more than just a carpool.

Mrs. Goldfarb didn't understand. "I don't know what you see in that crotchety old man," she said.

My mother didn't understand. "Next thing you know you'll be going to shul with him," she said.

Michelle didn't understand. "When's the wedding?" she teased.

I didn't fully understand what we saw in each other, either. But we saw each other.

After that first ride, I kept the stereo off during our brief car trips. I couldn't imagine the rabbi getting down with M.I.A. or the new Rufus Wainwright.

Once, as I drove him up the hill after work, I asked him if he ever listened to music.

"Not anymore," he said. "Music is for young people."

"Then what about when you were young?"

He stopped and pondered the question for a moment, as if it had been years since he'd even thought about music.

"Many years ago, I did," he said. "Sophie used to play records in the store—we had a hi-fi behind the counter."

"What kinds of things would she play?"

"Whatever records we were selling: cantorial recordings, Hanukkah music, sometimes old Yiddish songs."

I must have turned my nose up at this dull and predictable

list, because the rabbi quickly continued: "Sometimes she played the Barry Sisters," he said. "Sophie loved them."

"Never heard of them, sorry," I said.

"They were very famous," he said defensively. "They sang Yiddish jazz."

I wasn't impressed. "Did you listen to any *popular* music?"

"The Barry Sisters *were* popular."

"That's not what I mean."

"You mean did I listen to any secular music?"

"Yeah, I guess. Like stuff that was on the radio." I was trying to imagine him doing the Twist, snapping along to Motown, arguing about which Beatle was his favorite—or whatever people did in the sixties.

"How about Sammy Davis Jr.?" he asked.

I looked at him to see if he was kidding.

"Sammy Davis Jr.?" I asked. "You?"

"Why so surprised?" he asked with a satisfied smile. "Sammy Davis Jr. was very popular when Sophie and I got married. And also a Jew."

"I just didn't think you'd have liked that kind of thing," I said.

"Benji, I'm not made of stone," he said. "I also used to drive around in a car, like you, with the radio on. 'What Kind of Fool Am I' was a wonderful, wonderful song. Do you know it?"

I shook my head. He shook his, too. "So young," he said.

He started to sing: *"What kind of man is this—an empty shell?"*

I almost went off the road as the rabbi channeled the Candy Man.

He stopped when I started to giggle.

"Frank Sinatra did this song, too," he said. "But he was no more Sammy Davis Jr. than I am."

I was stunned. "What else did you listen to?"

"Well, I remember putting on an Allan Sherman record once," he said.

"He was a comedian, right?"

The rabbi started to sing again: *"Hello Muddah, Hello Faddah . . ."*

"Right, right," I said.

"Also a very popular record in the early sixties—and of course he was Jewish, too," the rabbi said. "Sophie never thought he was funny, but I did."

"And you used to play these in your store?" I asked. It seemed so out of character, since the store always felt so serious to me.

"No," he said. "That wouldn't have been appropriate. We played them at home. In private. Just the two of us."

I pulled into his driveway.

"Do you still have those old records?" I asked.

"I don't know—I haven't thought about them for ages. I don't even know if I still have the phonograph," he said. "Maybe in the basement somewhere. Come inside and you can help me look."

As we got to know each other, I got increasingly curious about the rabbi's life. Fiddling around on my computer one afternoon, I Googled some of the musicians he'd named. He was right: The Barry Sisters had been popular. And Sammy Davis's version of "What Kind of Fool Am I" was better than Sinatra's.

Then I Googled the rabbi's name.

Nothing. Like he never existed.

Not so unusual for someone his age, I figured; even my parents only popped up online a handful of times—a brief mention in a community paper when they won a raffle to benefit the National Zoo, a photo of my father speaking at a county council meeting about a new highway he opposed. So I wasn't surprised.

But then I Googled his bookstore, and again found nothing. That, I thought, was simply bad business.

"You don't have a web page?" I asked him that evening.

"I don't know what that is," he said.

I explained it to him, but to the rabbi, I was speaking a foreign language.

"Benji, I don't know from computers," he said.

"Don't you have one in the store?"

"Linda Goldfarb does whatever needs to be done with that," he said. "I never understood it."

"You really should have a website for the store," I said, explaining that it might increase his business and raise his store's profile.

"Eh, I don't have the time to worry about such things," he said.

I offered to make a page for him. "Nothing fancy," I said. "No online sales, no e-mail or anything. Just a simple page with directions to the store, the address and phone number, and maybe a bit about the history of the store and what you sell."

He mulled this over. "I can't afford to be starting up all these new things," he said.

"I'll do it for free," I offered. "Seriously, it won't take long, and it won't even cost you fifty bucks to register the URL."

"The what?"

"Never mind."

"Okay," he said. "I trust you. I have no idea what you're talking about, but if you say it's a good thing, I trust you. Some things in this world, I suppose you know more about than I do."

It didn't take more than a few days to set up. There were no bells and whistles, no drop-down menus, no animated menorahs. Just the basics about the store, presented—if I did say so myself—in tasteful fashion: blue and white background, a few photographs I'd taken of the store displays, a picture of the rabbi and Mrs. Goldfarb side-by-side looking almost like they liked each other. There was a map to the store, a list of their most popular items with thumbnail images, and a history of the business told in first person and signed by the rabbi. It was simple, but definitely polished and professional looking.

I pulled up the page on the bookstore's computer one day at lunch. Mrs. Goldfarb was impressed. The rabbi seemed pleased, although it was clear he still didn't quite understand who might ever see this information, or how they could find it on their own computers.

"Wait, I forgot the best part," I said.

At the bottom of the page, a gold Jewish star stood alone without any text.

"This is a little hidden feature, just for those in the know," I said. I clicked on the star and music started to play on the computer. The Barry Sisters. I'd downloaded a greatest hits collection.

"It's a very nice song," Mrs. Goldfarb said. "But who will ever know it's there?"

The rabbi didn't answer. He just looked at me, smiled, and winked.

I burned a CD of the Barry Sisters after that, and every day in the car, I'd play a different song. Sometimes a particular tune became a catalyst for a story from the rabbi's early days in Maryland—a story he'd continue in my office or in his living room.

"You really want to hear about this ancient history?" he asked once and only once.

"I do," I said. It was true. Besides, the rabbi's spirits lifted each time he recounted these stories. He'd never had anyone to tell them to.

The music, to be honest, wasn't quite my speed. A bit hokey, overly cheerful; a little went a long way. But I loved looking at the Barry Sisters online, seeing their period-perfect album covers and publicity shots where they appeared in matching dresses and matching hairstyles, beneath multi-colored block lettering. As a designer, I couldn't get enough of the visuals, even if the songs themselves quickly wore thin.

I mentioned this to the rabbi one day, when he remembered a certain song from their LP *Shalom*.

"I've seen that one online," I said. "They're getting off a plane carrying huge bouquets of flowers."

"Yes, we sold that one in the store," he said. "I remember it. That wasn't just any plane, Benji, it was an El Al plane."

"All I remember is what a wonderful image it was. So sixties."

"You weren't alive in the sixties."

"When I see pictures like that, I can almost imagine what it was like."

Later that week, when the rabbi got in my car at the end of the day, he handed me a rolled-up promotional poster of the Barry Sisters. It was dusty, torn, and discolored from age.

"I found this in the back of the storage closet," he said.

"You just happened to find it? After forty years?"

He shrugged.

I unrolled it across the steering wheel, careful not to rip it further. It was beautiful.

I thanked him.

"I don't need it anymore," he said.

"I'll hang it in my office," I said.

"Let's go home," he said.

One Wednesday morning in mid-August, I pulled into the rabbi's driveway and found the front door still closed. I checked my watch; I wasn't running early. I waited for a few minutes.

Nothing.

This wasn't like the rabbi. He was usually waiting in the doorway. I tooted the horn, but got no response.

I got out of the car and walked up his front steps, pulled open the screen door, and knocked.

No answer.

I knocked again. Still no answer.

I rang the doorbell. This time I heard a voice inside, shouting from a distance: "Who's there?"

"It's me, Rabbi," I answered, confused.

"Me who?" the voice replied, closer.

"Benji. Benji Steiner."

The door opened a crack and I could see the rabbi scanning me from head to toe with squinty eyes. I pushed the door open wide and found the rabbi as I'd never seen him: in loose pajamas and a rumpled bathrobe.

"I'm here to drive you to work," I said, walking past him into the foyer, letting the screen door swing shut. "Are you feeling all right?"

"Of course, I'm fine," he said, but it was clear he was not. "Did I call for a car?"

"Rabbi, I drive you to work every day," I said. "Don't you remember?"

Obviously he did not. But he pretended to understand. "Then I should go get dressed," he said, turning to go upstairs.

I followed him upstairs to a part of his house I'd never seen before. There were just two rooms, one on each side of the landing. One was his bedroom, with bookshelves covering every available wall, and an unmade bed beneath a double window. The other was a mirror image, filled with more books, a small desk, and an old couch—his study. Lined with still more bookcases, the hallway between the rooms was lit by a single overhead light, marking the entrance to the bathroom—which was decorated with pink wallpaper and pink fixtures, the only room in the house without any books.

Outside the bathroom, two framed needlepoint pictures hung on either side of the door: one of an apple tree, the other of flowers, both with Hebrew writing along the bottom in neat red stitching.

I was trying to make out what the pictures said—my Hebrew, which had never been good, was quite rusty by this point—when the rabbi came up behind me.

"Excuse me," he asked, "but what do I wear to work?"

I called an ambulance.

Holy Cross Hospital. What kind of a place was that for a rabbi?

The doctor said it sounded like the rabbi had suffered a ministroke. He would need to stay in the hospital for a couple of days for tests, but he'd probably be fine.

Most likely, however, he would never recall the events of that morning.

Sure enough, by the next evening when I visited him after work, he was awake and alert, and he knew exactly who I was when I came in.

He pushed aside his food tray, which held a kosher hospital dinner, the kind where every item is individually wrapped and sealed and stamped three times: kosher, kosher, kosher.

"The doctor tells me that you brought me here," he said. "This I do not remember. I remember going to bed in my house and waking up in this bed instead."

I pulled up a chair and recounted the previous morning's strange scene.

"Amazing," he said. "You tell me it happened, and I believe you. But I do not remember."

"How do you feel?"

"Well, the food is bad and the bed is uncomfortable and the nurses keep taking blood for some test or other. And then Linda Goldfarb came to visit me." He rolled his eyes.

"I told her you were here."

"Yes, this I suppose is necessary. But she brought me these awful flowers"—he gestured to a basket of mums on the bedside table—"and they smell just as terrible as her perfume."

"I'm sure she was trying to be nice."

"Flowers you bring to a dead person," he said. "Or a wife."

I was glad I had opted against flowers on this visit.

"You'll come again tomorrow?" he asked.

I said I would.

"Would you stop by my house and bring my reading glasses and my prayer book? They are on the desk in my study."

"Why do you need them?"

"Tomorrow is Friday, and tomorrow night is Shabbat. I will need my glasses and my siddur to daven."

"The doctor said he wants you to rest."

He waved off this notion with the back of his hand. "Benji, there is an authority higher than the doctor."

I paused to see if he'd elaborate, but he didn't; apparently that's all that needed to be said.

"You've never broken Shabbat, have you?" I asked.

He shook his head.

"Why not?" I asked.

I couldn't begin to understand why the rabbi was so rigid in his observance, keeping every letter of the law even when it was inconvenient, uncomfortable, or unhealthy.

"Your question is a strange one to me, Benji," he said. "You ask why I do not break Shabbat. But I wonder why you do not keep it."

"Too many rules," I said.

Judaism was a religion of a million rules; no matter how hard you tried, you were bound to break most of them. This, I was convinced, was a way of maintaining communal guilt and shame—making sure we all felt that we came up short. It was a trap. I had decided years ago, when I left my parents' house to go to college, that I wasn't going to play by those rules anymore.

"You are looking at it upside down," he said. "Judaism is not only about refraining from doing bad things. It is also about doing good things. Shabbat is not only a day when you do not work, it is a day when you *do* rest. Keeping kosher is not only about rejecting *treyf,* it is about eating the way God has decreed. You see restrictions. I see opportunities. Opportunities to get closer to God, to become the man He wants you to be, to live your life as a good Jew."

This sounded like one of my Hebrew school teachers' speeches. I wasn't buying it.

"Thanks, but no thanks," I said. I didn't mean to be rude, but I wasn't in the mood for a lecture on observance.

He was taken aback, probably unaccustomed to having people reject his spiritual guidance.

"You're not interested in being a good Jew?" he asked, incredulous.

"I'm not interested in all those rules," I said.

"Benji, the rules apply to you whether you obey them or not," he said. "You can't just pretend you're not a Jew."

"No offense," I said, "but I'm a grown-up and I'm pretty sure I can do whatever I want."

He blinked several times, as if trying to wake from a dream. Then he returned my snideness in kind: "So being a Jew doesn't mean a thing to you?"

"I didn't say that," I said, slumping back in the chair. "It means a lot to me."

"What does it mean, then?"

I was silent. I honestly didn't know the answer, not in any sense that I could put into words.

"You are lost," he said.

"No, not exactly. . . ."

"Yes, you are lost," he repeated. "But you can find your way back."

"I'm not going to become Orthodox," I shot back quickly. My mother must have gotten to me, after all.

A look of confusion spread across his face, but it soon softened into an amused grin.

"Benji, you do not have to keep kosher or become *shomer shabbes*," he said. "But you need to find out what about Judaism has meaning for *you*—the place where you feel connected to your faith."

"I don't really feel connected anymore," I said.

"Then you must reconnect. You must not give up on your faith," he said, growing serious and shaking his finger at me. "My Sophie lost faith in God. With what she endured, it's no wonder. Anyone might lose faith. But did she stop lighting candles on Shabbat? No. Did she stop keeping kosher? No. Did she stop going to shul? No. The Nazis tried to take all of that away from her, and after she came to America, she swore that she would continue to practice her religion as long as she was free. She did not find her faith again in an instant. But she maintained her rituals, and the meaning eventually returned. She was a woman of great faith—greater than my own, because her faith had been tested so terribly. She questioned, she doubted, but she did not cast aside her religion like an old coat that has grown too heavy."

I was listening quietly, taking it in.

"And neither will I," he announced as a sort of grand conclusion. "So please, Benji, the reading glasses."

"I'll bring them tomorrow," I said, getting up to leave.

"And tell Linda Goldfarb that she doesn't need to bring me any more flowers."

The third date. There has to be something, at least the spark of something, to get to the third date.

I hadn't gotten to the third date for a while. But my first two dates with Christopher, the Hill staffer, had gone well: an evening of Shakespeare at the Carter Barron Amphitheatre downtown (his idea) and an afternoon of duckpin bowling at a shopping center in the suburbs (my idea). Both dates had been followed by moderately priced meals and moderately tasteful kissing in the car.

Here's what I had learned about Christopher so far: He grew up outside Omaha. He had double-majored in English and political science at Northwestern. He could bench-press more than I could, but I could kick his butt at duckpin bowling. (Admittedly it wasn't a fair contest; I'd grown up in an area where duckpins were the norm, while he had never even heard of such a thing.) He had good, progressive politics—better than his moderate, farm-subsidy-loving representative—and he was out at work. I also knew that he was active in his church; I didn't know the details or even truly understand the differences between all the Protestant denominations, but I did know that he could never stay out late on Saturday night because he had to get up early on Sunday.

I also knew that he wasn't the sleep-around type. He was hunting for a husband. And he had me in his sights.

At least until our third date.

I met Christopher after work at a romantic restaurant near Union Station. Nouveau comfort food. Mix and match silverware on the table and Billie Holiday on the stereo set the tone: offbeat but homey.

Christopher had been having a slow week since Congress wasn't in session, so we spent most of dinner talking about the rabbi. I had mentioned him to Christopher before, but for obvious reasons, there was a lot more to talk about this time.

"So tomorrow I've got to go to his house and pick up a few things for him," I said.

"Isn't there anyone else who can do it? That woman he works with?"

"He doesn't exactly like her."

"A relative?"

"All he has are some nieces and nephews and none of them live here."

"So you're like his personal assistant now?"

"I'm just helping him out."

"If that's what you want to do."

Christopher asked about my own Jewish background, and I gave him the whole synopsis. From growing up Conservative—synagogue, bar mitzvah, planting trees in Israel—to giving it all up when I went off to school.

"I still do a few things, mostly for my parents," I told him: Passover seders, Hanukkah parties, going to services on the High Holidays. "But mostly I don't miss it."

I didn't tell him about the rabbi's suggestion that I start picking up the rituals I'd left behind. He didn't seem to want to talk about the rabbi.

"What will you do if you have kids?" he asked.

"What do you mean?" I hadn't really thought about kids. I still felt like a kid myself.

"I mean, would you raise them the way you were raised? Send them to synagogue and Hebrew school? You've rejected all those things, but you had to learn about them first before you could make that decision. What would you do with your kids?"

I stopped to think about it for a moment, chewing my Cornish hen.

"I'd definitely want them to know they were Jewish and understand what that means," I said.

"How would you do that?"

"Well, I guess we'd observe the holidays. And maybe I'd send them to Hebrew school—I don't know. I had such a rotten time with it, but maybe I could find a better synagogue."

"You'd send your kids there, but you wouldn't go yourself?"

I hated the idea of pretending to like going to synagogue just so my kids would go, too. But even more, I hated the idea of dropping them off and making them do something I wouldn't do myself.

"I suppose if I sent my kids there, I'd have to go with them," I said. "At least until they were bar mitzvahed. Then they could make up their own minds."

"So they'd get bar mitzvahed?"

"Oh yeah, that much I do know." I said it with certainty, but honestly, until that moment I hadn't even considered the concept. But yes, now that I thought about it, that much I did know.

Christopher was looking down at his goat cheese ravioli.

"Benji, I don't think this is going to work."

"What are you talking about?"

"You're Jewish."

"Yeah, but I told you, I'm not religious."

"You might not be observant, but you're more religious than you think," he said. "And anyway, it doesn't matter if you're not religious. I am."

I was accustomed to hearing Jewish people talk about the difficulties of interfaith relationships. I had never bothered to wonder if non-Jews had the same problems. Apparently, they did.

"Look, I really like you," he said. (Nothing good ever followed such an opening.) "But I'm looking for someone to settle down with, someone I might want to start a family with, have kids with. And part of that is someone to go to church with, and celebrate Christmas with. Being Christian is too important to me to give it up. And you don't realize it, but being Jewish is too important to you to give it up. I would never ask you to. But that means this won't work out."

I'd love to say that Christopher was an asshole about all

this, that he made some anti-Semitic crack or said he couldn't imagine looking at my hook nose every morning over the breakfast table. But in truth, he was sweet about it.

We skipped the crème brûlée and kissed on the street. A kiss good-bye.

I was getting frustrated. With Pete, it hadn't bothered me so much when things didn't work out; his rotten politics made him someone I was glad to stop seeing. But Christopher was different. I really liked him. We hadn't broken up over a fight or because one of us met another guy. We broke up because of who we were. Or, more precisely, because of who I was.

I wanted to talk to someone about it, so I drove to Dupont Circle and called Phil, asking him to meet me at one of the bars on Seventeenth Street. It was reasonably busy for a weeknight. Video screens were showing one of those reality shows where everyone's competing to be the top chef or top designer or top hair stylist. I tried to look away and pay attention to Phil, but like all gay men, I found myself unable to resist the lure of Bravo. Our conversation had to be segmented and squeezed into the commercial breaks.

I was telling him about my third and final date with Christopher while I nursed a beer.

"You don't even think about religion when you're dating, do you?" I asked. "I mean, I know you're not only going out with other Catholics."

"Not an issue at all," he said. "You've seen most of the guys I've dated. White, black, Asian. Irish, Latino, Greek. I suppose some of them grew up Catholic, but who cares?"

"What if you had kids?"

"I'm pretty sure two guys can't get pregnant."

"You know what I mean."

"I'm not planning on having kids, so that's not an issue," he said. "And honestly, I don't really care what religion a guy is, as long as he's not real religious. I don't think I could handle a guy who wanted to go to church every Sunday, whether he was Catholic or Methodist or whatever."

"How about Jewish guys?"

"I've dated Jewish guys. Remember Marty Gold? That was cool. But he wasn't, you know, super Jewish."

"What do you mean?"

"He didn't go to synagogue or wear one of those things on his head."

"Right," I said. "How about me? Could you date me?"

"Benji, we're just friends," he teased.

"Not *me*, specifically," I said. "Could you date someone as Jewish as me?"

"You're not that Jewish," he said. "Or at least you didn't use to be."

"What do you mean?"

"Well, you've been spending all that time with the rabbi," he said. "And putting all that Bible stuff in your ads. I don't know. You talk a lot more about Jewish stuff lately."

"That's funny, because I really don't feel all that connected. But I guess it's always been a part of me," I said. "You don't stop being Jewish because you stop going to synagogue. You don't go to Mass anymore, but you're still Catholic."

"Only kinda-sorta," he said. "I mean, it's not like a magazine subscription where you actually cancel your subscription, so technically I suppose I'm still on the mailing list. But that's about it."

"I guess being Jewish is different," I said.

"Guess so," he said.

"It's screwing up my love life," I said. "Chosen people, my ass. I can't even get a date."

Over Phil's shoulder, I spotted a guy across the bar checking me out. Nice hair, unnaturally neat eyebrows, cute enough. But he was standing with a group of friends, discussing the television show and making predictions about which contestant would be eliminated at the end of the hour.

He looked over at me during an advertisement and caught my eye.

Then the show came back on, and he and his friends were rapt, all eyes on the video monitors, offering running commentary on the program.

I debated whether I should go up and talk to this guy, or call it a night and head home. On the one hand, I reasoned, I should just write off the night as a dud and cut my losses. On the other hand, I thought, maybe I could salvage the night by meeting someone new and forgetting about the gentile who'd just dumped me.

When I finished my beer, I headed to the men's room, walking right past Mister Winky. "How's it going?" he asked as I brushed past. I put on my butchest voice and said: "Good. Good." Before I could think of where to go from here, I noticed that all his friends were watching me, probably trying to figure out if I'd be eliminated before the end of the hour. I became suddenly shy. "I was just going to the bathroom," I said, and excused myself.

Standing at the urinal, I kicked myself for walking away. Wasn't I good enough to make it to the next round? I resolved to go right back and join their little group when I was done.

But before I had finished, Mister Winky walked into the men's room and stood at the urinal next to mine. "Hey there," he said.

"Hey," I replied, staring at the wall.

I finished my business and zipped up. He hadn't even started his business. Or so I thought. I looked at him and he smiled, then turned slightly to reveal the erection in his hand.

"Want to go in there?" he asked, motioning to the empty stall in the back of the bathroom.

I did not. "That's not really what I had in mind," I said, and walked back into the bar, past his friends, waved good-bye to Phil, and kept going out the front door.

That wasn't the first time I'd been propositioned at a urinal. The first time was many years before, by Avi Pinsky.

Avi had the biggest dick of all the Gefilte Fish.

We were all roughly the same age, boys who just finished seventh grade, bunking together at Camp Millwood, a Jewish boys' sleep-away camp in Capon Bridge, West Virginia. Officially, our bunk was known as the Guppies. The older boys were also named after fish: Minnows, Catfish, Bass. At least those were our official bunk names. The standing joke was that we were all named for fish with links to Jewish culture. Herring. Whitefish. Lox. In the joke, the Guppies were the most Jewish fish of all: Gefilte Fish.

Some of us Gefilte Fish had already started our growth spurts and looked like we might have our driver's licenses; others still looked like elementary school kids. I was somewhere in the middle. My voice had not changed, but my feet had grown three sizes in six months, and I'd outgrown every item of clothing from the previous summer.

Avi already looked like a sixteen-year-old. He had blond whis-kers on his chin. At five foot eight, he towered over the rest of us. And his penis was so oversized, it looked like something he bought at a gag shop, like bug-eyed X-ray glasses or plastic Mr. Spock ears.

I knew this because Avi proudly showed off his new trophy every night in our bunk. After the counselors made sure we were in bed, they'd head down to the pool to do whatever counselors did at night: smoke pot, listen to music, talk about campers behind their backs. That's when Avi, the clown of our group, entertained the rest of the bunk. Typically, in the nude.

Sometimes his nudity was incidental, the un-costume he wore as he went with a flashlight from bed to bed, teasing each kid, mocking one camper's mannerisms or making up stories about another's mother. Other times, his penis was the center of the show; it often served as his puppet in a sort of X-rated version of Shari Lewis and Lambchop, but with a lot more talk about tits and pussy. His shtick was quite popular, and always got Avi lots of laughs. I was often one of those laughing, despite myself.

This time, though, I was not laughing, because Avi decided to pick on me. Probably because I'd ratted him out that afternoon for smoking a clove cigarette behind the bunk; now I'd have to pay.

"Hello, Benji!" Avi was doing his penis-puppet routine, which involved him speaking in a high, squeaky voice while he held the head of his penis in one hand, using his thumb and index finger to open and close his urethra like a mouth, while his other hand held his flashlight, trained on his dick like a spotlight. "I want to be your friend!"

My bunkmates were laughing. I was trying to ignore Avi, but it's hard to ignore someone who's pointing his penis at your face.

"Awwww, won't you say hello?"

I gave in and muttered, "Hello."

"I think we're going to be great friends, Benji!"

"Uh-huh."

"We have so much in common!"

"Hmmm?"

"Yes, we're both total pricks!"

That got lots of laughs. Even I chuckled.

"And Avi tells me you're a real dickhead!"

I stopped laughing.

"Do you think we can be friends?"

The squeaky voice was getting to me. But I didn't say anything.

"Pleeeeease?"

I kept quiet.

"If you don't want to be my friend, maybe you want to meet my brother. He's a real asshole, just like you." With that, Avi dropped his penis and started to turn around. I knew what was coming; Avi had farted on at least half the guys in our bunk already that summer.

"Okay, okay, we can be friends," I said.

"Great," said Avi. "Let's shake on it."

I looked into Avi's eyes, but he wasn't looking back. He was looking all around the bunk, checking the audience response. I looked back at his dick, waving in front of my face. I decided to end this teasing, to call this clown's bluff. I reached out and grabbed Avi's penis in my right hand.

"Nice to meet you," I said, shaking my hand.

This was the first time I held another man's penis. In a moment, I took mental measurements: how soft it felt, how it filled my hand, how much it weighed against my palm.

Avi froze and looked down, astonished, and quickly pushed my hand away.

"Eww, you fucking freak!" he shouted. The squeaky voice thing was over—Avi's budding baritone was back. "You grabbed my dick! I can't believe it. You really are a fucking fag! You grabbed my dick!"

Avi leaped back into his bunk bed, flipping off his flashlight.

My bunkmates were staring at me in the dark, as if I was the freak, instead of the naked guy jumping around waving his dick in other guys' faces. "What'd you do that for?" one of them asked.

"I figured it'd shut him up," I said. This wasn't a lie. But it wasn't really the reason I grabbed him. I wanted to know what it felt like, to reach for it, to hold it, to be that close.

"Sick, Benji," said another kid. "You touched another guy's dick."

"What a fag!" Avi called from his bed.

"Avi, you're the one who told him to touch it," said yet another camper. "Maybe you're the fag here."

And that, once and for all, shut Avi up.

The next day, all the Gefilte Fish were talking about what happened. Because a lot of guys were sick of Avi's teasing, the story that finally became the official version portrayed Avi as a bully and me as the guy who stood up to him. I was happy not to sound like a creepy homo in this version, but it wasn't completely accurate.

Avi and I weren't speaking. It's not that we were giving each other the silent treatment; we were just avoiding each other. But later that week, I was in the poolhouse bathroom when Avi caught me by the urinal. There was nobody else around. Stepping up to the urinal next to mine, he pulled out his dick again and looked at me.

"Hey, Benji," he said in a normal voice. "You want to touch it again?"

I scanned his face and mulled the question. Was this another joke, a trap to prove once and for all who the real fag was? Would Avi pack up and run as soon as I touched him, telling everyone what had happened? Would anyone believe Avi if he told? I got the benefit of the doubt once; would I get it again? And what if it wasn't a trap? What if he let me touch it for more than a second? What if I never wanted to let go?

What did I want? Why wasn't this a simple question?

"No," I told him, leaving him alone in the bathroom, but still re-membering how it felt to hold him in my clutching fingers.

I ducked out of my office around lunchtime on Friday and stopped by the rabbi's house. He'd given me his house keys, so I let myself in.

It was the first time I'd been in his house alone. Free to look around at my leisure.

The books fascinated me. There were so many—thou-sands, surely, spread throughout the whole house—that I lit-erally didn't know where to start. When I looked closely, however, I noticed that the rabbi did have a sort of system, a rhyme and reason that dictated which books went where.

Books of scripture and religious commentary crowded his office—these volumes looked like they'd been frequently read, their spines cracked and often crumbling. The living room had books on Jewish history, ancient and recent, in English and Hebrew and a few in Yiddish; the Holocaust made up a predictably large segment of these books. The dining room held oversize books of photography and art, cof-fee table books about Israeli archaeology and bygone shtetl life in Eastern Europe. Cookbooks, naturally, crowded the kitchen, covering recipes for every Jewish holiday, representing Jewish communities from around the world: *Hanukkah Specialties from Morocco, Passover Cooking Israeli Style, Shabbes with Bubbe: My Grandmother's Recipes from the Old Country,* and so on. (These books had been gathering dust, I surmised, since Sophie had passed away.) When I dared to enter the bedroom, its bed still unmade, I saw shelves of how-to and why-do-we-do-such-and-such books—about weddings, funerals, educating children. There was also a single shelf of poetry books—Jewish poetry—on one side of the bed. Were these Sophie's books? Did she get a shelf for herself, I wondered, and did the rabbi ever read these poems over her shoulder in bed?

The rabbi and I had no books in common in our respective homes. No surprise here—my own tastes ran to David Sedaris and Augusten Burroughs, Barbara Ehrenreich and Al Franken, Dennis Cooper and Michael Cunningham. But what surprised me was how different the rabbi's collection was from my parents'. In my parents' living room in Rockville, there was a fairly extensive collection of Jewish books, but in a very different vein. Fiction by Philip Roth, Bernard Malamud, and Sholom Aleichem was predominant. Their photo books contained nostalgic paintings by Marc Chagall and sepia-toned photographs from Ellis Island. Their cookbooks had titles like *Kosher Chinese Cuisine* and *The Modern Israeli Kitchen.* There was a copy of the Old Testament and a battered siddur that I'd used in Hebrew school, but that was about as far as our liturgy went. And their bookshelves held a host of non-Jewish books, from the Tom Clancy novels my mother devoured to the Civil War histories my father preferred, with the occasional biography of Bill Clinton or Martin Luther King Jr. thrown in for variety.

Two Jewish households.

I went to the rabbi's study to fetch his things. Alone in the room, I could have opened his drawers, rifled through his papers, discovered his most shameful secrets. But what kinds of secrets could an eighty-something widowed rabbi have? A resin-coated bong? A stash of Asian porn? Not Rabbi Zuckerman, I figured. This man didn't have any secrets.

I grabbed his glasses and his prayer book and left, locking the door behind me. Then I took the mail out of the mailbox at the end of his driveway and headed to Holy Cross.

The rabbi was napping when I arrived, but he quickly awoke when I sat down in the chair by his bedside.

"The doctors say I should be released very soon," he said. "Not tomorrow—I told them I would have no way to get home on Shabbat. But maybe Sunday."

"That's good news."

"Yes. I am tired of this place. Awful food. And this ridiculous gown. And no books."

I asked if the tests had revealed anything.

"They do not see any permanent damage," he said. "But they also said that these things often happen more than once."

"And that is the bad news," I said.

"The good and bad often come together," he said. Very sagelike, I thought.

I handed him his glasses and his siddur, which brought a smile to his face.

"I brought over your mail, too," I said.

He put on his reading glasses and I began announcing his mail piece by piece as I handed him each item, like I was his personal mailman.

"Bill."

"Bill."

"Valpak coupons."

"PBS solicitation."

"Bill."

"Bank statement."

"Preapproved credit card application."

I had only one piece of mail left in my hand, a small lavender envelope with a handwritten address made out to Zisel Zuckerman. The rabbi's first name was Jacob. I held up the letter for a moment and asked him, "Who's Zisel?"

His arm shot out at me with surprising speed and snatched the envelope from my hand. He tore it in half and tossed it in the wastebasket next to his bed.

"Benji!" he snapped, a scowl on his face. "Don't be a snoop!"

CHAPTER 6

By the time he left the hospital, the rabbi was back to his old self mentally. But physically he seemed frail, weaker.

The doctor told him that he needed more rest and that he should think about taking some time off from work. He wasn't convinced.

I visited him the Sunday he came home and told him that the doctor was right: He should take a break from work.

"How can I stay home? It's my store," he said, sitting in his usual spot on his sofa.

"It's only temporary," I answered. "Just a little time off."

He shook his head. "I can't."

"You must have taken time off at some point," I said. "When's the last time you got away from the store?"

"Oh, Sophie and I used to go away a lot," he said. "She loved it. If I ever said that I couldn't leave because I needed to work, she used to tell me, 'Even the good Lord, *baruch hashem*, set aside a time to rest.'"

"Where did you go?"

He rattled off a list of destinations. Los Angeles, where he had two nephews. New York, of course, to see Sophie's family. Israel, many times. London. Paris. Montreal. A kosher cruise once, through the Caribbean. And, as might be expected for Jews of a certain age, Florida. Over and over.

"Who used to watch the store while you were away?"

"Linda Goldfarb."

I raised an eyebrow.

"Sophie trusted her," he clarified. "And I trust her, too."

"That's not how it usually sounds," I said.

"She has worked for me for many years, Benji. Of course I trust her," he said. "That does not mean that I must also *like* her."

"I see."

"Although she is much easier to like when she is far away."

A smile crept across his face and I saw that he was softening.

I told him I'd drop off any mail or important papers at his house at the end of each day so he could keep an eye on things.

"What if, God forbid, there should be an emergency?" he asked.

"If there's an emergency, just call me and I'll come pick you up," I said, although I couldn't imagine what might constitute an emergency at the bookstore. Dust on the dust jackets? A strike at the yarmulke factory?

"That's very nice of you, but . . ."

As he spoke, he leaned forward to get up off his sofa, but quickly found that even this simple task was not so simple. He tried a second time, and a third before I reached over and offered my hand to pull him up and steady his balance. He was silent for a moment, embarrassed.

"Okay, Benji, I'll try," he said, conceding. "Just until I get my strength back."

The first day the rabbi stayed home, I stopped in the bookstore late in the afternoon to fetch the mail. Mrs. Goldfarb stopped what she was doing—putting together a special display of shofars and honey dishes and greeting cards for the High Holidays, which were coming early that year—and stepped behind the front counter. She put three bills in a manila folder, and then she wrote the day's total sales on a piece of memo paper, which she folded in quarters and slipped into the folder, as well.

"I don't know how you managed it, Benjamin," she said. "I've been telling him for months to take some time off, and he's never listened to me."

"Doesn't it mean more work for you?" I asked.

"That's a small price to pay," she said without elaborating.

I couldn't quite figure why they didn't get along. Mrs. Goldfarb had once told me that she and the rabbi were just "two very different people," but I didn't buy it. Maybe the real problem was that they were too similar: bossy, opinionated, strong-willed. But I didn't dare suggest that to her.

"If you don't get along, why do you work here?" I asked.

"It wasn't always like this," she said. "When Mrs. Zuckerman was alive, this was a very nice place to work. She was a wonderful woman. And he was a whole different person when she was around. But ever since she died . . ."

She trailed off. I didn't say anything.

"Years ago, he couldn't have run the store without her," Mrs. Goldfarb continued. "Today, he couldn't run the store without me. We both know it. That's what keeps me here. And that's why he resents me."

"I don't know if he resents you," I offered.

"Benjamin, please. I can handle it. He's a very angry old man. But you, he seems to like," she said. "Oh, that reminds me. He wanted me to give you something."

She took a small dish off the counter and handed it to me. It was ceramic, with a single red apple in the center and tiny yellow bees around the edge.

"Sorry I didn't wrap it for you," she said. "I told him I would."

"What's this for?"

"It's a honey dish. You dip apples in it. For Rosh Hashanah."

"I know it's a honey dish, but why are you giving it to me?"

"Rabbi Zuckerman called this morning and asked me to give it to you for him," she said. "As a gift."

"That doesn't sound like him."

"You're telling me. In all the years I've known him, this is the very first time he's ever given away something from his store as a present."

I studied her for a moment, to see if she was pulling my leg. She wasn't. She shrugged.

"First time for everything," she said.

I held out the dish and rubbed my thumb over the apple.

"I don't get it," I said.

"You don't?"

I shook my head.

"You're like the grandson he never had."

The rabbi wasn't the easiest person to thank. I tried, but he was difficult.

"Mrs. Goldfarb gave me your present," I said that evening as he scanned the day's bills.

"It's nothing, Benji," he said without looking up, "a tiny gesture."

"Yes, but it's really not necessary."

"It is necessary," he said. "You need a honey dish."

"Why?"

"Because you didn't have one," he said. He put the bills down and peered over his glasses. "Am I right?"

He had me there, circular logic and all.

"Now you do. And now you can have a sweet new year."

I smiled. "Well, thank you."

He nodded and went back to his paperwork. And without a word, the subject was closed.

* * *

Even though the rabbi wasn't going to work, he got dressed every day in the same slacks and button-down shirt he would have worn to the store. I viewed this as a positive sign.

Some afternoons when I stopped by, he'd invite me in and we'd chat. Other times, he was in the middle of something— typically reading upstairs in his study—and he'd take the papers from my hand with a quick "thank you" while we stood in the doorway, then I'd simply turn around and drive home.

Either way, his strength was improving and his spirits seemed fine. Calm and relaxed.

He was even making jokes. Once, just after Labor Day, when I handed him the day's bills, he held them up to his nose and sniffed them. I asked what he was doing, and he said, "I'm just checking to see if Linda Goldfarb is smoking in the store."

"I'm sure she isn't," I said, although I didn't honestly know.

"She's probably too busy popping open bottles of champagne because I'm not there," he said.

I tried to reassure him: "No, I'm sure she's—"

"I don't mind," he said, interrupting me. "I'm so happy not to see her every day, I'd be drinking champagne myself if my doctor would let me."

He smiled, and I realized that he was putting me on.

"Fortunately, at my age, good old-fashioned ginger ale pretty much does the trick," he said. "I pour a bit of Canada Dry into a wineglass before dinner and drink a toast to Linda Goldfarb in absentia, and it's almost like New Year's Eve in here. Actually, it's better than New Year's Eve. It's like Sukkot!"

"I think those bubbles are going straight to your head," I said, joining him in a chuckle.

"You know, Benji, maybe this was a good idea after all, taking some time off," he told me as we sat in his living room. "I haven't had a vacation in ages."

Vacation. It wasn't the word I'd have used to describe the rabbi's situation. For most people, "vacation" involves lounging on a beach with a cocktail, toes digging tracks in the sand. Sitting home alone, taking blood thinners, studying Talmud or Torah or whatever the rabbi was studying—that wouldn't be what most people would call a vacation. But I went along with it.

"What was your favorite place to go on vacation?" I asked.

"Sophie loved Miami Beach," he said. "We bought a condo there about fifteen years ago. We were getting too old to schlep our luggage from hotel to hotel every time we went, so we got our own place. We would go down every Passover, and for a week every January, and over Thanksgiving. Sometimes just for a long weekend, too, if the cold weather got bad."

"Sounds like a nice place," I said.

"It is," he said. "It was. Sophie used to talk about retiring there."

I couldn't imagine the rabbi retiring. What would he do? Play shuffleboard with the other old rabbis?

"When's the last time you went?" I asked.

"I haven't been there since Sophie passed away. I could never go back."

"Well, you could always—"

"Never," he interrupted, poking the air with his index finger, pointing straight up. "End of discussion."

"He's taking advantage of you, Benji."

My mother. On the phone.

"He's not taking advantage of me, Mom. This whole thing was my idea."

"Then maybe you're the one who needs to see a doctor," she replied. "To have your head examined."

"What's the big deal? It's hardly out of my way to drop off his mail."

"So you're a rabbi's servant now?"

"He doesn't have anyone else, Mom."

"Maybe there's a reason for that."

"I'm sorry I brought it up."

"Benji, it doesn't make any sense what you're doing. What he needs is a home health aide or something, whatever they're called. You know, a nurse to keep an eye on him."

"He doesn't need a nurse."

"You said he was in the hospital."

"Yes, he had a little stroke, but he's fine now."

"And you're suddenly an expert in strokes? I didn't realize you were premed at Maryland."

"Come on."

"Look, he's got you running his errands for him, driving him around, delivering his mail. And what's he paying you?"

I paused. "Nothing."

"Exactly. He's taking advantage of you."

"It's not like that."

"Explain to me how it's not."

"I can't explain it, Mom. I guess I kind of feel sorry for him. He's all alone, with no real friends, and no relatives nearby. All he really wants is someone to talk to once in a while."

"So let him pay a shrink."

I stopped to think of a better way to get through to her.

I began: "If you died and—"

"God *forbid!*"

"Yes, if you died, *God forbid,* and Dad was all alone, wouldn't you want someone to look in on him and make sure he was okay?"

"Now you're talking nonsense."

"Why is that nonsense?"

"Because you live just a few miles away. He wouldn't have to turn to a stranger. He'd have you."

"Well, in the meantime, I suppose the rabbi has me, too."

She was silent. We were at an impasse.

"Fine, so he can have you," she said, changing the subject. "Can we borrow you just for one day? Your sister is flying in for Rosh Hashanah, with that husband of hers."

"His name is Richard, Mom."

She ignored me.

"Will you be coming to services with us?" she asked. "Or will you be going to the Orthodox shul with your rabbi this year?"

Apparently, we had progressed into sarcasm.

"Actually, I was thinking that this year I'd have a voodoo ceremony for Rosh Hashanah. Something with witchcraft and chanting and animal sacrifice."

"Nothing you say surprises me at this point, Benji," she said.

"Of course I'm coming to services," I said. We went through this every year.

"Good. Get a haircut before then."

"You haven't seen me in weeks. How do you know I need a haircut?"

"I'm your mother," she said, and hung up.

Michelle was trying to figure out her plans for Rosh Hashanah, too.

She called me at my office midafternoon, distraught. About Dan. She said she needed to talk to me after work, and before I hung up, I'd been roped into dinner and a movie at Union Station, not far from her office.

I'd played this role before, so even when I was still on the subway heading downtown to meet her, I already knew what the evening would involve: We'd meet in the food court and order cheesesteaks, but eat them open-faced to save a few calories, and she'd ask me how my day was. I'd have about six minutes before she got tired of listening to me and then she'd change the subject and spend the rest of the meal going on and on about her latest boyfriend troubles. I'd nod along, eat most of the french fries, and cut her off when it was time for the movie. We'd see some kind of stupid Hollywood comedy; we'd both laugh out loud while it was showing, and then talk about how lame it was when it was over. By then she'd be feeling better and she'd apologize for unloading on me. She'd give me a kiss and we'd go home and go to sleep.

I'd been helping Michelle in similar ways, with a dozen other boyfriends, for years.

I thought I might get more than my usual time at Union Station because I had something juicy to share: I'd scored a date that afternoon with a model from one of my Paradise ads.

"Let me guess," she said, after a quick gasp, as we carried our dinner trays to a booth. "Blond."

"That's the best part," I said. "He shaves his head. No hair at all!"

I hadn't honestly entertained the possibility that one of my models would hit on me, but Frankie had been pretty obvious about it. When I told him he needed to take off his shirt for a test shot, he looked me straight in the eye and said, "I will if you will."

"Did you do it?" Michelle asked.

"I'm a professional," I protested. "And by that I mean: Yes, I did. But I kept my pants on."

"For now."

"We'll see what happens without all those cameras around."

Michelle reached across the table and squeezed my hand. "Well, I'm glad one of us is having fun," she said, shifting the spotlight back to her as she launched into a story about Dan and one of his previous girlfriends.

"So he says that he just *happened* to bump into her last week and he just *happened* to be on his way to lunch and so he invited her to come along and she did and what's the big deal," she said as I mooched her fries. "And I'm like, 'The big deal is that she's your freakin' *ex*-girlfriend and you're not supposed to be going on dates with her.' And he's all, 'It wasn't a date,' and I'm all, 'If it wasn't a date, then why didn't you tell me about it for a whole week?' And he says, 'Because I knew you'd overreact.' Like the whole thing was my fault. Can you even believe him?"

Sitting here watching Michelle have a meltdown about what seemed to me like an innocent lunch, I *could* believe him. But I didn't mention that to her. Not that she paused long enough for me to interject anything anyway.

"So I told him that if he wanted to see her so much, maybe he should take *her* to the Redskins game this Sunday, and have *her* help him pick out new work clothes this weekend, and go home with *her* for Rosh Hashanah."

"Is she Jewish?" I asked.

"Of course she's Jewish. God, are you even *listening?* I was supposed to bring Dan home to Philly for Rosh Hashanah next week. I was going to introduce him to my parents. But now I don't know what to do."

"I'll go home with you," I joked. "And Dan can spend Rosh Hashanah with my parents. That could be his punishment."

She smiled, and her tirade derailed. "Your parents are great, Benji."

"Okay, then *you* spend Rosh Hashanah with them, and I'll take Dan to Philly to meet your parents, and he can be my boyfriend from now on."

Her eyes narrowed a bit. "He's cute, right?"

"He's cute," I said. "Cute and straight. And he's obviously into you, going to meet your family. Guys don't take that kind of thing lightly. I should know—I'm a guy, remember?"

She picked at her sandwich, which was getting cold.

"I'm sure he'll apologize," I said. "Once you start taking his calls." She had turned off her cell phone to avoid talking to him.

"And then what? That's it?"

"And then you forgive him," I said.

"Why should I?"

"Because forgiveness is what the High Holidays are all about."

She pursed her lips.

"You've been spending too much time with that rabbi," she said.

On Rosh Hashanah, my whole family planned to go to services together. Rachel and Richard had flown in the day before; they were staying with my parents in Rockville, despite the fact that my folks didn't much care for their son-in-law.

I drove over in the morning, singing along with the radio as I cruised up Rockville Pike, the eight-lane main drag where I spent most of my free time in high school. Some of the stores in the back-to-back strip malls had changed—a cell phone dealer where Blockbuster used to be, a Payless instead of a Fayva, an enormous new Barnes & Noble—but the basics were the same as they'd been for years: multiplex movie theaters, fast-food joints, Old Navy and Einstein's Bagels and three branches of Starbucks. "Everything you could ever want is right here. I don't know why anyone would ever need to go into the city," my mother used to say—and I used to agree with her.

While it was only a few blocks off the Pike, my parents' development was much quieter. Two-story colonial houses lined curved streets and shaded cul-de-sacs. Wide front yards were neatly mowed, the shutters neatly painted. The long white driveways revealed what type of people lived in these homes: While the occasional minivan or SUV, and even the odd sporty coupe, could be spotted, the bulk of the cars were the kind that middle-class families everywhere drive—neither bottom of the line nor top of the line, valued for their roominess and gas mileage and safety record, but with a hint of imported style. Camrys, Accords, Jettas, as well as a handful of Volvo hatchbacks, in muted blues and reds.

I pulled in behind my parents' new Altima and walked across the front yard, past the flowerbeds my mother now had professionally tended.

My sister met me at the door with a one-armed hug. Even though we'd grown closer as adults, after we'd both left home, we were never the type for fawning kisses and extravagant affection. "You look nice," she said. I shrugged; I was wearing my only suit, the same one I'd had since college, the same one I wore every Rosh Hashanah.

Richard, the warmer of the two, hugged me harder and said, "Man, it's good to see *you*." I surmised that their visit wasn't going well.

"We're going with Benji, we'll meet you there!" Rachel called upstairs, where my parents were still getting dressed. And off we went.

On the drive to synagogue, they griped about my parents, who never quite understood what Richard's job as a consultant for tech companies entailed; they kept asking when he was planning on getting a "real" job and how they'd ever start a family if he was "out of work." He explained that compared to most people with full-time jobs, he was bringing in more money and working fewer hours, which actually left him with more time for a family, but they didn't get it. They badgered my sister about having children—in quips that were only half-kidding. She was almost thirty. If she waited much longer, they told her at every opportunity, she'd miss her chance. ("You can always go back to your little gardening job later," my mother would tell her, referring to my sister's job managing a plant nursery. "But you won't be able to have children forever.")

I was lucky, I realized. My parents and I mostly got along. They'd never complained about my work—they were even largely supportive when I opened my own office—and they never pressured me about relationships or kids. Aside from my mom's occasional peevish lecture, they stayed off my back. "That's because you're the favorite," said Rachel, who'd never quite gotten past her childhood resentments, despite our adult detente. "Their only son. And their baby." I usually tried to avoid dredging up our prepubescent tensions, so I told her it wasn't true. But it was, partly.

Waiting for my parents in Congregation Beth Shalom's parking lot, we saw a lot of familiar faces, people Rachel or I had gone to Hebrew school with, or friends of our parents. We both got a lot of attention—Rachel because she lived thousands of miles away, so seeing her was a rarity, and me because I might as well have lived thousands of miles away considering how infrequently I showed up at synagogue.

We saw the Siegels, who lived around the corner from my parents and used to invite us over for barbecues when we were little. And Mrs. Horowitz, whose son Dean dated Rachel in tenth grade; he was living on Long Island, we already knew, doing something that made him very wealthy, and living in a very big house with a wife and kids. And Miriam Goldstein, who went to Hebrew school with me, walking in with Howie Goldstein, who was also in our class and was now, since that spring, her husband. ("I wonder if she thinks she's using her maiden name or her married name," I whispered to Rachel. "Or maybe she hyphenates: Miriam Goldstein-Goldstein.") Plus a random collection of people who knew us well enough to gossip about us, but not well enough to remember any of the actual, relevant details of our lives.

Each of the conversations went something like this:

"Rachel Steiner, is that you?"

"It's Rachel Silber now, but yes, it's me."

"Oh, it's so nice to see you! You look just wonderful. And I remember your husband . . ."

"Richard."

"Of course, Richard. We met last year. How's life out in . . ."

"Seattle."

"Right, Seattle."

"It's great. I'm still working at the nursery, and Richard's still working with tech companies."

"Microsoft?"

"Well, he's a consultant, so he works for himself."

"Oh."

Richard would pipe in: "Microsoft is one of my clients."

"How nice. And little Benjamin, my goodness, I hardly even recognize you. It seems like your bar mitzvah was just yesterday. How have you been?"

"Fine," I'd say.

"Still no ring on that finger?"

"Nope."

"Well, you're still young, probably dating a different girl every night of the week. Am I right? They're probably knocking down your door, you're so handsome."

This was one of the many reasons I didn't like to go to my old synagogue. I'd come out years before, when I was in college. All of my friends knew, my family knew, and even most of my parents' friends knew. My parents were fine about having a gay son, for the most part. But they were still a bit uncomfortable telling "everyone"—meaning, they were fine telling people privately that their son was gay, but they weren't ready to come out publicly. In my world, I did what I wanted and everyone knew I was gay; but Congregation Beth Shalom was their world, not mine, and I deferred to their sense of what was appropriate. I didn't exactly lie, but I kept my mouth shut. So when I was faced with questions about why I hadn't gotten married yet, I'd answer with something like this:

"I just haven't met the right person yet."

I hated it.

My parents arrived and we filed inside. We had assigned seats for the holidays—the expensive seats, not the folding chairs lined up in the back of the room—and it took us a while to find them. My father sat on one end, next to my mother, who sat next to Rachel so the two of them could pass judgment on every other woman's outfit. Richard sat next to my sister, and I sat on the other side of him, because I honestly didn't mind my brother-in-law a bit.

I spotted Mrs. Goldfarb across the room, sitting alone. I nodded at her and she gave me a little wave.

The service was endless, just as I remembered it. Stand up, sit down. Pray silently, sing together. Read responsively in English, sing responsively in Hebrew. For hours and hours. And I was trapped, sitting against the wall. I couldn't sneak out without climbing over my entire family, and if I'd tried, my mother would have shot me a look that would have stopped me in my tracks. So I sat there, noticing how the men—wearing dark suits and conservative ties, traditional prayer shawls and unremarkable shoes—expressed their individuality through their yarmulkes: blue-and-white crocheted with a star of David, shiny crimson satin probably from someone's wedding, chic gray suede, burgundy and gold with a Washington Redskins design. I wondered how many of these designs Mrs. Goldfarb sold in the bookstore. It would surely have been more interesting than selling black yarmulke after black yarmulke to customers from B'nai Tikvah.

The choir, a bunch of old ladies selected more for their spare time than their musical talent, added a note of atonality to the proceedings. And the man blowing the shofar looked like he was about to keel over from the strain; he was red and sweaty and short on breath. It was not what you'd call a lively service.

But the low point was the sermon. It was the only time of the year when Rabbi Adler, who had led the congregation for some thirty years and was making noises about retirement, had pretty much the entire synagogue as a captive audience, upwards of a thousand people. He could have talked about so many things: the war in Iraq, peace in the Middle East, global warming, the following year's presidential race that was already kicking into high gear. He even could have stuck specifically to religion, talking about the crumbling wall separating church and state in America, or interfaith dialogue with Muslims and Christians.

Instead, Rabbi Adler took this rare opportunity to exhort his congregation to come to synagogue more often. A guilt trip, aimed squarely at the people who had skipped services since the previous High Holidays. And Rabbi Adler wasn't the greatest speaker in the first place; my mother could have given a better guilt trip in five minutes and had plenty of time left over to talk about real issues while the sisterhood handed out grape juice and petit fours.

My parents had been talking a great deal about how the Conservative movement was changing. It was about time, as far as I was concerned; my father liked to talk about how the Conservative movement played a key role in the civil rights struggles of the sixties and helped redefine women's role in Judaism in the eighties, but all I saw was a stagnant movement that hadn't kept up with the changing times for as long as I could remember. My father said they finally had some new faces leading the movement and policies around gay issues in particular—marriage, ordaining rabbis—had started to shift.

So the movement was changing. That didn't mean Rabbi Adler was any more enlightened as an individual. I had heard his opinions on gay issues several years earlier.

*   *   *

Everyone preparing for a bar or bat mitzvah at Congregation Beth Shalom was required to attend Saturday morning services regularly, to learn the prayers. So I sat there every week with my parents, wearing my brown loafers and my red tie and my blue blazer, listening to Rabbi Adler.

Before long, I learned the service pretty much by heart, and I took my cues from each page number Rabbi Adler announced.

Page 128: Beginning of the Torah service. Close the prayer book and pick up the Chumash, *which contains all the Torah portions along with translations and commentary. Flip pages until you find something interesting to read—either a familiar Bible story or an incredibly arcane commandment that has apparently generated centuries of rabbinical philosophizing.*

Page 139: The Amidah. *Stand silently for ten minutes, rocking back and forth, bending occasionally at the knee. Look around the sanctuary to see who else isn't really reading the prayer.*

And so on. Very little changed from week to week, other than the sermon.

Oftentimes, Rabbi Adler would pull a lesson out of the Torah portion and spin it into a speech. Other times, he'd focus on a less ancient subject by plucking something from the week's headlines: peace talks in Israel, universal health care, the Redskins' playoff hopes. He tried, given his limited skills as an orator, to keep things interesting.

But one October morning, he gave a sermon I'd never forget— about homosexuality. Here, the Bible and the Washington Post *were in synch: The Torah portion that week was from Genesis, and included the story of Sodom and Gomorrah. And that week in the* Post, *the debate over gays in the military had made headlines on the front page and the editorial page.*

Rabbi Adler wasn't some crazed right-winger ranting about sodomites. No, he spoke calmly about "homosexuals" and the ways they were trying to undermine traditional institutions, from the family to the military, the schools to our houses of worship. He spoke of a "homosexual agenda," and the general decaying of moral stan-

dards in America. He said he had compassion for homosexuals' sad plight—he meant AIDS, although this went without saying—but did not believe in giving them "special rights."

"If you want to see what happens to a society where our codes of morality are turned upside down, where perversion is treated as a reasonable choice, you need look no further than today's Torah portion. The Jewish community does not turn away people struggling with sin, whether they are homosexuals or adulterers, drug abusers or common criminals. But neither can we pretend that their sins are not sins. On this question, when it comes to homosexuality, the Torah says there is but one answer."

Not yet thirteen years old, I wasn't out of the closet. I wasn't even sure that I was in any closet yet. But I did have an inkling that Rabbi Adler was talking about me.

I knew that I didn't have any interest in girls. I knew that when I was alone in bed at night, I thought about other guys—guys I had seen in the gym locker room, or on television, or at the mall. I knew that this wasn't something I should talk about with anyone, not my parents or my sister or my best friends.

And I knew that in several weeks' time, Rabbi Adler would be on the bimah *with me, congratulating me on my bar mitzvah, welcoming me as a full member of the community, even as he had already, proactively, unknowingly cast me out.*

Rabbi Adler wrapped up his sermon, and then, as if his pronouncements had been utterly casual, he returned to the service.

Page 157: "Ein Keloheynu." *Such a pretty song. This means the service is almost over—time to get fidgety.* Am I really a sinner? I haven't even done anything yet.

Page 158: The Aleynu. *Closer, closer. Stand up, stretch your legs, and don't forget that funny bow in the middle.* So it's like being a drug addict—maybe there's a way to quit. Although I haven't even done anything yet.

Page 162: "Adon Olam." *At last, the end of the service. Cake and coffee to follow in the social hall.* I wonder if there's a way to stop the dreams.

We all filed out of the sanctuary into the social hall, where my parents loaded up their plates with cookies and cake and started chatting with some of their friends. I grabbed a minibagel and walked outside to sit on the steps on the side of the synagogue.

Joanne Gruber was already sitting there. She was in my Hebrew school class, too. And like me, she was a bit of a geek: braces, short frizzy hair, plastic-rimmed glasses. Joanne and I weren't really buddies, but we got along well enough. We'd known each other for years.

"What's going on?" I asked.

"Just waiting for my parents."

"Are they inside?"

"No, they drop me off and pick me up," she said. "And they're usually late."

As bad as it was being dragged to synagogue with my parents every Saturday—I complained to no end that it was unfair that Rachel, a senior in high school, didn't have to go—I knew that it'd be even worse if I had to come without them.

"I can't wait till this bar mitzvah prep is over, so we can stop coming here every week," I said.

"When's yours?" she asked me, motioning for me to sit down with her on the steps.

"December," I said, taking a seat. "Invitations went out yesterday."

She paused. "Am I invited?"

"Yeah."

"Cool. You're invited to mine, too. It's in January."

She looked pleased. I offered her half of my minibagel, which she declined.

We talked for a few more minutes, about our eighth-grade teachers, the new Nirvana album, the other kids in our class.

Then Joanne asked me if I had a date for the Homecoming dance at school the next weekend. Of course, I didn't. Joanne asked me if I wanted to go with her.

I looked at her. She was nice enough, and smart enough. The fact that she wasn't one of the "pretty" girls in my class didn't matter much to me, because I didn't like the pretty girls. I didn't even like looking at the pretty girls—eyeliner and hair clips and expensive sweaters didn't draw my eye, and neither did the pretty girls' chests, which had apparently developed with superhuman speed over the summer.

Joanne wasn't the problem. I was. Boys at school already called me "gaywad" and "fag" because I sang in the chorus, ran and threw and jumped "like a girl" whenever we played sports during gym, and made the crucial mistake of hanging an ad for the movie Benny and Joon *in my locker; I took it down after one day, but the "Benji loves Johnny Depp" taunts had lasted for months. Would showing up at the Homecoming dance with Joanne Gruber make my problems better or worse?*

"Forget it," she said after an awkward moment. "We should just skip the stupid dance. I mean, who cares?"

"No, no, I'll go," I said.

Now she looked very pleased.

My father opened the door behind us. "There you are, Benji. We were looking for you. You ready to go?"

I looked back and nodded.

He went inside. I scooted off my step and turned to follow him. But before I did, I leaned down and gave Joanne Gruber a kiss.

She was caught by surprise, but didn't pull back.

It was the first time I kissed a girl. Right there on the steps of Congregation Beth Shalom. And I felt nothing but the braces on her teeth.

The Monday after Rosh Hashanah, the bookstore reopened, so I stopped by to pick up mail and paperwork for the rabbi when I was done with work, and then headed up the hill. He was in a good mood and invited me in for a slice of an apple cake from the kosher bakery; since the rabbi had been such a loyal customer, the owner had delivered the cake himself.

"It is not as good as Sophie used to make," he said, offering me a plate. "But it is sweet, and that is the important part."

He wished me a happy new year in Hebrew—that much I could decipher—and then something else that didn't sound familiar. I nodded my thanks.

I asked how his holiday was. I knew it was his first Rosh Hashanah as a widower. But he seemed less maudlin than I'd seen him in weeks. He told me he had walked to shul each day. I gave him a scolding look, to remind him that such exertion was not good for him, but I didn't say a word.

And that was it. His big holiday: walking to synagogue a couple of times and a few slices of store-bought apple cake.

He seemed happy. Perhaps he didn't expect anything more elaborate.

"And you?" he asked tentatively.

"I went to services with my family," I said. He seemed relieved—could he even imagine a Jew *not* going to services on Rosh Hashanah?

"At Congregation Beth Shalom," I continued. Did a Conservative synagogue count?

"In Rockville. Linda Goldfarb's congregation. Rabbi Adler," he said, as if reciting information off an index card. "He sends us many customers."

I didn't detect any disapproval in his voice at all. Maybe he was more open-minded than I thought. Or maybe, I thought, religion is religion but business is business.

"And how was his service?" the rabbi asked.

Without going into detail, I said simply: "Boring."

"How can such a service be boring?"

"It just was. It always is."

"But how? We look back on our deeds from the past year, we ask the Lord, *baruch hashem*, to inscribe us in the book of life for another year. It is a time to think deeply, to pray that we are worthy of another year on this earth."

I wondered what Sophie did that made her unworthy of another year. But I didn't dare say that aloud. I wondered if the rabbi prayed for another year alone on this earth, or if he secretly wished to join his wife before the next High Holiday season. But I didn't dare say that, either.

"I guess I'm just not a synagogue person," I said, a bit sheepishly.

"You don't have to go to synagogue to be a good Jew," he said.

I looked at him quizzically. This wasn't what I was expecting to hear from a rabbi. An Orthodox rabbi.

"Benji, this is a new year. It is a chance to start over, to give your faith another chance. You don't want to light candles. You do not want to go to synagogue. Fine, this I understand. But I also know that you are a kind person, a good son, a young man with strong morals, a true mensch who does good deeds without being asked in advance or demanding anything in return. You do not know it, but already you are on the path of righteousness. You are already, in many ways, a good Jew."

"I don't feel like a very good Jew." This was true. I didn't keep kosher, go to synagogue regularly, donate money to B'nai Brith—I didn't do any of the things I was raised to believe were the most important things for a Jew to do.

"Then your journey is to find out how to connect your Judaism with your deeds," he said. "This means finding God in everything you already do, and doing everything with God in your heart. Once you have done this, then you will feel differently about synagogue, keeping kosher, lighting candles for Shabbat."

I had never heard the rabbi speak with such openness. I wished he had led our Rosh Hashanah services instead of Rabbi Adler.

I told him I'd think about what he said—and I meant it. After all, even if I wasn't sure the rabbi was the person to help me find my way as I tried to figure out how being Jewish fit into my life, at least he understood the journey I was on.

Then I said I had to get going.

"Michelle is coming back from Philadelphia tonight and I want to hear how her holiday went."

"Who is Michelle?"

"My roommate."

"You never told me you had a roommate," he said.

Gently, but with a matter-of-fact tone, I replied: "You never asked."

Apparently, the rabbi took this remark to heart, because the next evening when I stopped by, he invited me in for another slice of apple cake and this time, for the first time, he asked *me* a lot of questions.

He started with my family. I told him about my parents, and my sister, and growing up in Rockville. Public school, Hebrew school, having Mrs. Goldfarb as a teacher. (He found this last item particularly interesting: "Ah, so this explains your inexplicable bond!")

He asked about my work. I told him about my previous jobs, and opening my own office. I told him about a few of my clients: the gardening newsletter, the rock club posters. I didn't mention Paradise.

Then we got to the subject I think he most wanted to discuss all along: Michelle.

"You are not married, but you are living together?"

"Yes."

He shook his head.

"You said she is Jewish?"

I had mentioned her going home for Rosh Hashanah.

"Yes."

"Benji, I am glad she is Jewish, but you know this is still not right. Living together without being married. This is very serious. You don't keep kosher or observe Shabbat? You are the only one who can make this decision. But living with a woman who is not your wife is completely different—here you are not only breaking rules, but you are encouraging someone else to break the rules. And you are making light of a deeply sacred human bond."

"It's not like that," I said. "We're just roommates."

"I do not understand."

"Separate bedrooms. We just share an apartment."

"A man and a woman do not just share an apartment," he said. "With such intimacy, there is always temptation to do the wrong thing."

"Believe me, there's no temptation," I said.

"What do you mean?"

I could have simply come out and told him I was gay. But I didn't. I don't know why I hesitated. I wasn't ashamed of being gay. I wasn't deferring to my parents' sensitivities, the way I did at synagogue. But I did look up to the rabbi, as someone whose opinion mattered, someone whose feelings needed to be considered. This might be too much for him to handle, I told myself, and anyway, it wasn't necessary for him to know everything.

"Michelle isn't my type," I said, figuring that would suffice.

"And how do you know she is not interested in you?" he asked.

"Oh, we've been down that road before, in college. It, um, didn't work out."

He looked at me, confused. Did he know what road I was talking about? Did I need to spell it all out: the awkward kiss, the hurt feelings, the whole it's-not-you-it's-me speech? I decided to leave it at that.

"There are many things I do not understand about young people today," said the rabbi.

"Trust me, it works," I said. I considered making a reference to *Will & Grace*, but quickly realized it would go right over his head.

We continued to talk, and the rabbi kept the focus on me. We talked about the uncomfortable family dinner I'd endured on Rosh Hashanah after services. We discussed my relationship with Rachel and Richard. We discussed—very gingerly—the war in Iraq, the upcoming presidential primary season, and my connection to Israel. He kept the questions coming and I kept providing answers.

But some things I did not tell him. I didn't tell him that his apple cake had gotten stale. I didn't tell him that I was pretty sure I didn't believe in God. And I certainly didn't tell him that I had a date the next night—just days before Yom Kippur—with a tattooed skinhead named Frankie, a non-Jewish guy who was the half-naked model for my latest ad promoting Paradise, a venue where homosexuals gathered to drink excessively and pick one another up.

Some things, I reasoned, a rabbi just didn't need to know.

CHAPTER 7

Business picked up dramatically in late September, as the little website I started for the rabbi paid off. I sent it out as a sample of my work to land a new client, who offered me a job designing graphics for a start-up website where local bands would sell digital downloads of their music. Along with the perk of giving me a lot of new music to listen to, the gig paid well, and seemed likely to help me land other online jobs and expand my business.

Not that I really had time to do it. My plate was already pretty full and the website's deadlines were brutally short—it was set to launch before Thanksgiving. There were more than twenty bands involved and each one had had a page that required its own distinctive graphic design; it was a logistical nightmare. I figured I'd have to work nights and weekends for a couple of months to get it all done on time.

I didn't give up my other clients: the gardening group, the rock club, Paradise. By this point, most of this work had its own momentum and offered me regular paychecks.

I didn't stop visiting the rabbi—although I usually went back to the office after I dropped off his mail. He needed me: He wanted to build a sukkah, as he'd done every year in his backyard for Sukkot. I knew he couldn't do it alone, but I also knew he'd never ask for help. So I simply helped, unasked, for a few minutes every evening, screwing together the old metal frame, stringing fruit to hang inside, or laying fronds across the open roof. When the holiday arrived and we'd finished, I'd sit in the sukkah with him and share a snack from the bakery—at his insistence.

I didn't stop dating Frankie. The fact that I was working long hours didn't interfere with our plans, since he was a night owl who usually didn't even think about going out before ten. And going out with him was a great way to blow off steam. We didn't have long conversations at romantic restaurants; we were more likely to down several drinks and go dancing at noisy clubs until two in the morning, and then head back to his place and stay up for another hour or two, even on weeknights. Often, at the end of a long day, that's just what I needed. I certainly wasn't going to cut a hot man out of my schedule.

Something had to give. And that something, most of the time, was sleep.

By the end of October, I was exhausted. I'd catch myself staring into space at the office, half-awake. One more month, I'd tell myself. One more month.

"Man, you always poop out just when things are getting going," Frankie admonished me the fourth or fifth time I suggested leaving a club before he was ready. "It's like I'm dating an old man."

"You're never around anymore," Michelle would whine when I'd come home late. She was concerned. Or maybe she was just lonely. Either way, Dan started spending more time at our place on weekends, since they pretty much had the place to themselves.

"You're going to make yourself sick," my mother warned several times over the phone, claiming she could hear the exhaustion in my voice. I told her that I'd be able to take a breath around Thanksgiving. But she didn't like that answer: "You need to take it easy," she'd say, "before you give yourself an ulcer." Then she'd ask me over for Shabbat dinner, as if that was the most relaxing, fun thing I could possibly imagine doing. Once or twice, I said yes.

I knew things were serious when my sister called to invite me to visit her in Seattle for Thanksgiving. She had undoubtedly been prompted by my mother; Rachel and I preferred to communicate by e-mail, which made the time difference less annoying, so phone calls were usually saved for birthdays and the occasional "big news." There was no big news to report this time. "You can stay in the guest room and use my car," she said. "You've never been out here, you know, and Seattle has a pretty good gay scene from what I hear." She had never invited me to visit, which is why I sensed my mother's intervention. Still, it was tempting, despite the fact that I didn't really want my sister giving me listings of gay bars with directions printed up from Mapquest, and then asking me for the details in the morning over coffee. But who the hell wants to go to Seattle in November, when it's cold and dark and rainy? Thanks, but no thanks.

Unfortunately, I knew they were right. I was working too hard. I needed a break before I wore myself out.

The rabbi had a photo album open on his coffee table when I came to visit one evening.

He invited me to sit and look at some pictures with him. I politely demurred, even though I was interested. "I'm sorry, I really can't tonight," I said, standing in the foyer, my voice hoarse from lack of sleep. "I've got to get back to the office."

His eyes narrowed.

"You're working too hard," the rabbi told me. "Every night this week you've gone right back to the office after you bring the mail. And you're not sleeping enough. I can tell. This isn't right."

"What else can I do?" I asked him, covering a yawn with my hand. "It's my business."

"Benji, this is very funny coming from you."

"Why?"

"Why?" he echoed. "Because you are the one who convinced me to take time away from my business. You are the one who convinced me that there were things that were more important than work. And you were right."

He took a seat on his couch, eating salted almonds from the candy dish. His brow was unfurrowed, his shoulders relaxed, his eyes bright. He was positively peaceful, pure contentment wrapped in a gray cardigan.

"If I had not taken this time away from work, who knows where I'd be today," he said. "Probably back in that hospital. But thanks to you, I have been resting, thinking about other things besides work. And I feel better than I've felt in months."

In the beginning, it had been hard for him to distance himself from the store, but after the High Holidays, his attitude changed and he relaxed into his new routine. He'd recently begun talking about going back to work one or two days a week, but without any sense of urgency—maybe November, maybe December. He was a changed man.

"You taught me this lesson," he said. "And now I will try to teach you your own lesson in return. You need to take some time off from work."

"I guess you're right," I conceded. "I'll think of a place to go once work quiets down."

The rabbi took off his glasses, thinking for a moment.

"Wait one minute," he said, getting up and walking into the kitchen. I heard him open a drawer, fumbling around for a few seconds. Then he came back to the living room with his fist closed. He walked over to where I stood and opened his fist.

He dangled a keychain in front of me.

"What are these?" I asked, reaching out to take the keys.

"Keys to the condo in Miami Beach," he said.

I looked down at the keys in my open palm.

"I don't know," I said.

"Wait, I'll show you a picture," he said, fetching the photo album from the table. Standing with me by the front door, he flipped a few pages until he reached a pair of snapshots: one of Sophie standing on a balcony and one of the rabbi and Sophie together at a dining room table—Sophie looking at the camera, the rabbi looking at Sophie. In the first picture, clearly taken years earlier, Sophie stood tall, eyes bright behind her glasses, a broad smile spreading wrinkles across her cheeks, her short hair dyed that rust color that hair salons save for women of a certain age. In the other picture, her illness was already visible: She was thinner, paler, pink rouge doing little to disguise her pallor. Her hair was incongruously dark, brunette waves sweeping across her forehead; after noticing that it was identical to the hairstyle she had in the Florida photo on the rabbi's mantel, I surmised it must have been a wig, perhaps to cover the effects of her medical treatments. Her smile, whether genuine or simply a pose, was undiminished.

I wondered: Who took that photo in the dining room? And then I wondered: Who picked that wallpaper?

"I can't use your condo," I said.

"Why can't you?" he asked, closing the album.

I couldn't tell him my reasons: If I went to Florida for a vacation, I didn't want to be stuck in some old man's musty apartment. And it wasn't just his apartment—it was Sophie's, too. I didn't want to get more deeply involved in his grief by visiting a place so emotionally charged that he couldn't even visit it himself. I didn't believe in ghosts, but if ghosts existed, I was sure Sophie would be waiting for me in Florida.

But before I could answer, he continued: "It's a lovely

place, Benji. I cannot go, but somebody should use it. And it's the least I can do, after all you've done for me. So go."

"I appreciate the offer," I said, "but I can't."

He wasn't about to take no for an answer.

"Benji, when is your birthday?"

"December second," I said. "I'll be twenty-seven."

"Twenty-seven," he said to the ceiling, incredulous. "I'm old enough to be his grandfather."

I didn't ask him exactly how old he was, but I figured his math was pretty much correct.

"December second? Then the timing is perfect," he said, looking back at me. "Let this be my early birthday present to you."

Handing him back his key, I thanked him and told him I'd consider it. He nodded as if to say he already knew what the answer would be.

I hadn't been to Florida since eighth-grade spring break. That was the last time I saw my grandmother.

Grandma Gertie had been too sick to come to Passover that year, so the next week, my mom and dad dragged me down to her condo in Delray Beach, where she'd lived alone since Grandpa Jack died.

Aside from the metal entry gates topped with security lights and cameras, Grandma's retirement complex looked like a cheap motel: Six or seven rows of one-story attached condominiums radiated off the semicircular asphalt parking lot, strips of tan stucco separated by a cracked sidewalk and two thin ribbons of grass. The parking spaces were filled with Oldsmobiles and Lincolns; senior citizens still bought big sedans, American made. On the far side of the complex stood the clubhouse—where residents played bridge and bingo, or napped on the sofa next to a pair of unused exercise bikes—and the pool, surrounded by a six-foot chain-link fence.

It wasn't beautiful. But the weather was warm, the condo was easy to maintain, and my grandmother had befriended a few other women there. She didn't complain. Not about the noisy air-conditioning, or the neighbor's cat who was constantly digging up the flowers by her front door, or the cancer that had already taken both her breasts and showed few signs of giving up, radiation treatments notwithstanding.

Rachel, who was graduating high school the next month, was relieved of her family obligations, allowing her to spend spring break in Ocean City with her friends. So I slept alone on the foldout couch in Grandma's living room, awakened every morning at five thirty, when my grandmother would get up to read the paper. My parents, in the guest room, could sleep later—sometimes until nearly seven— but I was up at dawn with Grandma. Not because I wanted to wake up, but because I had to fold up my bed so she could read the paper on the couch.

This was not the image that most people conjured when they heard the phrase "spring break." But there I was: stiff-necked and sleepy, pouring prune juice for a sick old lady in an apartment that smelled of burnt coffee and farts and Glade PlugIns. Let the good times roll.

I was the youngest person at the Royal Floridian Senior Village, by several decades, except for a guy I saw by the pool one afternoon. He was a few years older, maybe sixteen or seventeen. Dirty blond hair, unkempt and shaggy, hung over his eyes. His skin was fair but sun-freckled. His feet, his hands, his Adam's apple, his baggy black swim trunks were all too big for his skinny frame. He looked about as excited to be there as I was.

We didn't introduce ourselves. He was with a man I assumed was his grandfather. I was across the pool with my father; my mother had taken my grandmother to the doctor. But he did nod in my direction, an acknowledgment of shared frustration, of both of us being somewhere we didn't want to be, somewhere boring and hopelessly uncool. I nodded back, lips pursed. I know, I know.

A couple days later, my parents had mercy on me and took me to the beach. Being at the beach with Mom and Dad wasn't exactly a thrill, but at least I had a few hours away from Little Old Lady Land. I spent most of the day in the ocean, neck-deep in the water, letting the waves carry me.

It wasn't until late afternoon, when we loaded up the rental car to head back to Grandma's, that I heard the news on the radio: Kurt Cobain was dead.

"Who's that, Benji? Someone you listen to?" my mother asked, turning to face me in the backseat. I shushed her and told her to turn up the radio.

"Nirvana," my father half whispered to her. He was always slightly hipper.

"Oh," my mother said, turning to me again. "You have some of their CDs, don't you?"

I shushed her again. "I'm trying to hear what happened, Mom!"

She turned back around with a harrumph. My father turned up the radio. By the time we got back to the Royal Floridian Senior Village, I'd learned that Cobain had shot himself.

"That's a real shame, Benji," my father said as he got out of the car in Grandma's parking lot. "I remember when John Lennon was killed—it was just a few days after you were born. . . ."

"Such a waste," my mother interrupted. "Drugs, I bet. They make people crazy."

I ignored both of them and strode toward the condo, scowling. I wanted to watch the coverage on MTV, but Grandma Gertie was watching some stupid game show on her only television set. Not that it mattered. She didn't have cable anyway. I took a shower.

I didn't talk at dinner. Grandma didn't ask any questions; either she didn't notice my silence, or my parents had already explained the situation. After dinner we sat in the living room and watched whatever was on network TV that night. I waited for the commercial breaks, watching for the news briefs.

I couldn't sleep that night. Kurt Cobain was dead, and I was stuck in the one place on the planet where nobody even knew who he was. Lying on the foldout couch in the dark, I could hear Nirvana songs playing faintly inside my head.

Or were they inside my head?

I got up and walked to the window and slid it open a crack. The music got a little louder. I picked up my T-shirt and shorts from the

*floor and put them on, then tiptoed to the front door and opened it
as quietly as I could, stepping outside barefoot.*

*From the sidewalk I could tell where the music was coming from.
I walked toward the parking lot and followed the sound to a silver
Buick Regal, parked, with its lights off. The guy who'd nodded at me
at the pool was sitting in the driver's seat.*

*He saw me standing there, and with one arm he invited me to
join him. He unlocked the car doors and I got in the passenger side.*

*He was smoking a cigarette. He'd kept the windows up to avoid
waking up the whole complex, but this meant the car was filled with
smoke. Nonetheless, I got in and shut the door. Sitting in a black
tank top and baggy black shorts, he was playing* In Utero, *Nirvana's most recent—and apparently last—album on the car's tape
deck.*

*He looked over at me. "My grandfather's car," he said. "Only
tape deck I've got. Fucking Walkman's busted."*

I nodded.

"Still can't fucking believe it," he said. "You like Nirvana?"

"Yeah."

"Unreal, right? Stupid asshole shoots himself."

"Yeah."

*He stubbed out his cigarette in the car's ashtray. From the looks of
it, he'd been there for a while. He extended a hand. "Jimmy," he
said.*

"Benji."

"Who you visiting?"

"My grandmother."

*"That's cool," he said. He reached for his pack of cigarettes and
held it out toward me. I shook my head.*

"Shit, man, what are you? Like thirteen?"

"Fifteen," I said, lying. Did he know it was bullshit?

*He took a cigarette out, then stopped. "I got a joint, too, man.
You wanna get stoned?"*

"I don't know . . ."

"Come on, man. It's good stuff."

He turned off the tape and took the key out of the ignition. He opened his door.

"Where you going?" I asked.

"Can't smoke a joint in my grandfather's car, dude. He'll smell the shit."

He shut his door and started walking across the parking lot. I got out and chased after him across the asphalt, toward the pool.

"Jimmy, it's locked," I called in a stage whisper.

He waved me off. It didn't matter if the gate was locked—he was climbing the fence.

This was pushing it for me. But what was my option—go back to Grandma Gertie's foldout couch? I climbed the chain-link fence and joined Jimmy by the pool.

Sitting on a plastic lounge chair, he lit up a joint and took a deep drag, then passed it to me. I took a shallow puff, held it in my mouth, and started to cough.

"I'll show you," he said. Then he taught me how to inhale, holding the joint up to my mouth, his fingers brushing against my lips, his eyes looking directly into mine through the flame from his disposable lighter. I got the hang of it. I always was a fast learner.

"Feel good?" he asked. And I did. After two or three hits, I'd forgotten about Kurt Cobain, and my sick grandmother, and my shitty spring break. All I was thinking about was Jimmy, who was now kicking off his tennis shoes and pulling his tank top over his head.

"Let's go for a swim," he said. And he smiled at me.

"I don't have a swimsuit."

"It's just us," he said. He unzipped his shorts and pulled them down.

In the dim glow from the lampposts around the pool, I could make out Jimmy's body: his skin pale, his smooth stomach and legs making the tuft of blond hair below his waistline all the more surprising. And on his hip, a small tattoo of two fish, one above the other, swimming in opposite directions.

I told myself I shouldn't stare, but I couldn't possibly look away. I sat frozen, my eyes fixed on his crotch.

"Like it?" he asked.

I swallowed and looked up at his face.

"Fish," he said. "Because I'm a Pisces."

He ran his fingers over the tattoo.

"My parents wouldn't let me get a tattoo," he said. "So I got one where they'll never see it. I mean, fuck them. I'm a senior already."

I nodded.

"Come on, it's warm enough," he said, jumping into the deep end. When he wasn't looking, I peeled off my clothes and lowered myself into the pool on a ladder.

He was right. It was warm, even at night.

Jimmy dunked himself under the water, emerging only a few feet in front of me, pushing his wet hair out of his face.

"Cobain was a Pisces, too, you know," he said.

I couldn't get a word out in response. Maybe it was the pot. Maybe it was Kurt Cobain. Maybe it was Jimmy.

While everyone else in the complex slept, Jimmy floated silently with his eyes closed, back and forth in front of me on his back, as if his body were a raft I could climb aboard. But I didn't move. I clung to the ladder with one hand, feet not touching the bottom, watching the water lap at his tattoo: two fish swimming underwater one second, two fish out of water the next.

Frankie had lots of tattoos. We'd been dating for weeks and I'd seen them all.

He was a tough-looking guy: shaved head, black boots, permanent scowl. Nobody would have guessed that he had a Hello Kitty tattoo on his butt. Which is exactly why he had one. "I can tell a lot about a guy with this thing," he told me. "Some guys think it's too faggy and it ruins their fantasy. And some guys pretend they haven't even noticed it. All of those guys are the wrong guys for me."

I had laughed the second I saw it; apparently, this was the right reaction, because I'd been invited to see it many more times. And every time, I laughed again.

Most of our early dates involved going out—to a bar, to a club, to a party—and staying up late. I'd crash at his place on Capitol Hill and head home in the morning. We cracked each other up, but we didn't really talk that much on our dates; it was hard to have serious conversations over the music and noise. But I sure liked looking at him. There's a reason he was a model.

When work picked up, though, I was too exhausted to keep up with Frankie. Sometimes he'd go to a party alone and I'd meet him in the city afterward. Or he'd go to a club with a friend and I'd join him a couple hours later. Then we'd go back to his place, but I'd usually fall asleep right away, before I'd even caught a glimpse of Kitty. I was no fun and we both knew it.

I started begging off dates with him, telling him to go out without me. A few times he convinced me to change my mind; a few times he didn't. Once or twice, he didn't even try.

But then Halloween came, and with it, a huge party in a warehouse on U Street. Some DJ I'd never heard of from Berlin was being flown in, along with a DJ from London I'd also never heard of. How could I resist? We'd bought tickets in advance, fifty bucks a pop.

When the day finally arrived, I just didn't feel up to it. It was a Wednesday, a work night, and I had a string of deadlines in the coming week. I called Frankie from my office and told him that one of his friends could use my ticket.

"You're not getting out of this one," he said. "It's Halloween. That's like gay Christmas."

"I'm Jewish," I said.

"Okay, gay Yom Kippur."

"That's not really a party holiday."

"Well, how the hell should I know?" he said. "Gay Hanukkah."

"Oh, *now* I get it," I teased. "I'll grab my dreidels and come right over."

"I hate you," he said sarcastically.

"Did you say you hate *Jews?*" I asked, still joking.

"Not all Jews; just you, Benji," he said, now getting peeved. "I never see you anymore. And it's Halloween, for Christ's sake. I even got us matching costumes."

"What'd you get?"

"Angel's wings."

"That's the gayest thing I've ever heard."

"They're perfect," he said. "Hardly any fuss. Just take off your shirt and slip these on. Easy to dance with—not too hot. And we'll match. Come on . . ."

The image of Frankie, shirtless, wearing fluffy white wings, was certainly a strong incentive to give in. But I knew I'd be yawning before the party really got started.

"I'm just too tired, Frankie."

"You know, there's an easy way to stay awake," he said. Apparently, he'd scored some crystal, more than enough to get us both through the night.

"I don't do that stuff," I told him.

"Have you ever tried it?" he asked.

"I don't need to try it to know that I don't do it."

"It's just one party, Benji."

"On a school night," I reminded him—although that concept was probably lost on Frankie, who, as a model who made most of his money posing nude for magazines and websites, didn't have any regular day job.

"This isn't some afterschool special," he said. "It's not like you're gonna turn into a meth junkie overnight."

"You're right," I said. "Because I'm not gonna do it."

"It's no big thing," he said. "I do it all the time."

All the time? I wondered if he'd done it when we were together. Would I even have known?

"Is that supposed to impress me?" I asked, a bit more snidely than I'd intended.

"I don't really care," he said coldly.

I was no prude: I drank, I smoked pot when the mood struck me, and I'd even dropped acid a couple of times at Maryland. But crystal was a different story. My parents would have shaken their heads in disapproval if they knew about the pot and the acid, but at least I could be pretty sure that they'd done the same things growing up in the sixties—even if they'd never admit it. But crystal? My parents wouldn't even know what it was, exactly. I knew: It was dangerous, addictive. *This is your brain on drugs, blah blah blah.*

Frankie gave up, called me an asshole, and hung up after wishing me a "happy fucking Halloween."

I slammed down the receiver and kicked my desk. I yelled at the phone: "Asshole!"

I thought about my options. I could call Frankie back and apologize—but for what? Having a real job? Not wanting to snort crystal? I knew where the party was; I could go and meet him there and just pretend nothing had happened. Or maybe I could show up and ignore him and try to meet someone new right under his nose. "Oh, I really wanted to come to this party," I'd say when he noticed me. "I just didn't want to come with you."

No, I thought, I don't want to deal with Frankie at all. Not right now and not again.

But just because I'd miss the party didn't mean I couldn't do something else.

I called Phil, who'd told me about a Halloween party in a friend's apartment downtown, a party I'd already told him I couldn't attend. I hadn't seen him much since I'd been dating Frankie; I hadn't been spending much time at bars lately—and those times when I had been at bars, I'd usually been with Frankie, so Phil had begged off. Phil didn't like him. "I don't trust him, Benji," he'd told me the night I introduced them. "He's bad news." I was belatedly coming to the same conclusion. With Frankie out of the picture for the night, Halloween suddenly seemed like a perfect time to re-connect with Phil. Except that he wasn't answering his phone and I didn't know where the party was. I'd missed my chance.

I called Michelle on her cell phone, but she was out with Dan at a costume party. "We're Bill and Hillary Clinton!" she told me. "Who's who?" I asked. She giggled and, without asking what I was doing for Halloween, told me she'd see me in the morning.

I called my parents, but they were watching one of those *CSI* shows that they loved; they were already annoyed at having to answer the door for trick-or-treaters who couldn't wait for commercial breaks, and they sure didn't want to waste more time on the phone.

"I thought you were going to a party with your *friend*," my mother said.

I hated how she used that word. My father would never have said it that way, so belittling. But I gritted my teeth rather than start an argument.

"That didn't work out," I said.

I heard their doorbell ring.

"The party or the *friend?*"

That word again.

"Both."

Their doorbell rang a second time. My mother shouted to my father, "Sid! Get the goddamn door! I'm on the phone!"

I guess he didn't move fast enough.

"Jesus Christ," she grumbled, then called out in a forced cheerful voice, "I'm coming! Hold on!"

I could hear her put on her phoniest happy-mom act as she handed out goodies to the kids: "Oh, you're a very scary monster! And what a pretty little princess you are! I think you each deserve *two* pieces of candy for having such won-derful costumes!"

Then the kids left and she was back to her old self.

"Benji, are you still there?" she asked as she closed the door. "Go home already!"

Then she hung up.

I decided I'd just as soon stay at the office and get some more work done. Right after I lay down on my couch.

"You are so totally pathetic."

This was Michelle's idea of sympathy. When she and Dan woke up and realized that I wasn't home, she assumed I'd had some fabulous night on the town, probably staying out till dawn with a bunch of queens in unbelievable costumes, really doing Halloween up right, before stumbling into the office hungover. She called me at work to hear stories about my amazing adventures.

She woke me up. I had fallen asleep on the couch—clothes on, shoes on, lights on—and my nap turned into an all-night affair. No trick. No treat. No miniature candy bars.

"I thought you were going to that party with Frankie," she said.

I explained.

"Well, you did the right thing," she said. "Your mom would be proud."

"Yeah, that's what I was aiming for."

"So what're you gonna do about Frankie?"

"I think that's done," I said. Our professional dealings were over; his Paradise ad was already running in the local gay paper. And as much as I was attracted to him physically, it didn't seem like we were a good match after all.

"He sounds like a bit of a party animal for you," Michelle said.

"And what am I, a librarian?"

"You're a nice Jewish boy from the suburbs," she said.

"Hot," I said flatly.

"It *is* hot. You're a great catch," she said. "You just keep getting caught by the wrong guys."

*   *   *

I clearly needed a change, a break from my dysfunctional routine: long hours working alone in my office, followed by frustrating dates with the wrong men.

The more I thought about Miami, the more it sounded like just what the doctor ordered—if I actually had a doctor who cared about my personal life. I could relax, catch up on my sleep, and even meet some new people. I'd heard stories about Miami's gay scene: fabulous beaches, fabulous bars, fabulous boys. Seemed like a good birthday present to me.

I e-mailed Phil for advice, since he'd been down there before. He e-mailed back within minutes, with the subject line: YES YES YES.

"Exactly what you need, Benji," he wrote. "But don't wait for your birthday. Thanksgiving is the time to go. Check this out."

He included a link to a website about the White Party— one of the biggest gay circuit parties in the country—that happened over Thanksgiving weekend. Thousands of men at some gorgeous mansion, with a bunch of celebrity appearances, and it was all a benefit for some local AIDS charities. Plus, a slew worth of *other* events had developed around the White Party, making that the ideal time to be down there.

I wrote back to Phil: "Looks incredible. But do you think it'd be fun to go alone?"

"Just because you go alone," he replied, "doesn't mean you'll be alone for long."

After work, I went to visit the rabbi.

He was sucking on a hard candy. I handed him a stack of mail, and when he put it on his coffee table, I noticed that he had a whole bowl of candy, surrounded by crumpled wrappers.

"Leftovers," he said, "from Halloween."

"I thought Jews didn't celebrate Halloween," I said—although what I meant was Orthodox Jews.

"We don't," he said—also meaning Orthodox Jews. "But Benji, not everybody is Jewish. And if my neighbors' children knock on my door on October thirty-first, what should I do? Read to them from the Talmud?"

I shrugged.

"It is not my holiday," he said. "But giving a child a piece of candy is not the same as joining his church."

He reached into the bowl and fished out a red sourball. He offered it to me; when I shook my head, he unwrapped it and popped it into his own mouth.

"Remember," he said, nudging the sourball into his cheek, "we do not all share the same beliefs, but we must all learn to live together."

I cocked my head at him. He was sounding downright progressive. I considered checking his forehead for fever.

"You sure you're not Reconstructionist?" I teased.

He laughed and rolled his eyes.

"Have you thought about Miami?" he asked.

I told him I'd decided to go over Thanksgiving, without explaining why.

He must have known that I'd accept, because the keys were already in his pocket.

He drew me a crude map on the back of an envelope and wrote down the condo's address. He explained where to park. He told me where he kept the sheets and towels. And he informed me where the nearest kosher market was.

"The condo is kosher, of course," he said, stopping and giving me a questioning look over the top of his glasses.

"I know."

"You know what this means?"

I did know. And I also knew that the rabbi would tolerate fewer broken rules than my mother.

"I grew up in a kosher house," I said.

He seemed relieved.

In reality, I knew that it was a moot issue; I'd be eating out, and avoiding even the possibility of accidentally defiling the rabbi's dishes with *treyf* food.

And just as surely, I knew I'd be sleeping on the couch, to avoid the possibility of defiling the rabbi's bed with my *treyf* self, fresh from the gay bars mere blocks away.

CHAPTER 8

I had to go shopping.

This was more important than work, at least for a few hours. If I was going to the White Party, I needed the right clothes.

I didn't own anything white, other than a few Hanes undershirts and a bunch of old sweatsocks. So I stepped away from my desk on a Saturday afternoon and hit the mall.

Michelle came with me. She was always happy to have an excuse to shop. And I knew she'd be brutally honest about what looked awful on me. That's what girlfriends are for.

"I can't believe you're staying in that old man's apartment," she said as we searched for shirts at Old Navy.

"It's a very nice gesture," I said, trying to convince myself as well as Michelle.

"Whatever," she countered. "I'm not saying he's not nice. I'm just saying it's weird."

"Look, it's a big weekend there. I'll probably be out most of the time. I'll just use the apartment to sleep."

"Or maybe you'll find someone else's apartment to sleep in," said Michelle, smirking.

"Not if I'm wearing this," I said, putting a particularly hideous item back on the shelf.

"How about that?" she said, pointing to a simple white dress shirt. "Goes with everything, and you might actually wear it again after this week."

"Nice, but too formal," I said. "I'll be dancing, and sweating . . ."

"Right," she said.

I plucked a lightweight, short-sleeved button-down off the sale table and held it up in front of me. Michelle reached out and tugged at the shimmery fabric, which stretched.

"Too queeny," she said.

"Excuse me?" I said.

"Oh, sorry to offend you," she said sarcastically. "I mean it's too girly."

"Too girly for what?"

"Too girly for *me*, and I *am* a girl," she said. "And certainly too girly for you."

I raised an eyebrow at her.

"Because you're so butch," she deadpanned.

"Damn right," I said, holding back a laugh.

"This is hopeless," she said.

"Let's go to the Gap," I said.

As we walked across the mall, Michelle nudged me with her elbow playfully. "You know, you haven't asked me what I'm doing for Thanksgiving," she said.

"I figured you were going to Philly."

"Nope."

"There's no way your mom and dad are letting you skip a family holiday. Mine would have a cow. And yours are twice as bad."

"Not if I have a good excuse," she said.

I didn't have to ask what the excuse could possibly be, because Michelle was about to burst.

"I'm going to Long Island," she said excitedly.

"What's on Long Island?"

"That's where Dan's from," she said. "I'm going home with him."

"To meet his parents?"

"Yup."

"Sounds serious."

"I know, right?" She sounded like she could hardly believe it herself.

"It's been, what, a year?"

"More than a year," she said. "I've never been with a guy long enough to think about anniversaries."

"Me, either," I said. "Unless you're counting in dog years."

"With the guys you've dated, dog years might make sense."

"Real funny."

"And I've never gotten to meet a guy's parents."

"Except mine," I said.

"That doesn't really count," she said.

Michelle was uncharacteristically nervous about meeting Dan's parents, so she kept chattering about it while we checked out my options at the Gap. We had better luck there: I found a white oxford with gray accents, a white hooded sweatshirt, a white T-shirt with a small "Gap '07" logo on the chest, and a pair of white 501s. Michelle found a pair of boxer shorts with orange and red turkeys, which she bought for Dan. We were both good to go.

I hadn't seen Michelle much lately, so I decided to play hooky—if you can call taking a break on Saturday hooky. I asked if she wanted to get tickets to a movie; the cineplex was just across the parking lot.

"Oh, I'm sorry, Benji," she said. "I'm already going to the movies tonight. With Dan."

I was disappointed. Another Saturday night alone.

"That's okay," I said, probably not concealing my feelings particularly well. "It's no big deal."

"Wait, I'll call him," she said, opening her purse and

searching for her cell phone. "You can come with us, I'm sure he won't mind."

"No, you two go," I said. "I've got work to do anyway."

"On a Saturday night?"

"Just for a couple more weeks," I said. "I'm not taking my laptop to the White Party. Although it *is* white. . . ."

Michelle and Dan went to the movies. I spent another night at my desk.

I finished a large chunk of graphics for the website and e-mailed it to the client for feedback.

I wrapped up the cover design for the next issue of the gardening newsletter.

I finished up the next ad for Paradise. The headline was "Heaven on Earth," and there was a photo of a shirtless hunk wearing white angel wings. I was inspired by Frankie's Halloween costume, the one I never got to see. I hadn't heard from him since that night. I wondered if he'd call me when the ad hit newspapers in December. Probably not.

The next couple of weeks were pretty much a blur: Work ate up almost all my time. I didn't see Michelle much, I didn't have a single date, I didn't go out downtown at all. A much-neglected Phil left me a voicemail: "I figure you've gotten married, or moved away, or died—and I'm calling dibs on your ticket to the White Party, no matter which of those three things is true."

Basically, the only people I saw were Mrs. Goldfarb, when I'd pick up the rabbi's mail, and the rabbi himself, when I'd drop it off. Since our chats had gotten shorter, I started to feel a bit like the mailman: Here's the mail, thanks, see you later. I could hear my mother saying, "I told you so," in the back of my head.

Of course, all my work did get done, and on time. I turned in the last bit of material for the website the weekend before Thanksgiving and spent a couple subsequent days tweaking a few minor details. The day before Thanksgiving, I was done; the site was ready to launch and I was ready to take a break.

"What's wrong? You are coming over tomorrow, aren't you?" my mother asked when I called from the office. "I know you've been working a lot, but tell me you're not going to work on Thanksgiving."

"Nope, I'm all done," I said. "That's all I was calling to tell you."

"Wonderful," she said. "Go home and get some sleep."

"It's not even dinnertime."

"So you'll save your appetite for tomorrow," she said. "And wear decent pants."

I set my e-mail to auto-reply, turned off the computer, shut off the lights, and locked my office door. I ducked into the bookstore, which was already decked out with silver streamers for Hanukkah. I picked up the mail from Mrs. Goldfarb, who—despite giving me a strange look a week earlier when I told her I'd be staying in the rabbi's condo—wished me a happy holiday and a good vacation.

The rabbi seemed happy to see me. He invited me in, and for the first time in weeks, I accepted. I sat in his living room and he brought out a glass of water and a dish of honey-roasted cashews—"fancy *shmancy*," my mother would say.

"So, you do not have to rush back to work?" he said.

"No, I am all done," I said. "Finished. So tonight I can sit with you."

"Wonderful," he said.

Although I was exhausted and really wanted to get home, I asked if I could see the photo album he had tried to show me weeks before, and a smile spread across his face. He dashed up the stairs like—well, not like a child, but like a far younger man, and returned with the album, a three-ring binder covered in faux wood-grain vinyl.

I sat next to him on the couch—for the first time—and he opened the album on the coffee table.

The album started with his wedding; it was as though this event marked the beginning of his remembered life. There were clear reasons why Sophie had no photos from her childhood, but I didn't quite understand why the rabbi's earlier years had been excluded.

There were photos of his parents, his father visibly stern and unsmiling. And pictures of Sophie's adopted American family. Photos of husband and wife in front of the bookstore on opening day, looking young and confident. A snapshot of Sophie standing behind the counter with Mrs. Goldfarb.

"When's this one from?" I asked, pointing to the picture of Mrs. Goldfarb.

"I don't remember exactly," he said. "It must be more than twenty years ago, I guess."

I figured he was right: Her clothes and makeup certainly looked like something from the eighties.

"That's about the time I was in her Hebrew school class," I said. He nodded.

We flipped through the pages slowly. Some photos were faded and brown around the edges. A few times there were blank spots on the pages where photos had fallen out or been removed.

"What happened to those ones?" I asked. But the rabbi dismissed me with his hand—as if he did not want to be sidetracked from sharing his life story—and turned to the next page.

Finally, he was able to tell stories about Sophie and their life together without choking up or losing the battle with his emotions. I supposed that this time at home had allowed him to spend time with Sophie—or the memory of Sophie—and come to focus on their life together as opposed to her death and his new life alone.

He told stories about trips they had taken, holidays they

had spent together, the early years when the bookstore was struggling. Most of the time, when I asked about the strangers in photos, the rabbi would respond: "Oh, she passed away many years ago," or "He died of a heart attack," or something along those lines. But if his album was filled with ghosts, their stories remained alive in his memory; he could recite all their names, and their spouses' names, and where they lived and what they did for work—and what ultimately killed them.

"You don't have to talk about all this if you don't want to," I said, thinking all this reminiscing about dead people might make him morose.

"I like talking about them," he said, a peaceful tone in his voice.

"Okay," I said. "Just checking."

He looked at me and paused, realizing that perhaps I was the one who was uncomfortable.

"I'm sorry, Benji, all this talk must get very boring for you," he said. "Listening to an old man go on and on about people you never met."

"No, no, keep going," I said. Inside, I wished I'd had the chance to do this with my own grandparents before they died, to sit down and simply listen to them explain their lives, to feel as close to them as I felt to the rabbi at that moment.

Toward the end, we came to the pictures he'd already shown me of the Miami condo. With the same awful wallpaper.

"Is that still what the condo looks like?" I asked, careful not to insult the décor directly.

"Yes," he said. "You will see for yourself very soon."

"I suppose so," I said.

He closed the photo album. "You are all ready for the big trip?" he asked.

"I think so."

"Florida will do you good," he said. "It always did me good."

"Yes, I'm very excited. I really need to get away."

"You could use the rest," he said. "You've been working too hard."

He sounded like my mother, but somehow more concerned and less scolding.

"Well, I don't know how much rest I'll actually get. . . ."

"What do you mean?"

I wasn't about to tell him about the White Party, so I kept it vague: "I hear Miami can get a little crazy."

He smiled. "Yes, I suppose it is a different place for a young man," he said. "For Sophie and me, it was a place to relax. No work, no phone to answer, dinner on the balcony. It was where we went for some peace and quiet. But you are right. You are not even twenty-seven and you are single. Peace and quiet are probably not what you are looking for."

I smiled back uneasily. Was I just overtired, or was the rabbi thinking unholy thoughts? Would he even have any notion of what Miami had to offer aside from kosher markets and storefront shuls?

"True," I said, without adding anything specific.

"You think of me as an old man who knows only Torah and Talmud, but I am not blind," he said with a knowing nod. "I am aware that most people go to Miami to look at the beautiful girls."

"Not exactly," I said under my breath.

"What do you mean?"

I hadn't intended for him to hear that, but I was stuck now.

"I'm not going to Miami to look at the girls," I said, and left it at that.

The rabbi looked at me, confused.

Maybe I felt that we had grown comfortable enough to have an honest talk. Or maybe I was simply too sleep-deprived to keep up my defenses, remaining opaque in my statements and obtuse in my replies. Either way, I finally just said it: "I'm gay."

"What?" he said, leaning toward me.

Had he not heard me?

"I'm gay," I repeated.

His eyes widened.

"You're homosexual," he said flatly, drawing out the "h" as if he could hardly bring himself to say the word. He shifted away from me on the couch.

"Gay," I said.

He sat back against the cushion and stiffened. "You never mentioned this before."

"It's no big deal," I said, hoping we could drop the subject and move on to something else.

"It is a very big deal," he said. "All this time I've known you, I never imagined something like this."

"Well, now you know," I said matter-of-factly.

The rabbi didn't say anything. He was stunned, still. And it dawned on me that this might not go well. I hadn't ever planned a coming-out speech for the rabbi, since I hadn't had to make a big announcement like this for years—since I'd told my parents. With them, I'd spent months going over how to phrase it, practicing with Michelle so I could antici-pate what they'd say. (Somehow, in all that rehearsing, I had perfectly guessed my father's characteristically cool and mea-sured response—"We're glad you told us"—but not my mother's initial self-centered disbelief: "If you're trying to play a joke on me, this isn't funny." She always did know how to catch me by surprise.)

With the rabbi, since I hadn't planned a speech, I also hadn't considered how he might respond, and how I might handle it. So I was winging it, at exactly the moment when I was most exhausted and least articulate.

"It doesn't change anything," I said.

He didn't reply. His brow furrowed and he scratched at his beard. He stared down at the carpet.

"It doesn't change anything," I repeated. "Right?"

"You lied to me," he said finally.

"When did I lie?"

"You told me you lived with a woman."

"I do. But I told you we're not a couple."

"Yes, but this was only half the story," he said. "You told me that you had tried to be a couple and it had not worked out. You did not tell me why. You did not tell me you were . . . this way."

I cringed at his tone, and the fact that he couldn't even say the word "gay."

"This changes everything," he said, rubbing his forehead with one hand.

"Why?"

He turned to me with an exasperated expression, as if he couldn't believe I'd ask such a stupid question. "The Torah says this is a grave sin."

I quickly remembered why I had hidden this from the rabbi for so long. Our growing ease together had lulled me into thinking that he was just like anyone else—ready to reason, ready to think for himself, ready to accept what he saw with his own eyes. While he played by the rules in his own life, he seemed to take a more open-minded view of how other people behaved.

But he was still an Orthodox rabbi, and some things, I supposed, would always be black and white. I had overestimated him as a man—or underestimated his faith.

"You really believe this?" I asked. And this time I moved away from him, scooting to the farthest edge of the sofa, turning to face him.

"I am sorry, but Jewish law is very clear," he said. "You are breaking God's commandments."

"I have broken a lot of them—you know that. I don't keep

kosher, I don't go to synagogue, I don't observe Shabbat," I said.

"Those are questions of conduct, and those I might at least understand," he said, stabbing a finger into the air. "This is an affront to God himself. You are breaking the rules of nature. The Torah says what you are doing is wrong."

"So did the Nazis," I shot back.

He inhaled quickly through his teeth and his face hardened.

"Don't you speak to me about Nazis," he warned, his tone growing sharp.

Thinking better of it, I backed off, but my tone also changed.

"Who are you to judge me?" I asked. "Are you so pure?"

He looked at me coldly. "I obey God's commandments."

"You believe *everything* the Torah says?" I asked.

He stared into my eyes. "Benji, there is no other way."

"And you honestly believe that I should spend my whole life alone and unloved because that's what it says in the Torah?"

"No," he said. "You should find a wife and live properly."

"Then God should have made me heterosexual," I said. Atheist or not, I could still speak his language.

"This is not God's fault, Benji," he said.

I hadn't had to deal with this kind of bullshit for years—not since one of the Christian student groups at Maryland held a protest outside a gay dance on campus. I knew that a lot of people had some ridiculously outdated ideas about gay life, but living in a liberal area as an openly gay man, I hadn't seen it firsthand for years. I usually had the luxury of dismissing homophobes as crazy idiots and getting on with my life. But this time, sitting face-to-face with a man I'd grown to trust and care about, I had to deal with it head-on. And I was pissed.

"I thought you told me that Judaism is not simply about

not breaking rules," I said, "but about what good deeds you do."

"We are not talking about eating meat with a *milchig* fork," he said. "The Torah says this is strictly forbidden! What good deeds have you done that could possibly outweigh such a sin?"

By this point, I'd had enough. I felt attacked, and I didn't see the need to spare his feelings anymore.

"I befriended an old man who had lost the will to live," I said, standing up. "A man with no friends. A judgmental old man."

"A man who never asked for your help," he interjected.

"A man who knows how painful it is to be alone," I said.

He took a deep, slow breath. I took one, too, and thought we might get past this anger and have a real discussion. I sat back down, across from him in my usual chair, so I could look directly at him.

"Being gay isn't just about sex," I began. "It's about relationships and finding someone to love and spend your life with."

His hands clenched into fists in his lap. "But the Torah says—"

I cut him off. "I'm not talking about the Torah. I'm talking about you," I said. "You can't tell me that I'll simply have to live without love forever. Is that really what you think?"

He paused, lips pursed. I wondered if he had any ideas, other than what the Torah told him.

"It doesn't matter what I think. And it doesn't matter what *you* think, either, about what you feel inside or what you think you want," he said. "You are supposed to find a wife and have children together. That is God's plan."

"You and Sophie never had children," I said.

"Don't talk about Sophie," he admonished me.

I didn't heed his warning; I thought the fact that I'd touched a nerve was a positive sign, and figured I might get through to him more effectively if I personalized the issue even further, so he could think about things in human, rather than religious, terms.

"What if you knew that Sophie was your *bashert*," I said, "but when you met her, someone told you that you were forbidden to be with her?"

His face grew red.

"I told you not to—" he began, but I cut him off.

"What if your rabbi had told you that the Torah commanded you to stay away from her? That your feelings for her were unnatural, or wrong?"

His fists tightened.

"Would you have listened?" I asked. "Could you have stayed away from her, no matter what anyone said?"

Beads of sweat formed on his forehead.

"Could you have denied what you knew was right in your heart? Could you have simply walked away and lived your life without her, alone and loveless?"

Even his ears started to redden.

"Of course not," I said, since he wasn't responding. "You can't change the way you feel, whether someone else tells you it's right or wrong. It's the same for me as it would be for you. What I'm looking for is the same thing you had. Except your *bashert* was a woman and my *bashert* is a man."

Here, something snapped. The rabbi shot up out of his seat and pointed his finger at the front door, shaking, spitting mad.

"How dare you compare my marriage with your disgusting perversion, this *abomination!*" he growled. "I want you out of my house!"

I had heard that awful word before.

It was 1995 and my whole family had taken a vacation to Israel. The ostensible reason was that Rachel had finished her first year at Boston University and was considering applying that fall to spend her junior year abroad in either Paris or Jerusalem. My parents were pushing for Jerusalem, and to help sway her decision, they took us both on a trip in August.

These were the heady days of Oslo, and an uncharacteristically optimistic air pervaded the place. The Palestinians were gradually taking control of the territories. The border with Jordan had opened that summer. There was even talk of progress with the Syrians. Peace, it seemed, was just around the corner.

I'd been out of Hebrew school for more than a year; I left after eighth grade, telling my parents that I didn't plan to go for confirmation, that a bar mitzvah was enough for me. (They weren't happy about it—"Your sister got confirmed," they'd tell me, as if this would change my mind—but in the end I got my way.) But all those years at Congregation Beth Shalom certainly paid off on this trip: It seemed like every day, my Hebrew school lessons came in handy. We visited Tiberias. We climbed Masada. We swam—or floated—in the Dead Sea. All the stories I'd learned came to life.

We had to split up when we visited the Western Wall. Men on one side, women on the other. When my father and I got past the entrance, an attendant handed us yarmulkes made of white paper, with staples holding them together. They were awful, but we both reluctantly put them on; was there a choice? We stood at the wall, surrounded by men—men in black hats, men with real yarmulkes, young men in army uniforms, old men with trembling hands. We touched the wall. Neither of us had a note to leave in the cracks. Neither of us prayed. It made no difference. We stood together for a moment, silent, not because we did not know what to say, but because nothing needed to be said.

Even a fourteen-year-old who wasn't sure he believed in God could feel the weight of the millennia.

But history wasn't going to sell Rachel. She wanted to see the "real" Israel—how young people lived, what they did for fun, what the country had to offer besides religious fervor and biblical landmarks.

So we headed to Tel Aviv, the heart of secular Israel, for a few days. We shopped for clothes at Dizengoff Center. We ate falafel on Ben Yehuda Street. We spent an afternoon at the beach, watching skinny people in scandalously small bathing suits playing paddleball on the sand and cooling off in the surf.

At night, we'd return to our rooms at the Hilton, overlooking the Mediterranean. One night, after having dinner in the old city of Jaffa, we had an unusually chatty cabdriver, eager to practice his English. He took us on a roundabout tour of Tel Aviv and gave us a running commentary about places we passed: such-and-such market, this-or-that tower. We drove around circles, observing fountains, architecture, gardens. As we got close to the Hilton, he pointed out one last site: Independence Park, right next to our hotel.

"But into this park you should not to go, special at night," he warned.

"Is it dangerous?" my mother asked.

"Not like your parks in America, no," he replied. "But is famous place for to meet homosexuals."

"Oh," said my mother. My father nodded. Then the cabbie muttered something in Hebrew. Nobody else asked what he'd said, so I asked.

"I do not know the word in English," he said. "I think it is 'abomination.' "

He said the word slowly, each syllable distinct, as if he was sounding it out in his head. Then he repeated it, his accent thick: A-bo-mee-na-shun.

He pulled into the circle in front of the Hilton and dropped us off. I jumped out first and headed inside quickly, trying to get away from the cabbie. My parents lingered longer, thanking him for the tour and offering him a generous tip.

Rachel and I had our own room and she planned to use this to her advantage. After our parents had gone to bed, Rachel decided she was going out on the town, alone. She had asked a girl who worked in one of the stores in Dizengoff Center where the college kids hung out at night and the clerk had written down an address and slipped it to her when Mom wasn't looking. Rachel figured this was her only chance to get out on her own. She stuffed a few shekels in her pocket and brushed her hair in the bathroom mirror.

"If Mom and Dad knock on the door, don't answer," she said. "We'll just tell them we were both asleep and didn't hear them."

"Do what you want," I said, looking out the window, trying to determine if I could see into Independence Park from our room.

"What's your problem?"

"Nothing."

"Right, nothing." Sarcasm. I'd missed that during her first year away from home.

"It's that cabdriver."

"What about him?"

Had she really not noticed what he'd said?

"He was an asshole," I said.

"I guess," she said, checking her watch.

"He's a cabdriver. Not a rabbi."

"Yeah, it was weird," she said. "But it's no big deal."

"Right," I said. "No big deal." Two can play at sarcasm.

"Look, I'm going out. Don't tell Mom and Dad. I'm supposed to be keeping an eye on you."

"I don't need a babysitter."

"You promise you won't tell?"

"Rachel, I'm not a kid. I can keep a secret."

She stepped back and took a long look at me, sizing me up, before she turned and headed out the door.

I stood in the window and tried to make out the men in Independence Park below—walking in alone, meeting, walking out together. Did they talk to each other? Did they have sex right there behind the trees? Did they think what they were doing was an abomination? Did they care?

With Rachel gone, I could have simply taken the elevator downstairs and walked out the front door and checked out the park myself. But I was too afraid. I stayed in the room, looking out the window, trying to catch a glimpse of gay life from ten stories up.

*   *   *

I drove home from the rabbi's house in a rage. I couldn't believe I'd been such an idiot, thinking that Rabbi Zuckerman was somehow enlightened. I'd believed that he had a willingness to bend, or at least accept things he didn't like: He might not have been thrilled that I didn't keep kosher, but that didn't stop him from trusting me to use his kitchen. He might have wished that I went to synagogue—any synagogue—but he never condemned my decision to avoid synagogue as sacrilege. He was probably miffed that I didn't keep the Sabbath, but he had never quoted scripture at me and called me a sinner.

Mrs. Goldfarb was right, I realized. He had some very old-fashioned ideas. Any flexibility I'd seen in him was only in my own imagination. I'd been duped. I felt betrayed.

And I was pissed. I couldn't go home and tell Michelle, because she'd already left for Long Island with Dan. So I headed downtown.

Even though it was a Wednesday night, the bars around Dupont Circle were mobbed, since everyone had the next four days off work.

Paradise was busier than I'd ever seen it. The manager found me in the crowd, though, to tell me he'd gotten the "Heaven on Earth" ad and liked it a lot. The knot in the back of my neck loosened just a bit. He gave me a shot of cinnamon schnapps on the house. That helped, too.

Phil rushed in a few minutes later and found me sitting at the bar.

"What's wrong?" he asked. "You sounded awful on the phone."

I told him about the fight with the rabbi.

"Fucking asshole," said Phil. He gestured to the bartender for two more shots.

"I really thought I knew him," I said.

"Can I be honest?" he asked. "I always thought it was kind of weird that you were spending so much time with a rabbi anyway. But I guess after tonight, that's all over. Maybe you can start hanging out with the hell-bound masses again."

I didn't reply. We downed our shots.

Phil checked his watch. "You gonna be okay?" he asked.

"Yeah."

"Because I've got to go," he said.

"You just got here," I said.

"I've got plans with Sammy."

"Who's Sammy?"

"The guy I've been seeing for three weeks," he said. "Man, you really have been out of it."

"I know. I'm sorry."

"Look, if you want me to stick around, I'll call him and tell him I've got to cancel."

"I'll be fine," I said. "Go."

Phil gave me a kiss on the cheek and a long hug, then turned and left. He never even asked if I was still planning to go to Miami.

I stood alone against the wall and checked out the crowd. Everyone seemed to be having a good time. There were crowds of friends standing around and talking too loudly. There were a handful of single guys standing on the side-lines, looking for an opening. And, of course, there were a few couples mixed in—perhaps longtime lovers, or perhaps new acquaintances—sipping drinks, eyes locked on each other's faces.

I wondered what the rabbi would say if he could witness the scene. Would he be shocked to discover how at ease these men seemed, how casually they laughed or told stories or sang along with the music? How utterly normal it felt for them? Would he see any of that? Or would he get red in the face and storm out quoting Leviticus?

I took a deep breath and tried to push the rabbi out of my mind.

One couple close to me was talking so quietly, it was

almost a whisper, yet somehow they could hear each other above the din, as if everyone else in the rowdy bar had vanished. They weren't touching, but they were so close: their hands holding their drinks, their whispering lips, their khaki-clad legs.

I looked at them longingly, until the one with his back to me turned his head to the side and I saw that it was Christopher. Looking as good as ever. Probably talking to his new future husband about where they'd send their kids to church.

If one observant Jew couldn't keep me from having a good time at a bar, one observant Christian could. For a moment, I considered tapping him on the shoulder and asking how he reconciled religious teachings with his homosexuality; maybe he'd found a scriptural loophole that I could bring back to the rabbi. But seeing the one guy I'd dated recently who I actually missed, flirting with a new man, I needed to get out of there more than I needed a Bible lesson. There's only so much a guy can take.

Shit, I thought as I fumbled for my car keys, I really do need to get away—because things here clearly aren't working out for me.

I was pretty sure the pilgrims didn't know from matzoh ball soup and I was absolutely positive that the Native Americans didn't welcome them with gefilte fish. But my mother had but one menu for a holiday meal: Passover, Rosh Hashanah, Thanksgiving. They were all the same.

Not that I ever complained. It was a good meal. And it did involve turkey, so it was still essentially true to the spirit of the day.

Thanksgiving had been a small affair for several years. Rachel had told our parents that she and Richard could only afford to fly east once a year and she'd left it to Mom to decide whether Rosh Hashanah or Thanksgiving was the most important. Mom's response—"If you leave Richard in Seattle, you can afford to come home twice without him"—was not taken seriously, even though she meant it. At any rate, in the end Mom chose the High Holidays, so we were a cozy little trio, just Mom and Dad and me, for Thanksgiving.

I was thankful that my hangover had started to recede. And thankful that my parents knew I'd been working long hours lately, so I had a valid excuse for looking as haggard as I did. But thankful or not, I wasn't really in the mood to deal with my mother.

"You need to take better care of yourself," she said as she brought the food to the table. "You look terrible."

"I know," I said gruffly. It was easier than arguing.

"You don't have to take on all this work," my father said. "If you're short on cash, I can help you out. It's better than making yourself sick."

"Thanks," I said. "I don't need cash."

"If you say so," he said, dubious.

"Sid, give him some money," my mother said.

"I told you I don't need cash," I repeated through gritted teeth.

"Just to get you through your vacation," she offered.

"Mom!" I barked. "Just drop it."

She sat back, hurt.

"Leave him alone, Judy," my father said, trying to avoid a fight.

My mother conceded. "Fine," she said. "But you'd better get some sleep in Miami. I *know* you need more of that."

What was it about old people and sleep? Did people really buy plane tickets and take time off work just to sleep?

"I will, Mom," I said. "Can we just eat now?"

"Fine," she said. "Pass me your plate."

Her food brightened my mood a bit. My mother found many ways to aggravate me, but her cooking was never anything but a comfort.

While we ate, she asked about my plans for Miami, and I kept my answers vague. I didn't bother telling her about the White Party; she'd only have given me some ridiculous lecture about something she saw on the *Today* show about the "latest" party drug—Ecstasy or cocaine or something equally passé. So I just told her I was looking forward to spending some time on the beach, or by a pool.

"We haven't been to Miami since before you and Rachel were born," my father said.

"I don't remember it being all that great," my mother added. "A bunch of old people and a bunch of old buildings. And the heat!"

"I think it's changed a lot since then, Mom."

"Eh, you can keep it," she said.

"There was that deli," my father said. "Wolfie's, I think. Is that still there?"

"I don't know, I'll check," I said. Leave it to my father to visit the country's most famous beach and only remember the best place to get corned beef.

"It's all full of Cubans now," my mother said. "That deli is probably some kind of a taco stand."

"Tacos are Mexican, Mom."

"You know what I mean."

Yeah, I knew what she meant. And I was thankful that there wasn't anyone else at the table to witness what she'd said.

"There's still a big Jewish community down there," my father offered.

"That's why the rabbi had a place there," I said.

"All Orthodox, no doubt," my mother said.

"Mostly," I said.

"Great," she said sarcastically. "I told you he was going to try to convert you."

"Oh, please," I said.

"Judy, don't start with him again," my father said, putting

a hand on her arm. "Benji's tired and he just wants to eat in peace."

"No, let me talk," she said, pushing his hand away and turning to me. "I know you think you're doing a mitzvah by looking after this old man, but I guarantee he doesn't think of it that way. He's going to try to turn you into one of them. That's what they do."

"Yeah, well, good luck with that!" I said. "I'm not turning Orthodox. I know that for sure."

"Still, I think you've been spending too much time with him, going to his house all the time," she said. "And now, staying in his condo. You're getting too close to this man, Benjamin. I don't trust him."

"You don't have to worry about that anymore," I said. "He kicked me out of his house today."

I explained the conversation, briefly, leaving out the parts where I taunted the rabbi and cheapened the memory of his late wife; I was already regretting those remarks. What was left was a back-and-forth where the rabbi basically condemned me for being gay and threw me out the door.

"I told you, they're all crazy," said my mother, satisfied.

But it was my father who was genuinely angered. "After all you've done for him, he's got the nerve to say those things to you?" he said. "Where the hell does he get off telling you how to live your life? He actually called you an *abomination?* He's living in the dark ages."

"Dad, remember, that's where the Conservative movement was until, oh, a few months ago. It's not like your rabbi is so enlightened."

"It's not the same thing at all," he said.

"Sounds the same to me," I said.

My mother brought the discussion back to practical matters.

"But wait, doesn't this mean that you're canceling the trip?" she asked.

"No, I've already bought the ticket."

"Then you'll have to get a hotel room," she said.

"You can't get a last-minute hotel room in Miami Beach for a holiday weekend," I said.

"Then what are you going to do?" my father asked.

"He kicked me out of his house," I said, "but he didn't say anything about his condo."

CHAPTER 9

The trip to Florida got off to a good start. The plane left on time. I had an empty seat next to me. And my flight attendant was flirtatious.

"Traveling alone?" he asked, more friendly than pitying, while he poured me a cup of Diet Coke.

I told him I was.

"Not for long, I bet," he said, handing me the cup and the rest of the can.

He was definitely handsome: somewhere around thirty, with short blond hair neatly parted on one side and a tiny silver stud in his left ear. That's about as much individuality as most airlines allowed—at least on the parts of the flight attendants that were visible to the public. His uniform was dark blue, some kind of polyester blend I guessed, but he wore it well.

He leaned over and whispered to me, "White Party?"

I nodded.

"Wish I could go," he said. "I'm continuing on to Caracas tonight."

"That doesn't sound so bad," I said.

"There are worse jobs," he said. "But after a while, you realize that the more time you spend flying around the world, the less you have to come home to."

"I wouldn't know," I said. "For me, Miami seems like a big trip."

"I'm sure it's gonna be very big for you," he said. "I'm Jamie."

"Benji," I said.

Someone a few rows back rang the flight attendant buzzer and Jamie had to run. We didn't get to chat again before we landed, but at least I arrived in Miami with a smile on my face.

I drove from the airport with the windows down, the late afternoon still warm and sunny. Following the map I'd brought, I took a route that was more scenic than direct, over the southernmost bridge into the heart of South Beach. I drove up Ocean Drive, the beach on my right, a row of hotels and restaurants on my left. The sidewalks were crowded with freshly tanned people, still donning sunglasses, ready for the cocktail hour. There were women in short shorts and bikini tops, but they were outnumbered at least five-to-one by the men, nearly all of them shirtless. They ranged from lean and muscled to beefy and muscled—men of all ages in remarkable shape. They rode by on rollerblades, or walked by in twos and threes, or sat in the outdoor cafés watching everyone else go by.

But the crushing intensity of South Beach didn't go on forever. Within fifteen blocks, I was out of the neighborhood—out of the compact area that gay men think of as the entirety of Miami, the part with the cutest little Deco buildings, and the hottest guys, and the coolest places to hang out. Instead, I was thrust into an area with more high-rises, less foot traffic, fewer guys showing off their muscles. Hardware stores, chain hotels, Cuban restaurants, beachwear shops.

And then, seemingly out of nowhere, when I turned onto West Forty-first Street and crossed Indian Creek, I was in yet another neighborhood. North Beach. The shirtless boys in baseball caps had been replaced by fast-walking men in dark suits and fedoras; the babes on rollerblades had been replaced by women pushing strollers, children pulling on their long skirts. Shabbat was just an hour or two away, I realized.

Even if the people had been invisible, it still would have been obvious that this was a Jewish neighborhood. On one block, a kosher Chinese restaurant stood between a kosher pizza place and a kosher deli; all three had neon signs with Hebrew letters in their windows. The Jewish Study Center stood opposite the Torah Time gift shop, and catty-corner from Jeremy's Judaica, where paper dreidels hung behind the glass door. I passed a tiny Sephardic synagogue, then a Bukharian synagogue, then a synagogue without any English signs at all to help me identify it.

It was like Glenbrook South.

Just two blocks off this main drag sat the rabbi's complex, a two-story block of condos with small balconies and modest grounds alongside the parking lot. Carrying my bags in from the rental car, I was hit by the smell of Shabbat dinner cooking in a dozen apartments. It smelled like home.

The rabbi's condo was upstairs, a simple one-bedroom, one-bath affair, with a galley kitchen, all of it covered in wallpaper that was supposed to be tropical—giant bamboo stalks on one wall, bright green palm fronds on another. The air was stale, so I opened the sliding doors and stepped onto the balcony. No ocean view. I went back inside to look around. No cable. No stereo. Just books. And seashells scattered around by the handful.

I was mere blocks from one of the hottest gay spots on the planet at that moment, but I might as well have been on the moon.

I dropped my bag in the hall closet, grabbed a towel, and took a shower, deciding to head back to South Beach as quickly as possible.

*   *   *

Bars in D.C. got crowded on weekends, but I'd never seen anything like this. The sun had barely gone down and there was already a line to get into Rascals, a small dance bar with a big reputation on Collins Avenue. Most of the guys didn't seem to mind; plenty of them had already had a few cocktails while the sun was still shining and almost all of them were with groups of friends, so they chatted and checked out the other patrons while they waited their turn to enter and cruise.

A group of seven or eight friends stood right in front of me on line. One of them caught my eye for a moment, while he was talking to one of his pals. A few seconds later, he looked again. And a third time.

When I finally got inside, I lost him. I couldn't find him upstairs by the dance floor or downstairs in the video bar. I did manage, after almost twenty minutes, to get a cocktail, although it was hard to find a place to stand and drink.

I was getting ready to give up and try another bar when he found me again.

"I've been looking for you for half an hour!" he said.

"Same here."

We made the usual small talk: What's your name? (He was Ed.) Where are you from? (Atlanta, he said.) Is this your first White Party? (Yes, for both of us.) Where are you staying? ("I have an apartment," I told him.)

His group of friends had their whole weekend all mapped out. Later that evening, dinner and a disco nap, followed by a dance on the beach that cost fifty bucks per person. Saturday, beach and gym in the afternoon, then the White Party, then the after-party, then the after-after-party. Sunday there was some big tea dance after brunch and then they'd all head back to Atlanta. They'd been in town for two days already and showed no signs of slowing down. They were going to have the complete White Party experience. As a group.

"That's too bad," I said. "I was hoping to have some one-on-one time with you."

"Yeah?" he asked. "Well, I can't bag out on them tonight, but I'm free right now."

"Now?"

"Yeah, I mean, we won't go out tonight for a few hours and I can skip dinner and just grab a burger somewhere later."

"Okay," I said, although I hadn't actually planned on going home with someone quite so soon. "We can go to your hotel."

"Oh, that won't work," he said. "I'm sharing a room. Can't we go to your place?"

I thought about it for a moment, while I watched a Robbie Williams video on the television screens, one where cowboys in fringed chaps rode bucking broncos in slow motion.

On the one hand, I knew the rabbi wouldn't approve. On the other hand, I knew the rabbi wouldn't approve.

But it wasn't like he'd find out about it.

As we left the bar, we could hear Robbie Williams singing above the noise of the crowd: *Come on, hold my hand, I want to contact the living . . .*"

Ed had locked his bicycle to a parking sign. He unlocked it and walked me to my car.

"It's a bit of a hike," I told him.

"That's all right," he said. "I'm right behind you."

He followed me back to the rabbi's condo. The streets were quiet already; hardly anyone walking around, no shops open, services finished for the night.

Ed looked around like he'd just been transported to a strange new world—a world where only the buildings had survived, a world where Friday night was the quietest night of the week and, most certainly, no one had heard of Robbie Williams.

Inside the apartment, his expression didn't change. This

strange warren of bamboo and palm fronds didn't seem to put him at ease at all.

His expression only softened when he spotted the brass menorah on the windowsill.

"So you *are* Jewish," he said.

"Um, yeah," I said.

"Cool," he said. "I thought you were."

I was confused. "What difference does it make?" I asked.

"I really go for Jewish guys," he said. "They turn me on."

He stepped forward to kiss me, but I pushed him back with one palm. "Why do they turn you on?"

"Well, they're really smart," he said, "and they have great senses of humor, and they make good boyfriend material."

I didn't say anything.

"Plus, they're really sexy," he continued, perhaps sensing that this would be a good thing to include if he was trying to get laid. "I love guys with dark hair and hairy chests."

He leaned in again for a kiss, but I kept my palm on his chest.

"Italian guys have dark hair and hairy chests, too," I said. "How can you tell the difference? We don't usually wear yarmulkes when we're out at bars."

"I can always tell," he said. "It's the eyes. Jewish guys have a look in their eyes that nobody else has. A sort of sadness."

"Sadness? That's what turns you on? I'm glad that our five thousand years of suffering have finally paid off."

I folded my arms over my chest.

"Geez, Benji, I'm trying to say that you turn me on."

"No, you're trying to say that all my *brethren* turn you on."

"I don't get what the problem is," he said. "I think Jewish guys are hot. Isn't that a compliment?"

I thought about it for a minute. Gay men have stereotypes about lots of people, I knew; so why is it that everyone else had a reputation that was primarily sexual—black guys' alleged endowments, Asian guys' purported submissiveness, Mediterranean guys' supposed libidinousness—while the Jews got stuck being valued for our brains and sensitivity? Then again, if a cute guy was after me, why did it matter exactly what about me turned him on?

"I guess so," I said.

"I mean, don't *you* think Jewish guys are sexy?" he asked, leaning in one more time. This time I didn't stop him.

As he kissed me, I thought about his question. Truly, my answer was no. But the more I thought about it, the more I realized that Ed being attracted to Jews wasn't really much different from me chasing after a string of gentiles.

He pushed me back onto the sofa.

"I think *you're* sexy," he whispered. "I want you to be my little bagel boy."

I pulled away from him.

"Now what's wrong?" he asked.

"Bagel boy?"

"I'm just teasing you," he said.

"Well, stop it," I said. "It's kind of gross."

Was I being oversensitive? Wasn't that also part of Jewish guys' personalities—a part that was less than sexy?

"Sorry," he said.

Don't be so touchy, I told myself. I figured kissing him was a good way to shut him up before he called me something else that could be construed as borderline offensive. His little matzoh ball. His potato knish. His fiddler on the roof.

It worked. But each time I closed my eyes, I could see the rabbi's face, spitting mad, telling me to get out of his house.

"Should we go into the bedroom?" Ed asked.

"Actually, I'm sleeping on the sofa."

"Why?"

"It's not my apartment," I said. "It's a friend's."

"But you're here alone?"

"Yes."

"So why do you have to sleep on the couch?"

"My friend asked me to."

"Why?"

"I don't know."

"That's kind of weird, don't you think?"

"Not if you knew my friend."

Ed looked around the apartment again. And this time, instead of noticing the garish wallpaper or the brass menorah, he noticed the shelves of dusty books, the doilies under the lamps, the jar of Metamucil on the table.

"Is this your grandparents' place?"

"No, I told you, it's my friend's place."

"How old is your friend?"

"I don't know," I said. "Maybe eighty. Or eighty-five."

Ed squinted at me. "Is this a joke?"

"My friend's a rabbi."

Ed looked at me, waiting for the punch line.

"I'm serious," I said, turning on a lamp and showing him some of the rabbi's books in Hebrew.

"You came down for the White Party and you're staying in your rabbi's apartment?"

"He's not *my* rabbi," I said. As if this made any difference to anyone but me.

Ed contemplated the situation as his eyes scanned the place.

"I don't think I can do this after all," he said.

"You're kidding."

"No, I'm not. It feels really weird to be doing this in a rabbi's apartment."

I felt the same way, but not for the same reason.

"Strange," I said, "I'd think that if you're into Jewish guys, then a rabbi would be the ultimate turn-on."

He didn't get it. So much for Jewish humor.

"I should go," he said.

Apparently, he liked everything about Jewish guys except their actual Judaism.

Ed turned around and walked out quickly but quietly, shutting the door behind him.

I only had a moment to process it all before I heard a knock at the door.

I looked around the condo, wondering what Ed might have left behind: cell phone, keys, a wristwatch. I didn't see anything.

As I walked toward the front door, the knock came again. And with it, a woman's voice, asking tentatively: "Zisel?"

She couldn't have been more than four foot ten, thin and gray-haired and on the verge of tears.

"Zisel?" she asked again, looking at me with confusion and dread.

"You must have the wrong apartment," I said.

Her tears now flowed freely.

"Where is Zisel?" she asked.

"I'm sorry, I don't know who you're looking for," I said. "This is Rabbi Zuckerman's apartment."

"I know," she said. "And who are you?"

"Benji Steiner," I said. "I'm a friend of his."

"And where is he?"

"He is in Maryland," I said. "At home."

"So he is all right?"

"As far as I know."

She wiped the tears away. "Oh, thank God," she said. "I was so worried. I haven't had news from him in so long, and then I heard someone upstairs and saw the lights go on during Shabbat and I didn't know what to think."

I would have invited her in, but it wasn't necessary; she simply walked past me into the living room.

"I thought—*kenahora*—that he might have passed away, and you had bought his condo," she said, taking the glasses on her granny chain and fixing them on her face. "But now I see nothing has changed. It's still Zisel's apartment."

She sat on the couch and made herself at home.

"I'm sorry," I said, "but who are you?"

"Oh, no, *I'm* sorry, I thought you knew," she said. "I thought he'd have told you. I'm Irene Faber. I live downstairs."

"Nice to meet you," I said. "Can I ask you a stupid question? Who's Zisel?"

She looked at me with a crooked smile. "Rabbi Zuckerman, sweetheart."

"But his name is Jacob."

"And nobody has ever given you a name that did not appear on your birth certificate?"

I never was big on nicknames, and the ones I was given—notably Barfy Steiner, which lasted through much of seventh grade after an unfortunate incident in Spanish class—were ones I'd just as soon have forgotten. But I got the point. Then I remembered the letter the rabbi had snatched from my hands when he was in the hospital. *Don't be a snoop!* And suddenly things started to click.

"You sent the rabbi a letter this summer addressed to Zisel," I said.

"I've sent him many letters, dear. And they're all addressed to Zisel," she said. "To me, he was Zisel long before he was ever a rabbi."

"How long have you known him?" I asked.

"More than sixty years," she said. "How long have you known him?"

"Just a few months."

"Ah, now I understand," she said. "Tell me, Benji Steiner, are you *shomer shabbes?*"

"No," I said.

"Good," she said. "Then make me a cup of tea and we can fill in each other's blanks."

*   *   *

"We both grew up in Jersey City," Irene told me, "although my family lived uptown and his lived downtown. My uncle owned a five-and-dime on Newark Avenue, not far from where the Zuckermans lived, and when I was in high school, I used to help out in his shop on Sundays. Jacob's mother would send him out every Sunday to buy a few things at the bakery and the greengrocer, and he'd come into our shop to spend a little of his change on candy. Just one or two pieces—licorice, or chocolate, or hard candies, or chewing gum. He couldn't buy more, or his mother would notice the money missing. But he always bought something. That boy had some sweet tooth, I remember."

An image of the rabbi sucking on hard candy flashed in my mind.

"I used to tease him about it," she continued, "how it was no coincidence that a boy with a name like Zuckerman— 'zucker' means sugar, you know—had such a sweet tooth. He'd just laugh. Until one day, we must have been about sixteen, he told me that the candy wasn't the only sweet thing in that shop. Can you believe it?"

I couldn't picture the rabbi flirting with a shop clerk. Or picture him as a smooth-talking teenage boy. But from the look on Irene's face, I could tell she could picture it still.

She saw my disbelief. "You'll have to trust me when I say that I was quite a pretty girl all those years ago. Long brown hair and quite a figure. Jacob wasn't the only boy who looked at me, if you get my meaning."

"I have no doubt," I said.

"Anyway, my uncle saw what was happening, and he thought that Jacob seemed like a nice young man, so he'd let me take a few minutes away from the counter on Sunday afternoons and Jacob and I would go for a walk in Van Vorst Park, maybe buy an ice cream or a soda. Let me tell you, he was one handsome devil. And always so polite. We'd see each other every week, only for a little while. But I guess you could say I fell for him. I thought he was just the cat's pajamas. And I told him one night that he was so sweet, even a name like 'sugar man' wasn't enough to describe him. I told him he was twice as sweet as any other boy. So I called him Zisel Zuckerman."

I looked at her blankly.

" 'Zisel' is Yiddish, dear," she clarified. "Do you speak Yiddish?"

"No."

"Of course you don't. Young people just never learned it, did they? Zisel means 'sweet little thing.' So you see, to me, he was sweet like sugar from beginning to end, from Zisel to Zuckerman."

"Ah," I said.

"He hated it. 'Zisel is what a mother calls her baby,' he'd say. 'Or what a man calls his sweetheart.' And I suppose he was right—it's what my grandmother called me when I was a little girl. It'd be like calling a grown man 'Sweetie.' He probably wouldn't like that much, either. But to me, he was always Zisel."

"That sounds romantic."

"It was," she said. "And besides, he had to have some kind of nickname. My father's name was Jacob, so there was no way I was going to go out with a boy and call him by my father's name. Imagine kissing your father! Well, I'm sorry, I haven't met *your* father, but still, you take my point."

Irene may have been little and old, but she was no typical little old lady, I could tell already. She'd been there five minutes and I'd already been forced to imagine the rabbi putting the moves on a teenage girl and my father kissing an octogenarian. I refilled her tea.

"So, my uncle knew what was going on, and he told my parents, who trusted my uncle to keep an eye on us," she said. "And Zisel's mother knew, because he had to explain to her why he was always late coming back with the groceries on Sunday afternoons. She stopped by the store one day to meet me, and to talk with my uncle, and I guess I passed the test, because we kept on seeing each other.

"But Zisel's father was another story. He was a horrible, strict man. He had grown up in Poland and never really left the shtetl behind in his mind. Zisel told me that in the house, his father always spoke Yiddish, and was very insistent about Jewish law. Zisel's mother was a much softer woman, who spoke English with hardly any accent, and listened to all the popular radio programs. Even though she also grew up in Poland, she thought of herself as very American. She convinced her husband to let Zisel attend the local public school, instead of a yeshiva. This wasn't easy, but she made sure that Zisel observed all the holidays and kept kosher and went to synagogue every week and knew all his prayers. He studied with his father every *Shabbes* afternoon. That was the only day he wasn't working in the bakery.

"But one day, Zisel's father demanded to know what was happening to his spare change from his Sunday errands, and Zisel told him. He thought his father would be pleased that he had met a nice girl—a Jewish girl. But he wasn't so excited. It's hard to explain, but we were from two different Jewish worlds. He lived downtown with all the immigrant families. They were poor, working-class, and Orthodox. They lived in crowded brownstones, a different family on every floor, one on top of another, and they went to Sons of Israel, the Orthodox shul on Grove Street right near City Hall. My family lived uptown. My father was an optician. We had a car and a house of our own and we went to the temple—the big Reform synagogue uptown. And we weren't immigrants. My parents were born in America. My *grandparents* were born in America. So Zisel and I were both Jewish, but we weren't really part of the same community."

I thought about the way the congregants from B'nai Tikvah had stared at me when I came to the rabbi's assistance outside their synagogue and the way my mother always talked about the rabbi like he practiced some other religion.

"Not much has changed," I said.

"Maybe," she said. "Sometimes I still feel like all these *frum* women down here look at me funny because I'm not as observant as they are. Not that I care anymore. But back then, everyone cared. The divisions were deep, and people viewed each other with suspicion. When Zisel's father found out he was dating me, it must have seemed like he had been completely betrayed by his wife and his son—they'd promised to maintain Zisel's Judaism, and now he was going around with this uptown, hoity-toity German Jew. Basically a *shiksa*, as far as he was concerned."

She took a breath.

"Remember, Zisel was the baby of the family, the only one born in this country. So his father thought this was his last chance to get things right, and apparently I was not the right type of girl. He forbade us to see each other. Zisel wasn't allowed to come into the shop, or to contact me at all. And at the end of the year, his father pulled him out of public school and sent him to a yeshiva in Brooklyn, which was basically a whole world away—Zisel's mother came to tell me. I cried and I cried, but there was nothing I could do. It was over. I thought I'd never see him again."

She paused for a sip of tea.

"But it wasn't over, apparently," I said. "You did see him again."

"Yes, dear, but not for a long time. I went to college and became a schoolteacher, and I married my husband Harold and we lived in New Jersey and raised three children. And Zisel became a rabbi and got married and opened the bookstore . . . well, this part I think you know."

I nodded.

"For sixty years, we didn't see each other. But when Harold died three years ago, I sold the house in New Jersey and moved down to Miami Beach. And who should be living upstairs?"

"Rabbi Zuckerman," I said.

"Exactly. And do you know why? Because it's *bashert*. Do you know what that means?"

"Fate."

"So you do know some Yiddish," Irene said. "Fate brought us together after all these years. Of course, he never believed anything was *bashert*."

I didn't tell her that the rabbi apparently did now believe it—because he'd used that word to describe meeting Sophie. And I didn't know if Sophie was a subject I should avoid bringing up.

"Listen to me, rattling on like a crazy old woman," she said. "You tell me, Benji, isn't it fate that brings people together?"

"I'm beginning to think so," I said.

I met Donnie when I was in tenth grade. We were both dancers.

I had always wanted to dance. When I was little, too little to know exactly what boys were and weren't supposed to do, I'd watch with envy when Rachel took classes in ballet or tap. Dance had everything: music, costumes, hand motions. I asked my parents if I could take tap. They signed me up for pee-wee soccer instead. Needless to say, I was rotten, and the coach was as happy as I was when I didn't return for a second year.

Once I was old enough to realize that boys who dance only set themselves up for ridicule, I resigned myself to the fact that my dance career would probably consist of doing the Macarena in my bedroom alone.

That equation changed when I reached high school. The idea of undressing in a locker room for gym class terrified me—or, rather, terrified and excited me in roughly equal measure—and our school had a strict gym requirement. There was only one way out: Take an accredited class outside school. I looked around for options and found a folk dance class at the Jewish Community Center in Rockville.

Chances of anyone besides my guidance counselor ever finding out about the class were slim to none; the jocks and meatheads who dominated my school didn't keep up on the folk dance scene, so I wasn't too worried about their taunts. I figured I'd finally found a way to get out of gym. And my parents were so happy that I'd be taking a class at the JCC, they didn't care if it was dance or ceramics or gunsmithing—it was something Jewish, a sign that their child who'd stopped going to synagogue wasn't giving up on their faith altogether.

I wasn't bad. At the end of ninth grade, the teacher asked me to join the JCC's teen dance troupe, which I did—since it still counted toward my gym requirement. And, because the girls outnumbered the boys in the troupe fourteen to one, I got parts in pretty much every single routine we did.

Our performances were mostly small affairs. We danced in the lobby of a retirement center for a dozen hard-of-hearing Jewish seniors. We did a five-minute routine as part of a Hanukkah celebration at the JCC.

By the spring, though, we were ready to participate in the Salute to Israel, an outdoor festival marking Israeli Independence Day that drew hundreds of spectators and included musicians, comedians, and dancers of all ages. We even had another teenage dance troupe coming in from Rochester to perform with us.

The kids in our troupe agreed to house the kids from Rochester, and since I was the only boy in our troupe, I hosted the only boy from Rochester: Donnie.

We set him up in Rachel's room, since it was empty now that she was off at college.

The van from Rochester arrived at the JCC while we were rehearsing. We stopped for a round of introductions, matching up hosts with guests. And when Donnie and I stood side-by-side, all eyes seemed to widen. It was like we were twins.

We both wore black high-top sneakers, baggy jeans, and Old Navy T-shirts. Our glasses matched, our haircuts matched. Our builds were similar, although he was slightly bigger.

"I'm seeing double," one of the girls in my troupe teased.

We both blushed and shook hands. "It's like looking in a mirror," Donnie said.

I had never met anyone who reminded me of myself. At school, I had my circle of friends, but what we mostly had in common was that we were all misfits in some way—and even in this group of guys, I had started to feel less secure as the rest of my friends started to date girls. When I was dancing, I was the only boy; while the girls never made me feel left out, I was never really part of their clique. But here was Donnie, two years older, confident, comfortable in his skin. He was a month away from graduation, getting ready to head to Stanford. This would be his last performance with his troupe, after three years.

Sitting across from each other on Rachel's bed, we stayed up all night talking. And not about our dance routines.

Donnie was gay. He was only out to a few of his friends in Rochester—not his parents, not the other members of his troupe— but it wasn't a total secret anymore.

"And once I'm away from Mom and Dad next fall," he said, "I can finally do what I want."

He knew exactly what he wanted. He had no problem imagining his life as a gay man: he'd have a boyfriend, a fabulous apartment, and maybe a cat, and they'd live in San Francisco. A total escape from his life so far in Rochester, which sounded surprisingly like mine, from Hebrew school to Jewish camp to visiting Grandma in Florida.

He described his future life clearly and concretely, as if he didn't have any doubt that it was possible. He was ready.

Why was he telling me?

Donnie asked me about my plans, but my plans at that point didn't stretch beyond high school. I knew I'd go to college, and I hoped that would offer some respite from my adolescent misery, but

I hadn't given much thought to what my life might look like after that. Maybe I'd been afraid to imagine it, afraid that picturing it— the boyfriend, the cat, everything I could only guess gay life in- volved—would make it too real.

A lot of things that might have happened that night didn't hap- pen. There was no attraction on that level, at least from what I could tell.

And even though I certainly had many opportunities, I didn't tell Donnie that I thought I was gay, too.

But I knew that night that fate had brought Donnie and me to- gether. Talking to him, I felt for the first time like things were going to be okay for me. Meeting him wasn't like looking into a mirror. It was like looking into the future.

Irene stayed and talked until midnight—about her family, about the rabbi, about the Jewish community in North Beach—when she went home to bed.

"I volunteer on Saturdays," she said. "And if I want to look presentable, I've got to get my beauty rest. At my age, every minute helps."

She pulled me down to her to kiss me on the cheek and headed downstairs. There was still plenty of time for me to go out, catch one of the pre-White Party parties in South Beach. But I wasn't really in the mood anymore. Instead, I stayed in, snooping around the rabbi's condo, looking for traces of the man Irene had known, the sweet, flirtatious Zisel she had loved.

I didn't find much. Bengay and Sanka and one box of very old raisins. Nothing revealing. I made up the sofa bed and went to sleep.

Saturday morning, North Beach was busy with people headed to their respective shuls. I got a couple of nasty looks—for wearing shorts, or driving a car on Shabbat, or going anywhere besides services, I'm not exactly sure—but I ignored them and headed back to South Beach.

An hour or two sunbathing helped me get a bit of a tan to offset the white clothes I'd bought.

An hour or two of shopping around Lincoln Road Mall allowed me to find the perfect shoes and the perfect cap, and the perfect postcard—with a photo of some serious Miami beefcake—to make Phil jealous.

An hour or two at the "Heatwave" pool party in the afternoon made me feel completely insecure about my body and made me wish I had another year to work out every day at the gym before that night's big event.

But I didn't have another year, so I made the most of it.

Even in my cutest white outfit, I was a bit apprehensive when I arrived at the White Party, but I exhaled after getting a few approving looks from other people in line. While other circuit parties often got a bad rap—for combining sex, drugs, and rock 'n' roll (or, in this case, house music) in such irresponsible ways—the White Party was another animal entirely. Spread across the grounds of a mansion called Vizcaya, the event included hundreds if not thousands of guests, yet managed to avoid feeling like a tacky, overcrowded club. A string quartet played classical music inside. Acres of gardens stretched back away from the building, with a performance space tucked away in the back, where the city's top caterers offered their food. Throngs of people, in blinding white, danced to big-name DJs. And, to top it off, as an AIDS fundraiser, it was all for a good cause.

I danced, I ate. I even got to hear Cyndi Lauper singing "True Colors," which was one of my favorite songs as a kid.

But I just couldn't get into it. After all the time and money I'd spent preparing and shopping, I couldn't seem to relax and enjoy myself. In a sea of beautiful men, the only person I could think about was Irene.

I left the party early and arrived on her doorstep still clad all in white.

She didn't seem the least bit surprised to see me standing there, at ten o'clock on a Saturday night.

"White Party?" she asked, pushing her glasses onto her nose, checking out my outfit.

"How did you . . . ?"

"Sweetheart, I volunteer at the Jewish Museum, smack in the middle of South Beach," she said. "So I do know a little bit about the scene down here. And I certainly know when the White Party is. It's all anyone in South Beach could talk about today."

"So you knew . . . ?"

"That you're gay?" she said. "I may need glasses, but I'm not blind."

"It's funny, Rabbi Zuckerman didn't know."

"We see what we want to see," she said. Then she opened the door and showed me into her apartment.

It was easy to see which furniture she'd bought when she moved to Florida (a generically modern, overstuffed beige couch; a small, pine dining room table that had probably come straight from IKEA) and which items had been hers for decades (an antique china hutch filled with gilt-edged dishes, matching table lamps with porcelain bases shaped like Oriental vases).

And there were framed photos on every available shelf or tabletop. Irene walked me around the living room and explained who was in each picture. Her late husband. Her kids. Her grandkids—at least a dozen different shots. The photos told the story of her family through the decades: vacations, graduations, birthday parties, school portraits.

On top of the television sat a color snapshot, in a Lucite frame. "My son took that picture about two years ago when he came to visit," she said. In the photograph, Irene stood between Rabbi Zuckerman and Sophie. All three were smiling. The women had their arms around each other's waists and were looking into the camera. The rabbi stood slightly separate, hands at his side, looking at Sophie.

"It's funny seeing the rabbi without his beard," I said.

"Zisel has a beard now?" she asked.

I nodded.

"He must have grown it when Sophie died," she said. "I guess he never shaved it off."

This was the first time Irene had mentioned Sophie by name, so I decided to pursue it.

"Were you and Sophie friends?" I asked.

"Of course we were," she said.

"Rabbi Zuckerman talks about her all the time," I said.

"I imagine he does," she said. "She was a wonderful woman, Sophie. Although of course I only knew her for a short time, and much of that time, she was sick. But when someone has a good soul, it doesn't matter if they're old or young, sick or not. You can tell."

I picked up the photo and examined it more closely. On second glance, it appeared that the rabbi wasn't looking at Sophie at all, but at Irene. Or was I seeing things? It was hard to tell from a slightly out-of-focus snapshot.

"When we were all together down here, the three of us became like a little family," she said. "Sophie and I would cook and the three of us would eat together. And when Zisel would go to shul, Sophie and I would sit on the balcony and talk."

"About what?"

"Well, I would talk about my children and my grandchildren, I suppose," said Irene. "And Sophie would talk to me about the bookstore."

"You didn't talk about the past?"

"Sweetheart, can you imagine that conversation? Neither of us wanted to talk about the past."

I felt like an idiot.

"But that didn't matter, we were friends," she said, pointing to a framed needlepoint hanging on the wall. "She made that for me."

I went to look at the needlepoint and Irene turned on another lamp so I could see better. It was an orange sunrise coming over a green hilltop and had something written on it in Hebrew. "What does it say?" I asked.

"I don't remember the Hebrew words," she said, "but it's a quote from Hillel: 'If not now, when?' I always liked that quote. Sort of like 'Carpe diem' for the Jewish crowd."

"I think the rabbi has a couple of things like this in his house," I said, remembering the pictures I'd seen upstairs in his house—one with flowers, another with apples, both with Hebrew writing on them.

"I'm sure he does. Sophie was an expert. She told me that she used to needlepoint in the store in between customers."

Without being invited to stay, I sat down on the couch. Irene sat in the chair next to me.

"Did Sophie know about you and the rabbi?" I asked.

"We never talked about it," she said. "But Sophie was no fool. She knew that we were friends when we were teenagers. Did she connect the dots? Probably. And she knew that we were close again down here in Miami. Did she connect those dots? Probably."

I looked at her in disbelief.

"Close?" I asked.

She paused. "You ask a lot of questions, Benji."

"I'm sorry," I said. "You don't have to answer. If it's too personal."

"At my age, most people I know want to talk about bowel movements and incontinence," she said. "Nothing's too personal."

She smiled and I knew I hadn't offended her.

"I'm just not used to talking about this," she said. "But yes, you might say we picked up where we left off."

"What does *that* mean?" I asked.

"Oh, it's not nearly as tawdry as you're thinking," she said. "Young people always go right to the sex, don't you? Dressed in white, but you've still got a filthy mind. When I say we had a little affair, I mean that we sort of picked up where we'd left off when we were teenagers—and we weren't having sex then, either! I was too young for all that then and I'm too old for it now. We just spent time together, a few minutes here or there, and talked."

"About what?"

"About all the years we'd missed. The years we might have had together. Even after all that time, we still loved each other.

"We never had more than a few minutes. He always got up early to daven and then he'd go to the bakery to get rolls for breakfast. He'd drop a couple of them by my apartment on his way home and we'd have two, maybe three minutes together. Or Sophie would take a walk to the beach to collect seashells and we'd have ten or fifteen minutes before she came back. It was never much. But it was a lot."

"Did Sophie ever find out?"

"No," said Irene. "But one afternoon, when they were down here for a whole week around Christmastime, Sophie wasn't feeling well—she'd been getting chemotherapy—and she lay down to take a nap. Zisel came downstairs and we thought we might have a whole hour together. A whole hour! He told me he still loved me, that he had never stopped loving me after all these years.

"It's not that we didn't both have good lives. He was happy with Sophie and they had a very nice life and a successful business. And I had been happy with Harold and wouldn't trade all my years with him for anything. But still, we knew we had both been denied what might have been for us. And regardless of what else happened, this was a tragedy. Because, like I told you, we were meant to be together. So that night, while Sophie was upstairs napping, we sat at my table and cried, both of us.

"And when Zisel went upstairs afterward to check on Sophie, he found her passed out on the bathroom floor. She had woken up feeling very sick, and started vomiting blood, and passed out right there by the sink."

"So what did you do?"

"We called an ambulance, of course, and Sophie went to Mount Sinai and got a transfusion and the doctor put her on some new medication and she came home a couple days later. But she was never quite herself after that. She never asked Zisel where he'd been that afternoon and he never told her. But he was convinced that God was telling him that what we were doing was wrong, that even though all we had done was talk, it was like he was breaking his marriage vows. So we had to stop seeing each other, even for a few minutes, without Sophie."

"And that was the end of it?" I asked. "It just ended, and you went back to being friends with both of them?"

"Mostly, yes," she said. "I didn't have a choice. I couldn't talk to Zisel about it in front of Sophie and he wouldn't see me alone anymore. And then they went back to Maryland, so it wasn't really an issue. But he did come once more to my apartment, many months later, when they came back to Florida."

"What happened?"

"He told me he had been praying a lot, and studying, trying to find a solution," she said. "And he had one. Even though he couldn't see me anymore while he was with Sophie, he told me that if, God forbid, Sophie should die before him, he would marry me."

"I don't get it."

"Well, in his mind, being with me while Sophie was alive was adultery," Irene said. "But if we were both—God forbid—widowed, then God wouldn't want two widowed people to be lonely and miserable, and then, and only then, would it be all right for us to finally be together."

"How much longer did Sophie live?" I asked.

"Just a few months," she said. "She got very sick, poor thing. May she rest in peace."

"So are you two going to get married?" I asked.

"Let's just say I've stopped looking for a wedding dress," she said with a flip of her hand. "After Sophie died, he stopped taking my calls, at home or at work. I send him letters, but he never answers. He hasn't come to Florida once since she died."

"He won't talk to you at all?" I asked. I knew the rabbi was stubborn, but this seemed unnecessarily cruel.

"I thought I'd lost him forever," said Irene. "Until he sent you here."

The trip home was uneventful—no flirtatious flight attendant, no whole can of Diet Coke.

The weekend hadn't turned out the way I'd planned at all. I had anticipated a few days of partying, hanging out on the beach with a bunch of guys, sipping fruity cocktails through silly straws. But while I'd dipped my toe into the gay scene, I'd actually spent most of my time in North Beach. And while I'd chatted with one or two guys, I'd spent most of my time talking to an old woman.

Irene made me see the rabbi in a new light. I wasn't ready to forgive him, exactly, but I felt like I had a better sense of what was going on in his mind. He was a man who lived his life by the rules—a man who had been punished every time he'd broken those rules; a man who punished himself for breaking them, as well. Still, despite his own black-and-white sense of propriety, before our fight, he'd never forced his ideas on me, never insisted that I live according to his code. In fact, he was the only person I'd ever known in a position of Jewish authority who hadn't told me I was a bad Jew if I didn't keep kosher or go to synagogue or pray regularly. Even though he made his own ideas clear, he'd listened, and for a while, he seemed to accept that I might not be the same kind of Jew that he was.

When it came to relationships, however, he was indeed a rigid man; some things, he seemed to think, were not negotiable. If he wouldn't permit himself to bend the rules, even after yearning for sixty years, he certainly wasn't going to allow some kid to break them completely.

When I got back to the apartment, Michelle was in the living room, watching television.

"How was Long Island?" I asked, even though her face already told me the answer.

"Awesome," she said. "His parents are totally cool—we stayed in his old bedroom and shared the bed."

"Your parents would never let you do that," I said.

"I know!" she said. "And I got to meet his sister, and his aunt and uncle, and his grandmother. The whole family. Everyone was really great and Dan and I had a fantastic time. Seriously, it was like the best Thanksgiving I ever had."

"I'm sure your parents would be thrilled to hear you put it that way."

"Right? I told my mom that Dan's mom's turkey wasn't anywhere near as good as hers, so she's happy."

"Smart," I said.

"And how about you?" she said. "I see a little bit of a tan on your face, so you must have gotten some sun."

"Yeah," I said.

"And was the White Party as amazing as you thought it'd be?"

"Yeah," I said.

"And did you meet anyone?" she asked with a smirk.

She laughed at my story about Ed and his Jew fetish, but by the end, I didn't think it was so funny. "I think I should give up on dating for a while," I said. "It's getting ridiculous."

"Come on," she said. "The whole time you were down there, you didn't meet anyone else?"

"I did, actually," I said. "But not the way you think."

I told her all about Irene and the rabbi's affair.

"No way!" she said. "This is like a total soap opera!"

"I know."

"So are you going to go tell the rabbi that you met his little mistress? His jilted woman? Or are you going to play dumb and pretend like you don't know a thing?"

"Actually, I don't know if I'm going to tell him anything," I said.

Michelle looked confused, and I realized that I hadn't seen her since before the holiday, and she didn't know the rabbi had kicked me out of his house. It had only been a few days since our fight, even though it seemed like much longer. I filled in Michelle, who was rapt.

"I knew that rabbi wasn't as hip as you thought!" she said. "I mean, Benji, come on. He's a rabbi. What did you expect?"

"More, I guess."

"So are you going to see him?"

"I don't know," I said. "I'm still thinking about that."

I took my bags to my room and picked up the phone. Message waiting. I checked my voicemail and found just one message waiting for me.

"Benjamin? It's Linda Goldfarb. I'm sorry to bother you at home, and I know you probably won't get this until you're back from Florida, but I thought I should call you. It's about the rabbi. . . ."

CHAPTER 10

"One of the congregants from B'nai Tikvah stopped by to walk Rabbi Zuckerman to shul on Saturday and found him on the bathroom floor," Mrs. Goldfarb told me in the bookstore on Monday morning. "He's the one who called the ambulance. It must have been an awful scene, because you know it takes a lot for one of them to use the phone on Shabbat."

"So what's wrong with him?"

"Another stroke," she said. "Much worse this time."

"Is he going to be okay?"

"We're not sure yet. He still can't talk," she said. "They're doing all sorts of tests to see if there's permanent brain damage, but even if there isn't, they're not sure how quickly he'll be able to recover."

"Do they know what caused it?" I asked. I knew he was supposed to be avoiding stress—could our argument have brought this on?

"They don't know," Mrs. Goldfarb said. "But you remember when he had his first episode, they told him that it might happen again."

I stood silently, replaying our fight in my head.

"I'm sorry you had to come home to this kind of news," she said, touching my arm.

"Me, too."

"I thought about calling you at the Zuckermans' apartment, but I figured there was nothing anyone could do," she said. "And I didn't want to ruin your vacation."

Funny, I thought, that she still talked about it belonging to the rabbi *and* Sophie. Although it made sense.

"Yeah, thanks," I said. "Not that it was really what you'd call a vacation. It was a pretty interesting weekend."

"What do you mean?" she asked.

I looked at her and it dawned on me that she'd known the rabbi for many years and probably knew much more than I realized.

I decided to test her: "I met his downstairs neighbor."

"Irene?" she asked.

Bingo.

"Yeah, Irene," I said. "Have you met her?"

"No," she said. "But we've spoken on the phone. She's quite something, isn't she?"

"You can say that again," I said, staying vague.

"So, what did you two talk about?" she asked.

I started to wonder if Mrs. Goldfarb wasn't testing me, too.

"About the rabbi, mostly," I said.

Mrs. Goldfarb nodded. But exactly what did she know?

"And about how he won't answer her letters or her phone calls," I continued.

Mrs. Goldfarb looked me square in the eye, waiting to hear what else I knew.

"And about how they had planned to get married," I said. She blinked.

"So she told you the whole story," Mrs. Goldfarb said.

"I suppose," I said. "Unless there's still more that I don't know."

"No, I think that's about it," she said.

Mrs. Goldfarb had heard about Irene for a few years. It wasn't the rabbi who first told her about Irene, it was Sophie.

Sophie who was so amazed to see how people's paths could diverge for years only to cross again unexpectedly, Sophie who was so delighted to make a new friend so late in life, Sophie who was so pleased to see the rabbi reconnect with someone from his childhood.

"Sophie talked about Irene quite a lot," Mrs. Goldfarb said. "Sometimes Irene would call her at the store to tell her about something that happened in Miami. And I remember Sophie spent quite a while making a big needlepoint for Irene—she only did that for people she really liked, because by that point, her eyesight wasn't so good and her arthritis was acting up and needlepoint was pretty difficult for her."

"Yeah, she told me they were friends," I said.

"Very much so," she said. "But I guess that's all over now."

"The rabbi won't even talk to her?"

"Not since Sophie died," said Mrs. Goldfarb. "At first, when Irene would call the store and the rabbi would tell me to say he wasn't in, I thought it was all just part of his grief. Like he was too despondent to talk to anyone. So I didn't think it was a big deal. I figured he'd get beyond that eventually.

"But then one day last spring, Irene called the store in tears," she continued, "and she said she wanted to talk to *me*. We'd chatted here and there over the years, but we'd never really had a serious conversation before. She was hoping I'd be able to explain to her why Rabbi Zuckerman had cut her off. I told her I didn't really know and that Rabbi Zuckerman really didn't talk to me about his personal life. So Irene told me her whole story."

"Were you surprised?" I asked.

"Definitely," she said. "But I could empathize with both of them. I lost my husband when he was very young, so I know what it's like to be widowed. I knew that Irene had been horribly lonely after her husband died and what a godsend it was for her to find the Zuckermans. And I knew that

Rabbi Zuckerman was going to have a very difficult time without Sophie—if you'd met her, you'd understand, she truly was his better half. What the rabbi was doing didn't make any sense. He wasn't just resigning himself to living out his remaining years alone. He was also leaving Irene all alone. Again!"

I thought about Irene. She seemed so strong and independent. But then I remembered how I first saw her, crying in the doorway, fragile and scared.

"It'd almost have been easier for Irene if she'd never met the rabbi again," I said.

"That's right," said Mrs. Goldfarb. "But here, she felt like she'd somehow been lucky enough so that she wouldn't have to be alone anymore and he went and abandoned her. Without even an explanation."

"So what did you do?"

"I told Rabbi Zuckerman that I'd talked to Irene and that I thought he should call her," she said. "He didn't want to hear it. I tried to convince him that calling Irene would make both of them much happier and it wouldn't be hurting anyone. But he didn't want to hear that, either. So then I told him that Sophie wouldn't have wanted him to be all alone."

I thought back on my fight with the rabbi and remembered how bringing up Sophie had been my ultimate error.

"That probably didn't go over well," I said.

"You got that right," she said. "He told me to mind my own business and stay out of his personal life. And he told me never to mention Sophie again. And I haven't."

"But you still talk to Irene?"

"Not for many months," she said. "After I had that talk with Rabbi Zuckerman, I called Irene and told her that I'd tried, but I didn't think he'd budge. Irene said she understood and she'd try not to get me more involved. She hasn't called since. I figured she finally gave up."

"Not quite," I said. "She's still sending him letters at home."

"How do you know?"

"I've seen his mail," I said. "But he throws them all in the garbage without reading them."

"See? Stubborn."

"Believe me, now I know just what you mean," I said. And I told her about my fight with the rabbi the previous week. I'd never talked to Mrs. Goldfarb about being gay, but I'd always just assumed she'd figured it out. After all, she knew me as a child; she probably knew I was gay long before I knew myself. Whether or not she'd already known for sure, or guessed, she didn't seem taken aback by this bit of information.

"You know, Benjamin, I really thought he'd be different with you," she said. "But I guess he fights with everyone. Sooner or later."

I didn't get much work done that day.

As I sat at my desk, staring at the Barry Sisters poster he'd given me, all I could think about was the rabbi. I wondered if our fight had brought on his stroke; after months of progress, with the rabbi finally learning how to relax and take care of himself, I might have unintentionally put him right back in the hospital with a ten-minute argument.

And besides, even if I wasn't the direct cause of his stroke, the plain truth was that I wasn't there when he needed me. I wasn't there to call the ambulance. I began to understand how the rabbi must have felt when he left Sophie alone: He was gone only for an hour, but that hour continued to haunt him almost two years later.

I may have forgotten the tunes to some prayers for Shabbat, and my Hebrew might have been rusty, but my sense of Jewish guilt was as keen as ever.

I called my mother—the one who'd done such a good job of instilling that guilt—and told her about the rabbi. For once, she didn't try to get in any digs about him or tell me why I should avoid all Orthodox people. She just listened.

"It's not your fault, Benji," she said. "You've already done more for that man than anyone could have expected. You can't be with him twenty-four hours every day. You're not his nurse."

"I know."

"And you knew he was sick," she continued. "You knew it was just a matter of time until he had another stroke, right? That's what you told me the last time he was in the hospital. So it's not your fault."

"I know."

"So if you know," she said, "then what's the problem?"

I explained that I felt guilty, despite everything I understood to be true.

"Guilt can be very useful," she said, "depending on what it makes you do."

"What do you think I should do?" I asked.

"All of a sudden you care what I think you should do?" she replied.

Touché.

"Listen," she said, "you know that I always thought it was a bad idea to get involved with that rabbi. But now you're involved, and it's up to you to figure out what to do."

She told me that she'd make a *misheberach*, a prayer for the sick, in synagogue that Saturday—which seemed like an unusually kind gesture until she added, "because I know you wouldn't deign to go to services and do it yourself."

Nice, Mom.

I couldn't figure out what I wanted to do. On the one hand, I was still angry about what the rabbi had said to me the previous week. I could put up with a lot, but that kind of thoughtless bigotry, veiled in piety and sanctimony, really got my hackles up. The rabbi and I had different views of our Judaism and how it informed our lives; so why did he get to judge my life by his standards, rather than the other way around?

On the other hand, if he really was like a grandfather to me, shouldn't I have been able to get past the arguments and forgive him? Wasn't our bond strong enough, after these months, to withstand a few harsh words—especially at a time like this?

I didn't have an answer yet when Mrs. Goldfarb knocked on my office door after five o'clock.

"I'm heading over to Holy Cross after work," she said, standing in the open doorway, one hand holding a lit cigarette just outside. "Do you want to go with me?"

I shook my head. "I'm not sure if I want to see him," I said.

She was taken aback. "Look, Benjamin, if you two are going to patch things up, somebody here is going to have to make the first move. And right now, Rabbi Zuckerman can't do it. So it's going to have to be you."

She waited for my answer, but I didn't respond.

"All right, not today," she said before she turned to leave. "But don't wait too long. You have all the time in the world. Rabbi Zuckerman might not."

I didn't go to the hospital that day. Or the next day. Or the next.

By Friday, Mrs. Goldfarb had stopped asking if I wanted to go. She still stopped by every afternoon to give me an update: "He's sitting up" or "He can hold a cup steady" or "He's getting a few words out." But no more talk of visiting hours at Holy Cross.

On Friday, I went straight home from the office after work. Michelle was already there, unpacking groceries.

"Still no visit?" she asked

"Nope," I said.

She nodded. "Still pissed, huh?"

"Yup."

That was it. No guilt, no pressure, no cross-examination. I

didn't know what Michelle really thought—or if she actually had an opinion one way or the other—about the situation. But I appreciated having someone who'd just listen without questioning me.

I went to my room and kicked off my shoes.

Michelle came in behind me and sat on my bed.

"I think I've got a solution to your problem," she said.

"The rabbi?"

"You are totally obsessed with him, aren't you?" she said. "I'm not talking about your rabbi problem. I'm talking about your *man* problem."

"I have a man problem?"

"Don't you? You're gonna be twenty-seven this weekend and you're still hopelessly single."

"Is that a problem?"

"Just because you don't have a biological clock doesn't mean that time is on your side," she said. "Twenty-one and single is cute. Thirty and single is pathetic."

"Is that from Confucius? Or *Sex and the City*?"

"Joke all you want," she said, getting sassy and snapping a finger in the air like she was a guest on *Jerry Springer*. "I don't gotta help you. I *got* a man."

"Okay, okay," I said. "Help me. Please. I need all the help I can get . . . with my *man* problem."

"I thought about it while you were away and I figured out what you've been doing wrong. You should be dating Jewish guys."

"Why's that?"

"You wouldn't be having all the problems you've been having . . ."

I could see her point with guys like Pete, with his vaguely anti-Semitic faux-liberal politics, and Christopher, with his I-like-you-but-I-*love*-Jesus issues. But Frankie?

"You really think the problem with Frankie was that he wasn't Jewish?" I asked.

"No, the problem with Frankie is that he's a tattooed, crystal-snorting skinhead," she said. "But can you name one tattooed, crystal-snorting skinhead who's Jewish?"

I thought about it.

"Actually, no."

"It's because their mothers would die of shame. And deep inside, they know that. And they care. That's what makes them Jewish."

"Funny, I thought it had something to do with synagogue. Or circumcision."

"Nope," she said, "it's all about Mom."

I wasn't convinced that it couldn't ever work with a non-Jew, that I should just write off ninety-eight percent of the men in America.

"You know," I said, "there might be some non-Jewish guys who aren't drugged-up porn stars, who have good politics, who are pretty darn cute, and who actually like dating Jewish guys."

"Like that guy you met in Miami?" she asked, folding her arms.

I flashed back on Ed. *I want you to be my bagel boy.* I shuddered.

"And if I date Jewish guys, all my problems with men will go away?"

"Well, not all of them, Benji," she said. "But it's a good place to start."

"It's that simple?" I asked.

"It's working for me and Daniel Solomon Moskowitz," she said.

"His middle name is Solomon?"

"Cute, right?"

"Very," I said.

She went back to the kitchen to start cooking dinner for Dan, who was on his way over. I sat on the bed and thought about what Michelle had said. Date a Jew. Seemed so easy for her. I couldn't remember her dating any non-Jewish guys, even though she wasn't, what anyone would call religious. Still, it's different for straight people—one of the few times they actually have it tougher. My parents would have had a fit if my sister married a gentile. In truth, they didn't like Richard much. He wasn't afraid to disagree with them, which they always read as disrespect. Plus, as far as they were concerned, he'd taken their daughter across the country, kept her from having the successful career they'd always imagined for her, and denied them the grandchildren they felt they deserved. But even with that lingering resentment, they'd been known to console each other by saying, "At least he's Jewish."

They'd never pressured me to date Jewish guys. For the most part, I was glad to have them stay out of my personal business. At the same time, this indicated to me that they took same-sex relationships less seriously. No awkward interfaith wedding to plan, no confused kids to worry about. No big deal one way or the other, just a couple of guys. Whatever makes you happy, live and let live.

They were accepting in a way that inspired jealousy in some of my friends with less liberal parents. But maybe they were *too* accepting—maybe they didn't hold me to the same standards because they didn't think my relationships mattered. I wondered: Would they even care if I brought home a Jewish guy?

I was dubious about Michelle's easy solution, but I had to admit that what I was doing wasn't working. I'd been dating non-Jews for years, and after a string of bad dates and forgettable hook-ups, what did I have to show for it? Another Friday night with no plans and no prospects.

I stayed home that night. But when I woke up on Saturday, I promised myself I'd find something to do that night. I couldn't stay home the entire weekend, alone in the suburbs. There's sad, and then there's hopeless.

I picked up the *City Paper* to see if there was anything interesting going on downtown—maybe a new movie, or a concert. Anything. And then one ad caught my eye. The gay synagogue in the city was hosting a Hanukkah party Saturday evening.

It was the kind of event that I would never have considered before. But maybe, as Michelle had suggested, that was exactly why I should go. It would get me out of the house and into a new environment, where I was virtually guaranteed to meet Jewish men.

Maybe all this time I'd been trying to find a boyfriend and trying to figure out how to connect to my Jewishness, I'd missed the possibility that they were connected.

I ripped out the ad, very cautiously optimistic. After all, I told myself, Hanukkah is all about miracles.

Hanukkah was never a big deal to me. Having a December birthday meant that I never even got real Hanukkah presents as a kid; I got those "combination birthday-Hanukkah" gifts that always struck me as a total rip-off.

There was one Hanukkah that had been particularly memorable, though, a decade earlier, during my senior year in high school.

Rachel was home from college for the first few days of her winter break. And she'd brought her boyfriend with her.

Even though Rachel and Richard went to school in the same city—he was studying computers at Northeastern, only a mile or two from Boston University, where she was majoring in history—they had met halfway around the world when they both spent their junior years in Israel. Their Middle Eastern fling had turned into a full-fledged American relationship and now she'd brought him home to meet the folks.

My parents were cordial. And why not? Richard seemed nice enough. Smart. Directed. Jewish.

We lit Hanukkah candles and sang "Maoz Tsur." Richard knew the words by heart. My parents nodded their approval.

But it wouldn't last. At dinner, we had barely finished the matzoh ball soup when Rachel decided she couldn't wait any longer.

"Richard and I have something to tell you," she announced. "We're getting married."

My mother nearly dropped the Pyrex platter of turkey she was bringing to the table. My father stopped breathing.

It was up to me to respond: "Uh, when?"

"Next June," said Rachel. "Right after we both graduate."

My mother, still standing, leaned on the table for support.

"I know, it's not much time to plan a wedding," Rachel said, seemingly oblivious to her parents' impending twin aneurysms. "But we don't really want a big wedding. We'll just have a small ceremony up in Boston, before we move."

My mother slowly sat down.

"Move?" My father had finally managed to get one word out.

Richard took over: "To Seattle," he said. "I've got a couple of job offers already. That's why we're going there this weekend—I've got some interviews lined up."

"Seattle?" My father again, in disbelief.

"I know it's far away," said Richard. "But it's the hottest spot for computer jobs these days. What they're offering me, I really couldn't make anywhere else."

My father looked at my mother. She looked at Richard, and in an instant I could see her turn against him. Her eyes hardened and her lips tightened. He'd blown it with her forever, I already knew.

She couldn't even speak to him at that point, so she spoke to Rachel: "But you don't even know yet where you'll be going for law school."

Rachel took a breath, looked to Richard, then back to Mom. "Actually, Mom, I don't think I'm going to law school."

My mother's head fell into her hands. "Oh my God."

"I mean, I'm not going right now," Rachel clarified. "I can always go later on. After we've gotten settled."

My father slammed his hands on the table. "This is nonsense!" he said. "You think you're in love? Fine. So what difference will a few years make? Rachel can go to law school—find one in Seattle, for all I care—and when she's passed the bar, if you still want to get married, great. We'll throw you a beautiful wedding. But this is nonsense. You are too young to get married and too young to throw your future away."

"I'm not throwing my future away, Daddy," said Rachel. "And I'm old enough to know what I want."

My mother looked up and said, "You're pregnant, aren't you?"

"I'm not pregnant," Rachel said.

"So what's the rush?"

"What are you talking about?" said Rachel. "By next June, we'll have been together for more than a year and a half. That's not rushing."

"It's too soon," said Mom.

"It's longer than you and Daddy knew each other when you got married," said Rachel.

"That's true," I blurted out. I wasn't trying to defend Rachel—I was just noting that she'd made a good point. My parents both shot me a sour look and I shut my mouth.

Rachel was starting to sob, so Richard took her hand and spoke calmly: "Mr. and Mrs. Steiner, I'm sorry that this all comes as a surprise to you, and I'm sorry that you're disappointed that Rachel's not going to law school right away. But we've already made up our minds. We're getting married in June. We hope that you'll come to the wedding."

My mother stood up, still not making eye contact with him, and said, "I need to lie down." She went upstairs and my father got up, without a word, and followed her.

We ate the rest of dinner quickly and while I cleaned up, Rachel and Richard went for a drive.

While they were gone, my mother came downstairs and told me that Richard would be sleeping on the trundle bed in my room—not with Rachel in her double bed, as they'd originally agreed. "This is still my house and I still make the rules," she said angrily, as her way of implicitly announcing that the rules could be changed at any time depending on her mood. "They can do whatever they do up in Boston. I don't want to know about it. In my house, unmarried people sleep in separate beds."

She made up two plates of food from the leftovers in the fridge and took them up to my parents' room.

When Rachel and Richard got home, I told them about the sleeping arrangements. Rachel rolled her eyes. Richard told her that my parents had already been through a lot that night and they shouldn't provoke them just for the sake of provoking them. "I'll sleep in your brother's room," he said. "It's just for a couple of nights."

In my room, Richard and I had our first chance to have a one-on-one conversation. And I liked him right away. He talked about his year in Israel and how much the situation there had deteriorated since my trip just two years before: it seemed like buses were blowing up every other day for a while after Rabin was assassinated. He told me about how he and Rachel met in a Tel Aviv disco—and how he started talking to her in Hebrew before he realized she was American. They'd done a lot of traveling together over there—the Sinai, Eilat, a weekend in Istanbul; Rachel had never told me these stories. He told me about the jobs he'd be interviewing for the next week. I didn't really understand what he was talking about, but it all sounded pretty cool to me: creating new software, everything from accounting programs to video games.

"Your sister's really excited about moving out west," he said.

"Yeah, as far from my parents as possible," I said.

"After tonight, I think they'd probably buy us the plane tickets," he said. "One way."

I told him that my parents weren't so bad—they weren't hippies who rolled joints with their kids, but they weren't strict drill sergeants, either. If their demands weren't flexible, they were at least reasonable most of the time. "They're just not used to anyone else getting their way," I explained. "Rachel and I would never stand up to them the way you did."

"Why not?"

"It's not like they'd hit us or anything," I said. "But we'd just feel too guilty."

"Yeah, I've been trying to help Rachel with that," he said. "She's getting better."

He made it sound like we had an illness, when I thought we were just being good kids. But maybe after a certain point, there's not much difference.

"Benji, you'll be going off to college next year, right?"

I'd already gotten into Maryland, with a partial scholarship.

"You won't be far from home, but you'll still be on your own," he said. "You'll need to take care of yourself and think about what you want, not what they want. You can't spend your whole life trying to make them happy. You've got to do what makes you happy and hope that they eventually get behind you. They can't get behind you if you don't get out in front and be your own person."

There was nothing specific in what Richard was saying, yet I felt like he was talking directly to me, like he knew exactly how I felt, like he saw me when other people looked right through me.

"Once you're out of here, you won't need to worry about what they think," he said. "You won't need to be their 'good little boy' anymore. You can be who you want to be."

It was time.

"I'm gay," I said. No preface. Right to the point.

I'd never told anyone before. But after knowing him for just a few hours, I was comfortable enough to tell Richard. Or maybe he was perfect because I hadn't known him for long; if he rejected me, it wouldn't much matter.

The silence stretched for one second. Two seconds. Three.

"I know," he said.

I started to sweat.

"How can you know? I've never told anyone. Rachel doesn't even know."

"She knows, too," he said. "She figured it out a while ago. She's been waiting for you to tell her yourself."

My face flushed.

"I don't get it."

Richard explained that they both had gay friends in Israel, and in Boston, and Rachel had talked to them about her suspicions: Why

*doesn't Benji ever go out with girls? Why is Benji interested in danc-
ing but not sports? Why does Benji listen to Erasure and watch
every film Johnny Depp makes? As their gay friends asked more and
more questions in return, they started to piece things together. It was
nothing definite, nothing more than a hunch. But Rachel had a feeling they were right.*

*Richard had set me up, prodding me. But I wasn't angry. I was
relieved.*

*Richard told me that things would be better in college and that
moving out of my parents' house would open up a world of possibilities. "Someday you'll come out to them, too," he said. "And
they'll be fine. Eventually."*

*"Are you kidding? I'm never telling them. I'm the golden child,
now that Rachel's on their shit list."*

*"They'll get over that, too," he said. I wasn't so sure. But he said,
"Trust me," and I did.*

*Then Richard hugged me. This, too, was something out of the or-
dinary in my family.*

*"If they don't get over it by next summer," I said, "I'll come to
your wedding without them."*

The Hanukkah party wasn't a complete disaster.

True, the DJ played crappy pop music that was nearly a
year out of date, and the few lights set up in the synagogue
social hall were pretty lame, and the table of soggy latkes and
chocolate gelt and Manischewitz wine—meant to be kitcshy,
I assumed—was closer to tragic. But there was one thing that
salvaged the night, and his name was David.

I found him fairly quickly: I saw him spitting half a latke
into a paper napkin and he smiled when he realized he was
being watched. He waved an embarrassed hello and I introduced myself. We were two of the youngest people in the
room and two of only perhaps a dozen who had come solo.
We soon realized that we'd probably have a better time if we
stuck together.

David was from Boston originally—Newton, to be exact—and had gone to school at Brandeis. He'd moved to Washington for law school, and had been working at a small firm for a few years since he'd passed the bar. His hair was curly and dark brown, his eyes intense and the same dark brown. He had a firm handshake and very straight teeth and he looked like someone who would have been more comfortable in a suit than he was in jeans.

We chatted in the hallway by the water fountain, about the presidential race that was about to kick into gear—specifically our mixed feelings regarding Hillary Clinton's candidacy, and our first impressions of Barack Obama.

"I like him, at least what I've seen so far," I said.

He agreed, but wasn't ready to abandon Hillary: "He's still too green," he said, "but maybe he'll be her running mate."

"Or vice versa," I offered.

"I wouldn't count your chickens quite yet," he said. "The primaries haven't even started."

A Madonna song came on—something from a few albums ago, but it was something—so I took him by the hand and led him back inside. We danced for a few minutes between a middle-aged lesbian couple and a gay male couple with matching moustaches, and when the song ended, we sat down on the edge of the dance floor to talk some more.

This time, I told him about the rabbi, and as I got deeper into the story, he gently put his hand on my knee. He listened intently and asked a few prodding questions; he never moved his hand.

And then, when I decided I'd had enough of light blue crepe paper and last summer's FM hits, I asked David if we could go somewhere else.

I suggested a coffeehouse near Dupont Circle and he agreed.

As I drove across town, I could watch him following me in my rearview mirror. Maybe Michelle was right, I thought: It wasn't so hard to meet a Jewish guy. Sure, the dance was pretty much a dud, but I did meet someone—someone with a job and a sense of humor and decent rhythm. Someone who was unlikely to dump me for being Jewish, or keep me around simply *because* I was Jewish. Someone my mother would like. For what that was worth.

We grabbed a table for two at Java the Hut.

"I've never been here before," he said.

"You're kidding."

"Seriously," he said. "I live in Georgetown and work downtown. I don't hang out in Dupont Circle."

"Yeah, I've never seen you out," I told him.

"I don't go out much," he said. "I'm not really into the scene."

"So of all places, why did you decide to go to this Hanukkah party?" I asked.

"Well, I'm a member."

"Of what?"

"Of the synagogue," he said.

"Oh."

"I've never seen you *there*," he said.

"I guess I'm not really into *that* scene," I said.

"What do you mean?" he asked. "You came to the Hanukkah dance tonight and you spent half an hour telling me about this rabbi you've befriended."

"To be honest," I said, "the dance was sort of my roommate's idea. She thought I should go somewhere to meet a nice Jewish boy."

"And you did," he said, smiling and taking a sip of his latte.

"So did you," I replied.

He tapped his coffee cup against mine.

"First time I've been in a synagogue since the High Holidays," I said. "And probably the last time until next year's High Holidays."

Now he frowned. "Oh, you just haven't been to the right synagogue," he said. "You should really give *my* synagogue a try."

Someone my mother would like.

He spent the next ten minutes telling about how great the gay synagogue was: same-sex commitment ceremonies, AIDS benefits, a gay rabbi. Parties and mixers where you could meet potential partners outside a bar. And during weekly services, they used a lot of the same tunes I'd recognize from Conservative services growing up, but with better gender politics in the English translations.

I wasn't sold. Shabbat services full of gay people weren't much more appealing to me than Shabbat services full of straight people. He wasn't any more persuasive about synagogue attendance than my mother had been. Or Rabbi Zuckerman.

"I used to feel alienated, too," he said, "I was really active in Hillel at Brandeis, but after college, I didn't feel any connection to the Jewish community as a single gay man. I tried to find the right synagogue here in Washington, but they were all so family-oriented—you know, Hebrew school and bar mitzvahs, and if you're not a part of that, then you're kind of invisible. So I stopped doing anything Jewish at all. I felt like I was drifting away."

I nodded. I'd never even been active in Hillel in college; even if it professed to being "liberal" and "open" to gay people, it always seemed like a dating service to me, aimed at helping Jewish boys and Jewish girls hook up. So I'd felt alienated for even longer than he had.

"But the gay synagogue really pulled me back in," he continued. "I felt like I found my community again."

"What about the gay community?" I asked.

"I don't really relate to most of that," he said. "The bars, the gyms, the whole thing. I mean, don't get me wrong—I'm out and everything. I've been out since I was twenty. But I've been Jewish my whole life."

As we finished our coffee, David explained how exciting it had been for him to realize that he could be a gay man, but still live the Jewish life he'd always expected. He went to synagogue every Saturday. He lit candles every Friday night. He didn't just observe Rosh Hashanah and Yom Kippur—he celebrated Purim, Sukkot, and a few holidays whose names sounded familiar but whose exact roots and placement on the calendar had long since vanished from my mind. He even kept kosher.

I listened politely until he was finished.

"You grew up doing all of this stuff," he said. "Don't you miss it?"

I thought about it for a few seconds, trying to imagine sitting next to David in synagogue, lighting candles together, checking the list of ingredients on everything in the grocery store to make sure it was kosher.

"Not really," I said. "I guess I'm just not that kind of Jew."

"He was just one guy, Benji," Michelle said while we waited to be seated for Sunday brunch. "I didn't say *any* Jewish guy would solve your problems."

"I know," I said. "I just got my hopes up—I went to that stupid party and met this guy right away. But he wasn't the right one, either."

"There are other Jews in the sea," she said.

"Maybe," I said. "Or maybe I'm supposed to be single."

"Lighten up, will you? It's your birthday. You're seriously ruining it."

The hostess showed us to our table, a quiet spot in the back; she probably thought we were on a date. We had never been to this restaurant—a trendy bistro on Connecticut Avenue that was out of our normal price range—but Michelle wanted to take me somewhere "special" on my birthday. Just the two of us.

So, in a way, it was a date.

"Nobody is *supposed* to be single," she said while I studied the menu. "There's someone out there for everyone."

"Now *you* sound like the rabbi."

She didn't like that much. "What did he call it?"

"*Bashert.*"

"Right."

"But the rabbi wasn't even being honest with himself," I said. "Who was his *bashert?* Sophie? Or Irene? Who was the one person he was destined to be with?"

"Maybe you can have more than one."

"No way," I said. "If one person can have more than one *bashert*, then there's got to be a lot of people who don't have any. Think about it."

She scrunched up her face dismissively. "I don't have to think about it. There's totally someone out there for you."

Looking at Michelle, I could tell she honestly believed this. And that was somehow heartening.

"Is Dan your *bashert?*" I asked.

"That's what I'm trying to figure out," she said.

We spent the rest of my special birthday brunch talking about Michelle's relationship. This wasn't unusual for us. But one thing was different: Michelle didn't have any complaints about Dan this time. In fact, any worries she had were due to the fact that she had never been in this situation before—a situation where instead of finding reasons to call it quits, she was trying to figure out what it meant to stay together. What was their next step? When would they be ready? How would she know? Would Dan know, too?

Michelle paid the bill—this was also unusual, but it *was* my birthday—and we headed outside. She was adjusting her scarf, trying to wrap it just right, when I heard someone call my name.

I turned around and saw a blond guy with a silver earring. He looked familiar, but I couldn't place him.

"I'm Jamie," he said. "From your flight to Miami . . . ?"

The cute flight attendant. He looked even better wearing jeans and plaid flannel.

"Right!" I said.

He gave me a hug and I introduced him to Michelle, who quickly excused herself to check her voicemail on her cell phone several paces away—a simple ploy to give us some space while still being close enough to eavesdrop.

He asked about Miami and I told him it was an "interesting" trip, without offering any specific details. I asked about Caracas and he said it was hard to remember, since he'd been on a half dozen trips since then.

"So, do you live down here?" he asked.

"No, I live out in Wheaton with Michelle." I braced myself for the next question: "Wheaton? Where's that?" But that wasn't his response.

"That's cool," he said instead. "I share a place out near White Flint. Other end of the red line."

Another suburbanite. And apparently unashamed.

Michelle was done "checking her voicemail." She walked back up beside me and hooked her arm through my elbow.

"Did he tell you it's his birthday?" she asked.

"It's your birthday? Hey, happy birthday, Benji."

"Thanks."

"Listen, I'm on my way to meet a friend," he said, "but maybe we can get together this week and I can buy you a belated birthday dinner?"

"That sounds great," I said. Michelle squeezed my arm. Real subtle.

"I'm off for a few days," he said. "So just give me a call."

He fumbled in his pocket, looking for something to write on. Michelle seized the moment, reaching into her purse and grabbing a pen and a scrap of paper. He wrote down his name and number, gave me a hug good-bye, and was on his way.

"You didn't tell me about him," Michelle teased. "I thought you only met that one guy in Florida—that 'bagel boy' weirdo."

"Yeah, I guess I forgot," I said. "I didn't even get his last name and I didn't know he lived in D.C., so I figured I'd never see him again."

"Quite a coincidence," she said with a smirk, as if she'd planned the whole encounter. "We come downtown to a place we've never been and he just happens to be walking down the sidewalk?"

I looked down at the paper in my hand and noticed—in addition to the suburban area code—his name: Jamie Cohen.

I held the paper up in front of Michelle's face.

"Bashert," I said.

My parents called that afternoon to wish me a happy birth-day.

"We got you one of those new iPods," my mother said, "the kind they advertise on TV."

"The one with the little video screen," my father added, talking on the extension.

"It's a combination birthday-Hanukkah present," my mother said.

December birthdays suck.

"Thanks," I said. "I've really wanted to get one of those." This was true.

"I don't know how you can see anything on that tiny little screen," my mother said, "but what do I know?"

My father asked about the latest news on the rabbi. I told him what Mrs. Goldfarb had told me. Secondhand news.

"You still haven't been to visit him?" he asked.

"No."

"Benji . . ." my mother said, with that disappointed tone in her voice.

"I thought you'd be happy," I said. "You didn't want me seeing him and now I'm not seeing him."

My father took over.

"Benji," he began. "I know how you feel. You're angry because of what he said to you. And I don't blame you."

I didn't respond.

"But you have to remember that the rabbi is very sick," he continued. "I'm not saying you should be taking care of him—he has doctors for that. I'm saying you should be taking care of yourself. And part of taking care of yourself is getting past this anger while you still have the chance. If you wait another week or another month, the rabbi might not be around, and you'll have to live with this unresolved anger forever. And on top of that, you'll have to carry around the guilt of knowing that you didn't see him while you still had the chance."

I already felt guilty—that I hadn't been there when he'd had his stroke and that I hadn't been able to bring myself to visit him in the week since I got back to Maryland.

"You never knew my father," he said, "because he died before you were born. But you've heard us tell stories about him."

I had, and they were never pleasant.

"Let's just say that he was a *difficult* man," my father continued.

"You can say *that* again!" my mother added.

I laughed. She's the one who had talked about him the most. Nothing positive.

"He was always telling me what to do, treating me like I was still a kid, even when I was a grown-up," he said. "What kind of car I should drive, how I should spend my money, where I should look for a better job."

Mom jumped in: "He always had all the answers."

I remembered the stories I'd heard since childhood, about his unsolicited bits of "advice" to my dad that had always started the same way: *Sid, you gotta listen to me . . .*

"You guys have told me about him," I said.

"I know," my father said, "but I don't think I ever told you about our last big fight."

"No," I said.

"After my mother died, he came to visit alone, and as usual, he started a fight in my own house. I had enough. I told him I was an adult with a career and a family and I wouldn't have him treating me that way anymore—and I kicked him out. We stopped speaking."

"For how long?" I asked.

"For good," he said. "My mother wasn't around to smooth things over anymore, so your Uncle Larry kept trying to patch things up, but neither of us would budge. When my father got sick a few months later and had to go into a nursing home, Larry handled it. I didn't visit him once. When he had a heart attack and went into the hospital, I still didn't go visit. And then he died. And we never had the chance to make things right."

"It sounds like he deserved it, though," I said.

"He did," my mother interjected.

"He probably did deserve it," my father said. "And yes, life was a lot easier for a while without him bossing me around all the time and making me feel like crap. But you know what? I felt better for a little while, but I've felt horrible for thirty years now. Horrible that I didn't try to bury the hatchet with him while he was still alive. Because now it's too late."

"I get it," I said.

"I'm not saying you need to be his best friend," my father said. "Make up with him, scream at him, or just forgive him and move on. Do whatever you need to do. Just don't wait too long to do it."

My father was never the kind to offer unsolicited advice, so I took this to heart. It had been a week. How much longer did I have?

"You're coming tomorrow night to light candles for Hanukkah?" my mother asked before we hung up.

"I'll be there," I said. Then, after a moment, I added: "But I might be a little late."

The rabbi looked awful. Worse than I'd ever seen him.

He hadn't heard me open his door, so I stood in the doorway and observed him silently. His beard was scraggly and unkempt, his hair uncombed, his blue hospital gown stained with whatever he'd had for breakfast and lunch. He was noticeably thinner, his paunch a thing of the past, the skin on his arms loose and blotchy.

"Rabbi Zuckerman?" I said.

He turned and looked at me, squinting beneath the bright fluorescent hospital lights.

His mouth opened, but no sound came out. Was he trying to conjure the right words to ask my forgiveness, or to throw me out? Perhaps he'd forgotten about our fight—or perhaps he'd forgotten who I was altogether.

Or maybe he just couldn't speak. Mrs. Goldfarb said he could manage a few words. But what does "a few" mean? He was never what anyone would call a man of *many* words.

"Rabbi Zuckerman," I repeated. "It's me, Benji."

"Ben-ji," he said, slowly and deliberately. No inflection, no glint of recognition or surprise or dismay. The simple act of getting two syllables out of his mouth was all he could manage. His brow was furrowed, not out of anger, it seemed, but out of sheer concentration.

Since I hadn't been thrown out, I approached his bed.

"I'm sorry I didn't visit you this week," I said.

He looked at me blankly. I could tell this was going to be a one-sided conversation.

"I'm still angry at you," I said.

He looked away from me.

"You said some awful things to me last time I saw you," I continued. "I don't know if you remember."

Still quiet, he turned back to face me, but he didn't open his mouth or raise a finger.

"*I* remember," I said, and I could feel my face getting hot as I recalled that awful scene in his living room.

But knowing he couldn't talk much made it much easier for me, since this couldn't escalate into a screaming match or an argument. We weren't going to pick up that argument where we left off. There was no way for him to attack me again, no reason for me to get defensive. I exhaled.

"But I didn't come here today to fight," I said. "I came because tonight's the first night of Hanukkah and I knew you'd want to light candles."

I reached into my backpack and removed the "travel-size" aluminum Hanukkah menorah I'd bought at his bookstore that afternoon and two blue candles. I set them up on his wheeled dinner table. I put one candle in the right-most candleholder and lit the other one with a plastic lighter I had in my pocket.

"This is against the rules, so we'll have to be quiet," I said. He looked at me with quiet disbelief and nodded.

I took the burning candle and lit the other one and started to sing the Hanukkah blessing.

"*Baruch atah Adonai . . .*"

The rabbi started to make noises, low staccato moans, attempting to sing along. I slowed way down and started over. He closed his eyes and sang along. He only got a few words right and this seemed to frustrate him; his right hand clenched into a fist. But when we were done, he opened his eyes and sighed. Then he pointed at me and tried to say something else.

I didn't understand.

He repeated himself, but I didn't understand again. He was, literally, talking nonsense.

He looked at me again, and this time a look of utter exasperation came over his face—not frustration at his lack of simple speaking abilities, but exasperation that I was being so stupid. That's when I knew that the rabbi was still in there somewhere, inside this elderly stroke patient. Nobody else could have made that expression.

"M-m-mah," he said. I nodded.

"O-o-oz," he said. I nodded.

"Ts-s-sur," he said.

"Oh, 'Maoz Tsur,'" I said. "You want to sing 'Maoz Tsur.'"

He shook his head and pointed his finger at me.

"Oh, you want *me* to sing 'Maoz Tsur.'"

He nodded. He couldn't sing along, we both realized, but he didn't want to skip this part of the holiday ritual. So I sang for him. Good thing I remembered the words. Hebrew school must have been good for something, after all.

"Maoz tsur yeshuati," I began, looking at the rabbi's face as I sang the cheerful melody. *"Lecha na'eh leshabeach."*

The rabbi didn't look back at me. Instead he stared straight ahead at the candles, tiny flames flickering in his eyes.

CHAPTER 11

I could smell my mother's latkes cooking in the kitchen, the scent of frying potatoes and onions drifting up the stairs to my old bedroom. I only had a few minutes before they were ready—and really, what good is a cold latke?—but I needed to make a quick call.

"It's bad," I said.

"How bad?" asked Irene.

"Bad," I repeated. "He can barely talk and he looks awful."

I told her about the rabbi's stammering, his shoddy appearance, how he cried. She listened, without interrupting to ask questions. While I talked on my parents' cordless phone, I played with the plastic dreidel Mrs. Goldfarb had given me that afternoon, spinning it on my desk and taking note of how it fell. *Nun. Nun. Gimel. Nun. Shin.*

I had kept Irene up to date by phone for a solid week, relating whatever Mrs. Goldfarb told me about the rabbi's condition. During that time, Irene had never once pressured me to visit him, nor had she ever asked why I wanted to stay away. As someone who knew how it felt to be snubbed by the rabbi, to be drawn closer only to be pushed away, she probably understood my feelings better than anyone else.

But as I sat at the desk in my old bedroom in my parents'

house, barely an hour after I first saw the rabbi in the hospital, I found that my feelings had changed.

"I'm glad I went to see him," I told her.

"That's good, dear," she said.

"I think you should go, too," I said.

Irene was quiet for a moment, clearly surprised by my change of heart.

"It's been a whole year since he's spoken to me," she said. "I don't know why he'd want to see me now."

There was no anger in her voice. Determination, perhaps, or resignation. But no anger.

"I honestly don't know what he wants," I replied. "But I think I know what he needs."

I went to Holy Cross again the next evening. The rabbi's hospital room stank of disinfectant and boiled corn. And it was quiet; was he the first hospital patient in history who didn't ever turn on his television?

"Benji," said the rabbi, still speaking in single words although his stammering was already starting to subside.

"I'm back," I said.

"Candles?" he asked.

I put my backpack on a chair and pulled out the menorah and the candles again. And once again, I recited the blessing and sang "Maoz Tsur" while the rabbi listened.

"I brought you something else," I said, while the candles burned on his table.

He raised his eyebrows, as if to say, "*Nu?* What is it?"

"I thought a lot about you when I was in Florida," I said.

I checked to see if he'd betray surprise that I'd actually gone to Miami after our fight. Nothing. Maybe Mrs. Goldfarb had already told him.

"I learned a lot down there," I said. "And I got some good advice. From Sophie."

Now he opened his mouth again. "Sophie."

"She made a needlepoint with a quotation from Hillel. Do you remember?"

He nodded.

"I think there's a lot of wisdom in those words."

"Benji," he said.

"You gave me a wonderful present for my birthday by sending me to Miami," I said. "And now I want to give you a present. For Hanukkah."

I walked over to the door and opened it and there stood Irene. She'd flown in that afternoon with a ticket I'd bought for her.

Seeing the rabbi in such a state must have shocked Irene—she hadn't seen him in quite some time. But she didn't let on; she looked at him as if he were still a handsome, smooth-talking teenager taking her for a stroll through Van Vorst Park.

"Zisel," she said, taking his hand as she stood by his bed-side.

"Irene," he said.

"If not now, when?" I said. And I turned to leave the two of them alone.

When Jamie asked me to pick a place for my belated birthday dinner—our first date—I named a couple of options in the District: a French place in Georgetown, a Caribbean cafe in Adams Morgan. "We both live in the suburbs," he said. "Why don't we just stay out here?"

Sharing a bowl of kimchi in a Korean grill in Wheaton, I told Jamie the whole story about the rabbi, and Irene, who'd arrived just a few hours before. I didn't want to bore him with tales about a couple of old people he'd never even met, especially on our first date, but he kept asking questions and prodding me to continue. So I did.

I waited for him to pull a Michelle, to interrupt and change the subject back to himself. But he never did. Not when our main courses arrived, not when the dessert arrived, not when the check arrived. He just listened, for an hour and a half.

"I'm not used to talking so much," I said as we left the restaurant.

"You seemed like you needed to talk," he said.

"Next time we'll talk about you," I said. "Promise."

"I really don't care what we talk about," he said. "As long as there's a next time."

The rabbi went home from the hospital later that week. Irene went with him.

She moved into his study, across the hall from his bedroom, sleeping on the foldout couch.

Irene arranged for a visiting nurse to come every day after lunch—to give the rabbi his medication, check his vital signs, and help him bathe—and a speech therapist who would help him regain his ability to talk. The rest of the time, she planned to take care of him herself, cooking his meals, washing his clothes, and, most importantly, keeping him company day after day.

Within a few days, Irene had the rabbi's schedule running smoothly and she walked down the hill to the shopping center one afternoon, while the others were attending to him. After she picked up a few things at the supermarket and the bakery, she stopped in the bookstore to chat with Mrs. Goldfarb, whom she'd finally gotten to meet face-to-face earlier in the week at Holy Cross. And when she was done with Mrs. Goldfarb, she came around to the back of the shopping center and knocked on my door.

A hug and a kiss and I ushered her in. My couch was too big for her; her feet dangled several inches above the carpet. But she made herself at home there.

"Oh, the Barry Sisters, I used to love them," she said, pointing to the poster.

"The rabbi gave that to me," I said.

"He was never big on gifts," she said. "He must really like you."

"Maybe he did," I said. "Before."

She told me about the rabbi's health, how he'd already progressed from single words to short phrases. While the stroke had caused aphasia—loss of the ability to produce words—the rabbi was recovering quite well and, she noted, he had never lost his ability to comprehend other people's words, spoken or written. He was physically weak—somewhat shaky on his feet, he spent most of the day in bed or sitting in his living room—but his spirits, she said, were strong and he was very nearly his old self again.

"He still davens every morning," she told me. "And he still spends hours a day reading his books. But that was always Zisel. Forever with his books. I guess even a stroke couldn't change who he was."

For better or worse, I thought.

I drove Irene back up the hill when we were done chatting. As we pulled into the rabbi's driveway, she asked me to come in, "just for a minute, to say hello."

"You know that I can't," I said.

"I thought you were past that," she said. "You visited him in the hospital."

"That was different," I said. "He made it perfectly clear that I'm not welcome in his house."

"But that was before all this," she said.

"I can't just pretend it didn't happen," I said, "forgive and forget."

She turned to face me from the passenger seat.

"That's not what this is all about, kiddo," she said. "Nobody's asking anyone to forgive or forget. Do you think I've forgotten what Zisel did to me? Or that I've forgiven him? Think again. I'm here because I love him—in *spite* of what he did to me.

"You should never forget what he said to you—only a fool forgets," she continued. "And forgiveness—that's something you get from God. Or your mother. You don't have to forgive him, or pretend this never happened."

I folded my arms. "So what *do* I have to do?"

"You need to understand him, and accept him on his own terms, and get beyond all this," she said. "You need to get over it."

"Get over it?" I asked, incredulous. "He condemns my entire life and I'm supposed to just get over it?"

"Sweetheart, if I can get over what he did to me, you can do it, too," she said.

She did have a point.

"And what about him?" I asked. "He gets to crap on everyone in his life and we all just look past it and keep taking care of him?"

"Oh, no, Benji, it's not like that at all," she said, index finger in the air. "There's plenty that he needs to get over. *Plenty.* And if you think I'm not telling him the same thing every day, then you don't know Irene Faber."

I sat for a moment, wondering what exactly Irene was saying to the rabbi as he sat on the living room couch.

"Come inside," she said. "You'll see."

I wasn't ready to go back inside that house. I told her: "Not today."

"You're just as bad as he is," she said gruffly, giving up the argument and grabbing her bags from my backseat. Then, looking at my face, seeing that I was more wounded than upset, she quickly softened: "I'll see you tomorrow, same time," she said, and she blew me a kiss against her brown leather glove.

"I just can't do it," I explained to Jamie that night over dinner at an Italian restaurant around the corner from his apartment. "I can't go back inside that house."

Jamie was a good listener. Despite my earlier promise, I found myself doing most of the talking on our second date. And once again, he let me.

My relationship with the rabbi was particularly intriguing to him. My feelings toward the rabbi had begun to shift. I wasn't feeling guilty anymore: I knew that I'd done everything I could to look out for the rabbi—and now that he had Irene or the nurse with him twenty-four/seven, he didn't need me checking up on his physical or emotional health. I wasn't even angry by this point. Yes, his words had stung, and yes, I was pissed that my months of friendship seemed to count for nothing in his Torah-blind eyes, but that feeling, too, had lifted after I confronted him in the hospital, however briefly. Just letting him know that he'd hurt me was enough to unburden myself.

By this point, I mostly pitied him. No matter how many times I'd thought otherwise, Mrs. Goldfarb had been right about him from the start: He was a rigid man who'd pushed away everyone who ever cared about him. He'd rejected every bit of kindness and sympathy, not only with indifference, but with snubs and dismissal. If he'd been left completely alone, he'd have deserved it; the fact that he had Irene by his side was actually *more* than he deserved.

"Everyone told me that I needed to make the first move," I said. "Well, I did. I went to see him in the hospital and I brought Irene here to stay with him. That's a pretty big move."

Jamie nodded.

"But I tell you, the next move is his. If he wants me to come visit him at home, he's got to invite me personally. He's the one who kicked me out, he's the one who's going to have to ask me back in. Irene keeps saying that it's all fine now, that I should just get over it. But it's not that simple."

"Why not?" Jamie asked.

"I'm still hurt," I clarified. "Look, I'm twenty-seven. I'm a grown man. I don't need to justify myself to anyone. I don't need to defend my existence as a gay man to some homophobic rabbi. He's not my dad. He's not even my *rabbi*. Who is he to judge me? Why do I care what he thinks?"

I was getting agitated. Jamie was calm. "Why *do* you care?" he asked.

I wasn't sure of the answer.

"Okay, before the fight," Jamie said, "why did you take such an interest in him?"

"I don't know," I said. "Maybe because he let me, and he trusted me."

"He treated you like family," Jamie offered.

"Only he didn't make as many demands," I said. "And he didn't tell me what *not* to do."

"He doesn't sound so bad," Jamie said.

"Great, now you're taking his side," I said.

"I'm not taking anyone's side. All I know is that if you hadn't met the rabbi, you never would have flown to Miami over Thanksgiving," he said. "I never would have met you, and I wouldn't be sitting here now thinking about how sweet you are and hoping that you'll want to skip dessert so we can go home already."

I looked into his eyes and realized I'd spent the better part of dinner talking about a sick old man when I had an adorable young guy sitting across the table from me. One had kicked me out of his house, while the other was inviting me into his.

I caught the waiter's eye and motioned for the check.

Jamie was unlike anyone I'd dated before, I soon realized.

He was funny and cute and bright—but I'd dated other men who possessed these qualities, albeit not usually all three simultaneously. We shared similar tastes in music, politics, and clothes, although, again, the same could be said of several erstwhile prospective boyfriends of mine.

What was different about Jamie is that he asked questions, real questions, and persisted until I gave him real answers.

Other guys had looked at my graphic design projects and said they liked them, sometimes offering a hint of enthusiasm or a relatively specific bit of praise. But Jamie was the first to ask why I'd made certain choices—why this color, why that font, why those images—in a way that showed real interest. He listened to my answers as I explained some basic principles behind my work, eager to learn more. And he wasn't afraid to be critical, in a gentle way, if he didn't like what I'd done.

He was equally curious about my personal relationships—and not just with the rabbi. He wasn't particularly close to his parents, who had recently retired and moved to Arizona; they weren't as intrusive as my folks just a few miles away, but they also weren't as accepting of their gay son. Jamie didn't have a Michelle in his life, either: His roommate was just a random guy he'd found online and he'd lost touch with his college friends, most of whom lived thousands of miles away.

Jamie had grown up in Minneapolis. Both his parents worked at the state university there: his father as a professor in the biology department, his mother as an administrator in the registrar's office. Mr. Cohen was Jewish, tracing his lineage to Lithuania by way of Toronto. Mrs. Cohen—née Lindstrom—was a Lutheran of Swedish heritage. Rejected by both families and both religious communities because of their interfaith coupling, the Cohens raised Jamie and his sister in a household that was both Christian and Jewish and yet neither at the same time. They had a Christmas tree, but never went to church; they ate matzoh instead of bread on Passover but never had a seder. Jamie had a bris, but no bar mitzvah; he went to a Christian private school and a Reform synagogue's Sunday school through sixth grade, when he switched to public school and got his Sundays back.

It was only when he got to Berkeley that Jamie embraced

his Judaism. He took a Jewish studies class, went to Shabbat dinners at the Chabad house on campus, checked out a few of Hillel's holiday events. There were always a few naysayers who told him that he wasn't really a Jew—because his mother was a gentile, because he'd never been bar mitzvahed—yet for the first time in his life, Jamie felt Jewish. Whatever that meant.

But the usual means of association weren't there: Synagogue was alien to Jamie, and he didn't have any personal connection to traditional holiday rituals. He wasn't about to join a JCC or subscribe to the local Jewish newspaper. So once he left Berkeley, and there were no more classes or events or Friday night dinners, he was on his own again. Questions remained, but he didn't have anyone to give him answers.

He found a group in Washington for "interfaith" Jews, but it was aimed at couples from different religious backgrounds—not individuals who had dual backgrounds. He went to the gay synagogue a few times, but that felt more like a place for gay people who already felt connected to their faith, who were just looking to transplant it elsewhere; Jamie didn't fit in.

Then he met me. Jamie found a source of information about Judaism—in *me*, of all people.

He'd ask questions about holidays and I usually knew at least the short version of the answer. He'd ask about Israeli politics, a Yiddish word, a seemingly incomprehensible restriction on behavior, and more often than not, I knew what to say. I was the answer man. *I'll take Judaica for four hundred, Alex.*

I helped him get in touch with his Jewishness. He helped me get back in touch with mine. And I liked that.

Jamie had to get up early for a flight to Mexico City, so I headed home around midnight. Michelle was waiting up for me in the living room.

She clicked off the television and ran over to give me a big hug.

"What's that for?" I asked.

"Oh, nothing," she said, completely unconvincingly.

She hugged me again and a grin spread across her face like I'd never seen before. She was bouncing up and down on her the balls of her feet, taking both my hands in hers. She was wound up so tightly, it looked like she might twirl around the room like a top just to relieve the tension.

"What's *up* with you?" I asked.

"Notice anything different?" she asked. I dropped her hands and took a step back to examine her.

"Different? It's not your hair. It's not your clothes . . ."

"Keep guessing," she said, slowly raising her hands in front of her face and wiggling her fingers until I noticed the diamond ring.

"Oh. My. God."

"We're engaged!" she screamed, throwing her arms around my neck.

I hugged her back and squeezed her tight.

"When did Dan propose?"

"Tonight at dinner. I was totally surprised. He'd worked it all out with the waiter ahead of time, so when he brought dessert out, he gave me a plate with this ring on it. I was like, 'What's going on?' And Dan said he wanted to marry me. And at first, I was like, am I on some kind of reality show? Have I just been Punk'd?"

Apparently, Dan had been considering popping the question for a few months; the trip to his parents' house for Thanksgiving was his way of seeing if his parents approved. And they did.

Somewhere in the back of my head, I knew that Michelle getting married was going to change my life in a profound way. We wouldn't be roommates anymore, wherever we'd both be living. I wouldn't get to see her every day. I hadn't spent so much as a week without her since we'd met; who could possibly take her place?

But I knew this was not the time to be thinking about my own impending loss, my own purely selfish concerns. Michelle was getting married—and to a pretty great guy. I was thrilled for her.

She started rattling off details about the wedding, all of them still tentative: "We might do it in June, or we might wait till next fall. . . . We'll do it in Philly, unless we can convince my parents to do it here. . . . We're thinking about a little ceremony, but then again, we have so many people we want to invite. . . ." Michelle was already talking in first-person plural.

"So I guess Dan's your *bashert* after all," I said.

She must have seen a hint of dejection on my face.

"No, actually, I decided that you're wrong," she said. "There isn't just one person for each of us. You *can* have more than one person you're destined to spend your life with. The same way your rabbi had his wife and Irene. I have two *basherts*: Dan and you."

That was Michelle's way of telling me that she wasn't going to abandon me, that we'd always be together in some way, even if we didn't share a home. I should have known that all along.

During our freshman year at Maryland, Michelle and I split about nine hundred pints of Ben & Jerry's ice cream—to relieve stress, alleviate boredom, celebrate handing in a paper, anything really. In a related vein, we started going to the school gym together to get rid of all that Chunky Monkey.

One afternoon, toward the end of our first semester—about a month after I'd come out to her and a few weeks into our intimately platonic friendship—we had really overdone it at the gym, taking an aerobics class that we had no business taking. "What does advanced aerobics mean?" Michelle had asked. "Like we can't take the fucking class until we have a master's degree?" We quickly learned that we were, in the world of aerobics, beginners.

Back in Michelle's dorm room, her back cramped up on her and I offered her a massage. An innocent massage.

She took off her T-shirt and lay facedown on her futon.

"This'd be easier without your bra," I said.

I reached down to unhook it. She turned and looked up at me.

"You're sure you're gay?" she teased, slipping the straps over her arms.

"I'm sure now," I teased back, tossing the bra aside.

There was nothing electric about the moment, but I felt an ease, a comfort with Michelle I had never experienced with anyone else.

I straddled her, in my gym shorts and tank top, and looked down at her body: smooth skin, narrow waist, soft shoulders. Ten thousand men on campus would have been ecstatic to be in my position.

I found the knot in Michelle's lower back and started gently kneading it. She sighed and relaxed into the futon.

We didn't even hear the key in the lock, as Michelle's straitlaced roommate, Kelly, opened the door. She gasped. Knocking me off her, Michelle shot up on the futon and covered her breasts with the pillow. I turned red. "I'm so sorry . . . I didn't realize . . ." Kelly said, backing out and closing the door behind her.

I started to giggle uncontrollably.

"What's so funny?" asked Michelle.

"She thinks she just walked in on something dirty," I said. "It's just funny because she doesn't know that I'm gay."

"No, it's even funnier," said Michelle, "because she does *know that you're gay."*

Apparently, while I'd been fretting over how to tell my roommate, my dormmates, my classmates, Michelle had been coming out for me. She'd already told most of the girls on her floor, who'd noticed how much time we spent together and had asked her what was up.

At first, I was peeved, but I quickly came to be grateful. Michelle gave me the push to come out by showing me that it wasn't such a big deal; for the most part, people didn't care one way or the other.

"But what happens if someone does care?" I asked her. "What if I tell someone and they're totally homophobic about it?"

"Then you tell them to go fuck themselves," she said. "This isn't high school, Benji. You don't need to waste your time trying to accommodate assholes anymore. Live your life, be yourself, and don't worry about those people. They don't like you? Good riddance."

I knew inside that she was right.

"And if they really hassle you, call me. I'll beat them up for you," she said, flexing her biceps. "Why do you think I've been going to the gym?"

I still had people willing to stand up for me, as I realized the next week.

The first snow came early that winter. Notorious worry-warts about any forecast of accumulation, Washingtonians were sent into an absolute panic with the news of a storm blowing through the area in mid-December, even if the weathermen were only calling for one or two inches, tops. The shopping center was crowded with people stocking up on milk, bread, toilet paper, and DVDs, certain they'd otherwise be stranded for days without any food or commercial entertainment.

The main parking lot was full by lunchtime and people had started parking in the employee lot around back, near my office. I watched them, wound up with predictable anxiety, out my window, while I finished the newest ad for Paradise, promoting the bar's two-for-one shots of orange vodka with the headline "Be Fruitful and Multiply" over a photograph of a shirtless hunk holding an orange standing next to his exact double doing the exact same thing.

Flurries started to fall in the afternoon, capping the golden bells and fake poinsettias that hung from the light poles in the parking lot. But Irene—herself a Washingtonian for just two weeks by this point—was not going to let a few snow-flakes change her routine.

"I haven't had a real winter in years," she said, shaking the snow off her sleeves in my office. "Don't even have a proper winter coat anymore, not to mention boots."

"So where'd you get those?" I asked, pointing at her feet.

"They're Sophie's," she answered. "He never cleaned out her closet."

I grimaced.

"Oh, come on," she said. "They fit me fine and she's not using them."

She sat down on my couch, boots dangling, dripping onto my floor.

"I brought you something," she said, reaching into her inside coat pocket and pulling out an envelope with my name on it. The block letters were deliberate but sloppy, like a child's.

I opened the envelope and found a brief note written in a neater cursive hand:

> *Benji:*
>
> *Hillel also said: Do not judge your fellow man until you are in his place. These are words both of us should heed. You and I have much to learn, and much to teach. Please visit. You are always welcome.*
>
> *Jacob Zuckerman*

"Is this your handwriting?" I asked Irene.

"I took dictation," she said. "The words are his."

I wondered if Irene had put words in his mouth or if the rabbi really had said these words of his own volition. But it didn't matter.

I also wondered how long it had taken the rabbi to get a few sentences out.

"Isn't this what you wanted?" she asked.

"Yes. It's just that I never thought he'd do it."

"Don't underestimate the man," said Irene.

"Did you put him up to this?"

"Do you really think I could make him do something he didn't want to do?" she asked.

"I guess you're right," I said.

I looked at her sitting in my office. Not even five feet tall, but a dynamo of energy and wisdom.

"Look, Benji," she said. "You think the rabbi has his head up his *tuches* when it comes to gay issues."

I did, although I'd never put it so colorfully.

"Well, I agree with you," she said. "I lived in Miami long enough to know a few gay people. And you know what else? One of my granddaughters is a lesbian."

"You never told me that," I said.

"You never asked," she countered. "I don't carry a big sign with me, telling the whole world, but I know firsthand what a wonderful young woman she is. And I've been telling Zisel for the past week that he's wrong about gay people, no matter what the Torah says, and that if he thinks you're an abomination, then he thinks my own granddaughter is an abomination, and if he really feels that way, then he should say that to my face and see what I do."

She made a fist—tiny and bony, but still intimidating.

"He's not a hateful man, Benji," she continued. "He just doesn't know any better. He only knows what they taught him in yeshiva. But he can still learn new things."

"How?"

"You, Benji," she said. "You're going to help him get over his ignorance. But first you have to go and visit him."

I stood for a few seconds, mulling it over. But I quickly realized that Irene was right and staying away wasn't going to help anybody.

"You win. Let's go see him," I said, standing up and grabbing my car keys off the desk. "Let's go to the bakery first. I don't want to visit empty-handed."

* * *

In only a couple of weeks, Irene had brought the rabbi's house to life.

Splashes of color dotted the previously drab living room: a vase filled with purple irises on the end table, a red afghan draped over the back of the sofa, a mound of green and orange sourballs in the candy dish on the coffee table. The mustiness was gone, replaced by the scent of clean laundry and fresh lemons. The drapes were open, the fading light of a winter afternoon filtering through the leafless trees outside.

"You've done wonders here," I said.

"A woman's touch, dear," she said. "Have a seat and I'll make you some hot tea."

I sat in my usual chair and noticed that the sofa now had two indentations: the rabbi's spot under the reading lamp and a second, smaller one on the next cushion. I imagined them sitting side by side in their stocking feet, the red afghan spread across their laps.

Irene put the cup of tea on the coffee table. "He should be finishing up with his speech therapist," she said. "I'll go check on him."

While she was upstairs, I picked up my teacup and walked around the house. The kitchen bore signs of recent cooking—a cutting board left on the counter, a roasting pan soaking in the sink. The dining room, too, showed signs of use, but not what I might have expected. The long table was covered in books, stacked high in a half dozen piles. The bookshelves in this room were mostly empty. Was the rabbi getting rid of his books or merely rearranging them? Or was this a project of Irene's?

The speech therapist came downstairs, carrying a notebook under her arm, and walked out the front door without noticing me. The rabbi followed behind her, taking each step at half her speed. He wore his usual clothes—navy slacks, white oxford—but they hung loose on his frame, and he wore bedroom slippers instead of hard-soled shoes. His hands gripped both banisters and he took each step with great deliberation, careful to steady himself on each stair before attempting the next. If a man in his eighties can look bad for his age, here he was.

Only one thing about him looked younger: He was clean-shaven for the first time since I'd known him.

I stood in the dining room, observing him for a few seconds, before he saw me.

"Benji," he said. No hug, no handshake.

"You shaved," I said, rubbing my own face.

"Irene's idea. It was time," he said with no further explanation. Then he hooked his hand under my arm and said, "Let's sit down."

I led him slowly to the couch and sat him down. In the time it took to complete this maneuver, Irene came downstairs, went into the kitchen, and brought out two plates with slices of the honey cake I'd bought at the bakery.

"Look what Benji brought," she said, putting the plates on the coffee table, along with a cup of tea for the rabbi. Then Irene excused herself, "to get dinner started."

"I am happy she is here," the rabbi said, the effort of making a complete sentence still apparent. "Thank you."

"She's an amazing woman," I said.

"And happy *you* are here," he said, gesturing in my direction.

"So am I," I said. This was true. It didn't seem possible that only a month had passed since the rabbi had screamed at me in this very room. The fragile man before me required all his strength to utter a simple sentence; how could he ever have shouted such poison?

"How are you?" he asked.

Was he making chitchat? Or was he trying to get me to talk so he could relax for a moment?

I told him all about the music website I'd been working on the last time we'd spoken—which was now up and running; he nodded along. I told him about Michelle getting married.

"And the apartment?" he asked.

"I guess I'll have to find a new roommate," I said.

I remembered how he had disapproved when I first told him about my living arrangements. This time, he didn't say anything derogatory at all. Maybe he was mellowing. Or perhaps his perspective had changed, now that he, too, had a female roommate who wasn't his wife.

Our small talk was pleasant enough, but by the time we finished our honey cake, we were done with the niceties.

He put his plate down and cleared his throat.

"Our argument," he said.

I wasn't sure he had the energy to speak in paragraphs and I didn't want to raise his stress level again, so I said it wasn't necessary to discuss all that now.

"Yes," he insisted. "I'll show you something."

He picked up a book from the end table and put on his reading glasses.

"*Pirkei Avot,*" he said. "Wisdom of the Fathers."

I had a vague memory from Hebrew school of reading some of *Pirkei Avot*—a collection of aphorisms from ancient Hebrew sages that is used as a guide for ethical living. But nothing specific.

He opened the book and pointed to one page, then turned the book around for me to see.

"Hillel, here—see?" he said. And there was the proverb that Sophie had used for her needlepoint.

He turned the book back to himself and flipped a few pages.

"You mentioned Hillel. In the hospital," he said, speaking in short sentences and catching his breath in between. "I came home. I read *Pirkei Avot* again. I found more wisdom."

He pointed to another passage and handed me the book. I remembered what he'd written in his note to me that afternoon—also Hillel. I thought that's what he was going to point out. But I was wrong.

"Read," he said.

I started to read to myself.

"Out loud," he said. "Please."

"Rabbi Tarfon?" I asked.

"Yes."

"Rabbi Tarfon said: It is not your duty to complete the work. But neither are you free to desist from it.'"

The rabbi looked at me expectantly, waiting for my reaction.

"I don't understand," I said. "What work is he talking about?"

"Being a good Jew," he said.

"I still don't understand."

He took a deep breath and summoned his strength.

"I said you had sinned," he said.

"Abomination," I said. "You called it an abomination."

"That is Torah," he said. "That is God's word. I cannot change it. You cannot change it. It is truth."

I wasn't liking this.

"But you were right," he continued. "A man who sins can still be a good Jew. You do mitzvot, good deeds. You are a good man. This is also truth. If sinners can never be good men, why do mitzvot? Why atone on Yom Kippur?"

"Exactly," I said. I wasn't happy about being called a sinner—again—but the rabbi did say I was right. That was something.

"However, here, I am also right," he said, pointing to the book. "Rabbi Tarfon. 'It is not your duty to complete the task.' You cannot learn *all* of Torah. Obey every law every day. Study and pray every minute of every day. Be a perfect Jew. You can never be perfect. But you are not free to stop trying. So you cannot do everything the Torah asks? This does not mean you may therefore do *nothing* the Torah asks. Sin is not an excuse."

I looked at him and thought for a moment.

"So what are you saying?" I asked.

"I am not perfect," he said, motioning toward the kitchen. He must have known that Irene had told me her whole story. "But I cannot give up my faith because of my failures. Neither can you. We are human. We fall short. But because we fall short, we need our faith even more."

I realized then that the rabbi had, in fact, dictated that note to Irene. Those were his words, not hers.

"If you're telling me to go to synagogue or observe Shabbat or keep kosher, we've been through this before," I said.

"No," he said. "I am saying: Do not walk away from your Judaism. No matter who tries to push you away. A synagogue. A rabbi. A foolish old man. Someone will always try to take your faith away from you. Or take you away from your faith. Do not let them win. Hold on to your faith. As much as you can. However you can."

Irene was standing in the doorway, listening silently.

"Take the book," he said.

"I can't," I said.

"Take it," he repeated. "We must start somewhere. Hillel speaks to your heart? So start with *Pirkei Avot*. Come visit me again. Teach me what you have learned. And I will teach you what I have learned."

"I don't know . . ."

" 'Do not say: When I have time I will study. Because you may never have the time,' " he said. "Also Hillel. Also *Pirkei Avot*."

Irene came up behind my chair and put her hand on my shoulder. And the rabbi looked at us and smiled.

I conceded: "Well, I guess I can't argue with Hillel."

CHAPTER 12

"So, he *is* trying to convert you."

My mother didn't much like the idea of the rabbi "teaching" me about Judaism; she didn't know exactly what we'd be discussing, but she was sure that his Judaism wasn't the same as hers and the rabbi was surely filling my head with Orthodox propaganda.

I tried to reassure her by telling her that I wasn't any more likely to start attending Shabbat services at his synagogue than I was to go to Congregation Beth Shalom. Or the gay synagogue. Or any synagogue.

"He's not going to change how I think," I said, sitting across from her at my parents' kitchen table over Friday night dinner.

"You're not going to start praying every morning, are you?" she asked, as if that was the most absurd thing she could think of.

"I'm an atheist, Mom," I said. "Who am I going to pray to?"

She threw up her hands. "An atheist!" she spat, as if she had now realized that there was one thing even more absurd than praying every morning: not praying at all.

Sitting next to her, my father was less dramatic, but no less confused. "If you're an atheist, why are you studying with that rabbi?"

"Isn't being Jewish about more than God?" I asked.

"Like what?" he asked.

"Community, family, tradition, culture, history," I said. "Codes of ethics. Social justice . . . should I go on?"

"No, I get the point," my father said. "But what brought all this on?"

I told him about the rabbi's speech, about how I shouldn't let someone take my Judaism away from me—and how I felt like I'd let that happen for so many years because I felt alienated at every turn. Other Jews had told me that I didn't matter because I wasn't observant enough, or Zionist enough, or committed enough to "continuity"—which was really just a code word for heterosexuality. Meanwhile, non-Jews saw me as too Zionist, or too invested in religion, or simply too culturally foreign to ever really blend in. Both sides would have been happier if I'd simply stopped calling myself a Jew. But I wasn't going to let them win. I was going to take back my Jewishness. On my own terms.

"I'm embracing my Judaism," I said to my parents. "I thought you guys would be happy."

They looked at each other.

"If you want to embrace your Judaism, you could just come with us to services," my mother said. "I don't understand what the rabbi has to do with it."

"No," I said. "I guess you don't."

I tried to change the subject by telling them about Michelle's engagement. It worked; they were both back on familiar ground.

My mother's first question: "Is he Jewish?"

I didn't know the answer to any of her subsequent questions: Will Michelle take his name or hyphenate? Have they set a date? Where will they live? Are they planning to have children?

She wasn't too annoyed that I didn't have all the answers. The first question was the only one that really mattered.

"I remember the first time you brought her home for dinner," my mother said. "You were both freshmen. You two made such a cute couple. I had this fantasy somewhere in the back of my head that someday she'd be marrying *you*."

In fact, when I'd come out to them at the beginning of my sophomore year, my mother's second reaction—after first believing I was playing a prank on her—was confusion: She was convinced that Michelle and I were an item, despite my insistence to the contrary. ("Michelle's not my girlfriend, Mom, I'm *gay*," I reiterated. She asked, without realizing how funny it sounded, "But does Michelle know?")

Sitting across the table from her now, I was amazed to realize that her fantasy of having Michelle for a daughter-in-law still flickered somewhere in her brain, despite how much she'd grown to accept me as her gay son. "Yeah, that wouldn't really have worked out," I said.

She shot me one of her don't-be-a-smarty-pants looks. "Well, God forgive me for fantasizing about my son falling in love and settling down," she said.

"That might happen," I said, "just not with Michelle."

My father's ears perked up. "Seeing someone?" he asked.

They never asked for too many details, but they did keep track of who I was dating.

"For a couple of weeks," I said. "His name is Jamie."

My father asked, "What does he do?"

"He's a flight attendant," I said. I imagined his disappointment; I'm sure he'd have preferred something like doctor or lawyer or civil servant.

"That's okay," was all he said.

I looked at my mother, who was conspicuously silent.

"And yes, he's Jewish," I said. This was true. Or half-true. Or true enough for me, anyway. I figured that'd satisfy her.

Instead, she shrugged her shoulders and said, "I didn't say a thing."

* * *

Despite my parents' misgivings, I developed a new routine with the rabbi. Once a week, I'd visit after work to discuss Judaism.

We started with *Pirkei Avot,* with more Hillel: "He who
does not increase his knowledge, decreases it." The rabbi intended this as a motivational slogan, something to prod my
further studies. I rose to his challenge.

Occasionally, we'd touch on a related subject that would
send the rabbi to his bookshelves to find another book,
something else to discuss. Sometimes it was a story I remembered from my childhood book of Bible stories, other times a
verse from the Talmud or rabbinical commentary that he
deemed relevant.

Once in a while, I'd come to him with a seemingly random
question about a holiday tradition or a custom that I didn't
understand. Why is it a woman's responsibility to light Shabbat candles? What does cheesecake have to do with Shavuot?
Why is fish considered pareve? These were usually questions that Jamie had asked me that I couldn't answer on my
own; I'd pose them again to the rabbi as if they were my own
questions and he'd answer them. Then I'd report his remarks back to Jamie, as if the rabbi were the Oracle of Glenbrook.

These were elementary discussions, I knew—things the
rabbi had probably talked about sixty or seventy years ago.
But he never talked down to me or treated my questions as
too obvious to warrant a response. He was a good teacher; his
years as a yeshiva instructor in Brooklyn proved useful. Usually, I left these sessions with a new book from his shelves,
something to pore over for a few days before our next meeting.

The rabbi, too, asked me questions. About being gay.

"I am afraid I do not even know what to ask," he said tentatively, at one of our first meetings. "About your . . . life."

I remembered a story from the Passover Haggadah about
four sons: a wise son, a simple son, a contrary son, and a son

who does not even know how to ask a question. "As for the son who does not even know how to ask a question," I said to the rabbi, quoting from my family's Haggadah, "you must begin for him." He nodded at the reference; I began for him, telling him about how I realized I was gay.

Eventually, he came up with his own questions: How was I so sure that I was *that way?* Did I ever *try* to change? Why did I feel the need to *talk* about it, to label myself? His questions were always general, and while he avoided using the word "abomination," he still couldn't bring himself to use the word "gay." My answers were similarly broad and I never spoke specifically about sex. But we understood each other.

The rabbi's questions about being gay were surely as elementary as my questions about being Jewish; I'd answered them all years before. But like him, I never spoke down to him or treated his questions as too obvious to warrant a response. It was the questions that mattered. I knew I'd never change his mind. But I tried to help him understand—to "get over it," as Irene might say.

Irene was delighted that I was visiting again, even if it wasn't every day. "He always looks forward to seeing you," she told me one day in my office. "He talks about it all week."

"That's because I always bring honey cake," I joked.

"Well, that doesn't hurt, either," she joked back. "The way to that man's heart is through his sweet tooth."

Mrs. Goldfarb admitted to being a bit surprised at the turn my visits to the rabbi had taken. "It's like you've come back to Hebrew school after all these years," she said with some disbelief when I saw her at the sandwich shop one day at lunch.

"He who does not increase his knowledge, decreases it," I told her. "That's Hillel."

She was somewhat stunned, but quickly came up with a retort: "I suppose your teachers must have planted those seeds of curiosity many years ago."

I didn't tell her that the rabbi was more patient than she'd been when I was her second-grade student. I just said, "A good teacher, you never forget," and left it at that. Let her think what she wants.

Work kept coming at a steady but reasonable pace through the winter. More ads for Paradise. More online work, thanks to referrals from my website launch the previous fall. I even picked up a bit of work for the bookstore, when Mrs. Goldfarb asked me to design the store's advertisements for the *Jewish Week*. ("Keep it clean, Benjamin," she told me, "no boys with their shirts off.")

In my spare time, I worked on a little project I was doing for free: designing invitations for Michelle and Dan's wedding. Here, too, I kept it clean.

Through it all, Jamie and I continued to grow closer. His work required him to leave town every few days—San Francisco, Lima, Detroit, Panama City—but he always came back to me.

We spent New Year's Eve at a great party at a disco downtown, on a double date with Phil and Sammy—still seeing each other, and still unwilling to visit the suburbs—with one of the hottest DJs from New York spinning. We left at a quarter after midnight so we could go home and be alone instead.

We spent a whole weekend in February doing door-to-door canvassing for Obama—my T-shirt said "Change" while his said "Hope"—and celebrated with champagne when he swept the primaries in Maryland, Virginia, and Washington.

We did Valentine's Day like a couple of giddy goofballs, exchanging heart-shaped balloons and heart-shaped candies and matching boxer shorts covered with hearts. I was hooked.

One day in the middle of March, Jamie came to my office to meet me for lunch.

"When's Purim?" he asked.

"Why do you ask?"

"The bookstore has a big window display," he said. "Just seemed so funny when everyone else's windows are full of shamrocks and leprechauns for Saint Patrick's Day."

"Welcome to Glenbrook."

"Right," he said. "So what's Purim again? Isn't that the holiday with the noisemakers and the big cookies?"

I knew there was more to it than that, but I also knew that I'd probably have described it the same way. "Hamantashen," I said. "The cookies are called hamantashen."

"Did your mom make them when you were a kid?"

I laughed. "My mother didn't bake much. She was more of an Entenmann's mom."

"Better than mine," Jamie said. "She used to bake these awful little Swedish cookies. Dry as dust, and they tasted like almonds and sand."

"Poor thing," I offered. "Sounds like child abuse. Or at least neglect."

"Want to make hamantashen tonight?" he asked.

"I've never done it," I said.

"Me, either," he said. "So we'll figure it out together. How hard can it be?"

Truth be told, it was pretty hard. Our first batch unfolded in the oven, leaving prune filling spilling out across the cookie sheet. The next batch burned on the bottom, and the one after that burned on the top after we'd moved the baking rack up too high. By the time we got a dozen decent hamantashen, our hands were blistered from the rolling pin and my kitchen floor was covered in flour.

But they were good. Even Dan and Michelle thought so; when they came home from a movie, they devoured five between them, standing in the kitchen doorway.

"Dude, that's good shit," said Dan.

"That's high praise," I told Jamie, translating.

"Thank you," Jamie told me, "but I know what he meant. I speak Dude."

"Hold on to this one," Michelle told me, gesturing toward Jamie. "He knows his way around a kitchen."

"You didn't see the first fifty," I said.

"You ate fifty of them?" she asked.

"No, they're in the garbage," I said.

Dan opened the lid of the garbage can and reached toward the burned cookies. "What's wrong with these? They're just a little burnt."

Michelle slapped his hand. "You're not eating those," she scolded. Taking Dan by the arm, she said, "Good night, you fabulous baker boys." And then she dragged him off to her room.

Jamie looked pleased. "We still have a few left," he said.

"I can't eat another one. I'm all pruned out."

"You could take them to the rabbi," he suggested.

"I can't," I said. "They're not kosher."

"Why? There's nothing in them but butter and sugar and flour. Prunes are kosher, aren't they? It's not like we filled them with ham and cheese."

"All right," I said. "They're kosher. But they're not kosher enough."

I stopped by the bakery the next evening and brought store-bought hamantashen to the rabbi's house, instead of the usual honey cake. I didn't mention my own baking adventure.

"So, Purim is coming," he said, biting off a corner of one of the triangular pastries. "You know the cookies. But do you know the story?"

"I know it's about Queen Esther," I said, opting not to tell him about my traumatic Esther masquerade as a young boy.

"And what else do you remember?"

"Haman," I added, pointing to the remaining hamantashen, which were supposed to represent his three-cornered hat. "Haman wanted to kill the Jews, but Queen Esther saved them."

The rabbi peered at me over his glasses, as if to say, "Is that all?" But instead, he said, "That is true. But there is much more. Maybe even a lesson for today. For you."

He recounted the story of Purim, details that I'd long forgotten. About Esther's cousin Mordechai's refusal to bow down before Haman, the king's righthand man. About Haman's plan to take revenge not just on Mordechai, but on all the Jews in Persia. About Esther's secret Jewish identity and the banquet where she revealed herself as a Jew to the king—risking her own life to save her people.

"It's like a suspense thriller," I said, nibbling on a cookie, thinking that the ones I'd baked were better. "All the politics and evil plots and secret identities."

The rabbi wasn't amused. "It's a serious story, Benji," he said. "About the importance of keeping your faith. Esther had power and wealth and could have given up on being Jewish."

"But being Jewish was too important to her," I interjected.

"Quite the opposite," the rabbi said. "That's why this is a good story for you. There is no evidence that being Jewish was important to Esther. She married a non-Jewish man, King Ahasuerus. She wasn't observant, or it would have been obvious that she was Jewish. We can assume that she didn't go to synagogue or keep kosher. Sound like anyone you know?"

"Go on," I said, one eyebrow raised.

"But when push came to shove," he continued, "she realized that her faith, and her family, was still a part of her. She risked everything for her faith, for her community. Even though she was not, on a practical level, part of the community. She could not completely leave that piece of her behind. Again, perhaps, like someone we both know."

"Yes, I get it," I said.

"Esther is a hero," he said. "Not because she observed every law or prayed every day. But she saved her people. And I don't think any rabbi anywhere would say she wasn't a good Jew."

He took another cookie and waited for my reaction.

"I think there is another lesson here," I said.

He chewed slowly.

"You asked me once why it was so important to come out, to tell the whole world about my quote-unquote private life," I said. "Purim is all about the importance of coming out."

He started to turn red.

"As a Jew," I clarified, before he could say anything. "Religion is what some people would consider a private matter. What you believe in your heart is your own business, but you don't have to run around telling everyone else about it. Of course, with some people it's obvious. Men wear yarmulkes, or they have *payes*, and that tells the whole world they're Jewish. But for most Jews, as long as they don't say anything, they can basically stay in the closet and nobody has to know. That's what Esther did. She stayed in the closet. And she was pretty happy in there for a while. She was rich and powerful and it seems like she had everything that anyone could ever want."

The rabbi's color had returned to normal, so I continued: "Her community needed her. As long as she stayed in the closet, she was safe, but the rest of her community was in danger. And that's when she realized that her own safety was an illusion, too. If she hadn't spoken up, she'd have been complicit in her community's murder. And she'd have lived in constant fear of exposure herself. Her closet would have become a trap."

He nodded. A good sign.

"Esther took a chance and came out," I said. "And once

the king realized that his own wife was Jewish, he understood that the plot against the Jews was wrong. Because he realized that she was one of them and they were just like her. It's hard to hate a whole group of people when you realize you already care about one of them."

"A very interesting interpretation," he said finally, brushing sticky crumbs off his shirt. "I suppose I am your King Ahasuerus?"

"In this particular case, yes," I said. "And I guess I'm your queen."

I cracked a smile, and after a moment, the rabbi's initial grimace turned to a reluctant, pursed grin.

Jamie and Michelle became fast friends. They shared certain passions—Britney gossip, *Desperate Housewives*, Major League Baseball—that left me cold, so they always had plenty to chat about whenever Jamie came over. And she constantly joked about having a tiny little crush on him.

"If he weren't gay . . ." Michelle said to me one evening after he left.

"Then he wouldn't be a very good boyfriend," I said.

"Maybe not for you," she said, winking.

"And you'd have to give Dan back his ring."

"Damn!" she said, snapping her fingers. "There's always a catch!"

Phil also approved. We didn't see each other as much, now that we were both "involved" and spending less time at the bars. But after all the evenings we'd hung out together over the years, I felt almost like he was my big brother. So even if we weren't together as often as before, we still e-mailed each other to keep in touch, and once in a while the four of us would meet for a drink.

"This one's different," Phil whispered to me one night at Paradise.

"How so?" I asked, having learned to trust Phil's intuition about these things.

"With the other guys you dated, I could only picture you together right there at that moment," he said. "When I look at you with Jamie, I can imagine entire photo albums of things that haven't even happened yet."

But my friends were the easy part. I wanted my parents to meet Jamie; I'd never dated anyone long enough to get to this phase, so I wasn't sure how to handle it. My mother didn't see anything complicated about the situation. "So bring him for Passover," she suggested.

Jamie had never been to a Passover seder before, so I prepped him on the basics. In my family, the seder wasn't a huge affair; since all my grandparents were dead, and Rachel and Richard held their own seder in Seattle, there were only three Steiners around the table every Passover. But others usually joined us: my parents' old friends the Frishmans; my second cousin on my mother's side, Nate, who was an undergrad at American University in the District, far from his parents' home in Chicago; and my Uncle Larry and his second wife, Linda, who lived outside Baltimore. Most of these people I only saw on Passover, so I wasn't too concerned about what they all thought of Jamie. But he was a social guy—he basically made small talk for a living—so the social aspect wasn't what had me worried. It was the seder itself.

We weren't a formal bunch, hung up on reading every single word of the Haggadah. But we did sing most of the songs and recite all the blessings, in Hebrew. Jamie didn't know any of this stuff and he'd forgotten what little Hebrew he'd learned in Sunday school as a child. He was worried that he'd look like an idiot.

So I went to the bookstore and bought a copy of the same Haggadah that we used in my parents' house and transliterated all the songs we'd have to sing together, spelling out all the Hebrew words phonetically in English. I shrank it down on a photocopier so Jamie could hide the cheat sheet inside his Haggadah. Then I taught him the melodies.

"It's a great plan," he said, "but I don't just want to fudge my way through this. I want to know what the seder is actually about."

For two weeks before Passover, we practiced the songs together—often over the phone, long-distance—and read through the Haggadah itself. He asked questions about the Passover story, and about how the seder was structured; I answered whatever I could and asked the rabbi about the rest.

By the time Passover came, he was prepared. And I knew more about Passover than I ever had.

I'd been worried about how my parents would introduce Jamie: Would they use the word "boyfriend"—which is what I was calling him by that point—or the more ambiguous term "friend," whose meaning depends on how long the vowels are stretched and how high the eyebrows are raised when it's said aloud?

I needn't have worried. When my mother introduced him to the others, she said simply, "And this is Jamie Cohen." Let them connect the dots.

Jamie was nervous at first and so was I, maybe more so. After all, if the seder was a complete disaster, he could walk away from my family relatively unscathed; I'd have to come back and face them alone.

But it wasn't a disaster. Jamie was well rehearsed. I led the seder and Jamie joined in all the songs, peering at his cheat sheet discreetly. Nobody would have guessed that it was his first time.

We had both relaxed when it came time for the festival meal, in the middle of the seder. My father cleared the table—putting the Haggadahs and the matzoh and the seder plate on the credenza—while my mother brought out her usual feast. This was the heart of the seder in the Steiner house, the part that really matters most.

"So I assume you're rooting for Barack *Hussein* Obama, like Benji is?" my mother asked Jamie. I recognized this as a gentle prod rather than a serious provocation. But it was Jamie's first time dealing with my mother and he was caught off-guard.

"Uh, well," he started. "Yeah, I guess."

"We're Hillary supporters," my mother said.

"Us, too," said Mrs. Frishman. Uncle Larry and Linda nodded along.

"Of course you are," I said, teasing, with a gesture toward my mother. "You're her core constituency: Jewish seniors."

"I am not a senior citizen," she shot back, feigning offense.

"Old enough for AARP, old enough for Hillary," I said. My father laughed.

Realizing this wasn't going to be a nasty fight, Jamie chimed in: "I just feel like it's time for a change. The Clintons had their time in office already."

"A pretty good time for this country," said my father.

"I'm not voting for 'pretty good,'" I said. "I'm voting for something better."

"And you trust this guy?" Uncle Larry asked.

Cousin Nate answered: "He's my senator and I trust him."

"I want to get out of Iraq and I want health care reform," said Jamie. "I don't think Hillary's the person to do it. I think Obama's the only chance we've got."

"I agree," said Nate. "But, you know, his stance on gay marriage isn't any better than Hillary's."

I looked at Jamie. "That's not an urgent issue just yet."

There was a moment of uneasy silence as the unspoken was made perfectly clear, but my mother quickly broke it: "I don't like that preacher of his, Jeremiah . . . what's-his-name."

"Jeremiah Wright," my father offered.

"A real bigot," she continued. "And that's who's giving him spiritual guidance?"

"I've heard your rabbi say plenty of awful things," I said.

My mother pursed her lips.

"It's not the same, Benji," my father said.

"Take a few sound bites out of context and it's not so different," I said.

The conversation then devolved into an argument over whose campaign had been nastier, whose strategy sounder. But in the end, everyone at the table agreed that whoever won the nomination would get their vote in November.

"We've got to get the Republicans out," my father said. "That's the main thing here and we can all agree on that."

Jamie looked at my mother and asked, "So you'll vote for Obama, if he wins the nomination?"

She nodded. "Jews don't vote Republican," she said plainly—meaning non-Orthodox Jews.

"A few of them do," Jamie said. "I mean, not me. But a few of them."

"Maybe a few who are so rich that they don't care about anyone but themselves," she said with disgust. Then she looked at Jamie and smiled: "But nobody I'd want at my seder."

Politics didn't last long as the main topic of conversation. Everyone at the table had travel-related questions for Jamie and he didn't let them down. He recommended a hotel in Puerto Rico for the Frishmans' upcoming vacation, gave my cousin the name of a popular dance club in London—where he was planning to spend the summer—and suggested a way for my Uncle Larry to save a bundle on his business trips to Boston by flying into Providence and taking the commuter rail instead of flying direct to Logan. By the time we were done with the turkey, all the guests had taken a liking to Jamie.

But my parents were the only ones who really mattered. He won them over while we ate dessert.

My father asked him if he liked traveling for work. "It must not be much fun after a while," my father said.

Jamie told him, "You're right, but whose job is always fun? What I love about my work is that there's always something for me to learn, always something new to see. You know, some people I work with never get past the airports and the hotels they stick us in. They just watch pay-per-view and use the hotel gym and wait until they can fly back as soon as they can. I'd rather get out and see where I am. Whether it's the Grand Canyon or the pyramids in Mexico, or finding a cool jazz club in San Francisco or a barbecue joint in Kansas City. There's always something to learn, if you're willing to go looking for it."

My mother asked, "So, if you've traveled so much, what's the place you've liked the most?"

Jamie didn't hesitate. "Israel," he said.

"Oh, us, too," my mother said. "We took the kids there when Rachel was in college."

"Benji told me," Jamie said, provoking a pleased look from both my parents.

"So what did you like best about it?" my father asked.

Jamie had told me about dancing at a fantastic disco in Haifa, and getting stoned on the beach in Eilat, and cruising Independence Park in Tel Aviv—years after I'd stolen a glimpse from my hotel window. But those weren't the kind of stories that would impress my parents. I hoped he realized that.

He did.

"I've never felt so close to my Jewishness," he said. "It's not just the ancient sites—the Western Wall or Masada or Rachel's tomb. It's the people. It's seeing people from all over the world, dressing differently and speaking different languages and eating different foods, and knowing that we're all connected."

"Very true," said my father, who still had a decidedly romantic view of the Jewish state—one that evoked images of flowers blooming in the desert while barefooted kibbutzniks danced the hora in a circle. Sure, he read news reports about armed settlers and racist politicians and Ethiopian immigrants living in poverty, economic problems and ethnic strife and ongoing military conflicts, but these never displaced the picture that had been fixed in his mind since the sixties.

Having already gotten my father in his corner, Jamie turned to my mother and added: "Plus, can we talk about the shopping in Tel Aviv? I got this Swiss watch for like twenty bucks on Sheinkin Street. I've seen the same one at White Flint for ten times that!"

"You're kidding!" my mother blurted out. "Let me see that watch."

He had them both in the palm of his hand before we ever opened the door for Elijah.

As we were leaving, my father shook Jamie's hand and told him, "I hope you'll come back and visit again." My mother kissed me on the cheek and whispered quickly in my ear: "I like him."

Someone my mother would like. The highest praise.

Jamie knew that he'd made a good impression. On the drive home, he said, "Well, I've met your parents, I've met Phil, and I've met Michelle. I guess the only person left to meet is the rabbi."

This wasn't the first time Jamie had expressed an interest in meeting the rabbi; he'd asked several times if he could join me for one of our "classes." I thought it might be too much for the rabbi to handle: One sodomite might be excused, but two? How much could one old man take? But Jamie was persistent.

As I'd told him many times before, I said I'd think about it. Jamie wanted to meet the rabbi and I wanted them to meet; I just wasn't sure the rabbi was up to it. Irene always said I shouldn't underestimate him, but I'd overestimated him once before. I didn't want to push it.

I dropped Jamie off at his apartment and went home. My place was empty; Michelle had taken Dan to her parents' house in Philadelphia for Passover. It was late, but I'd promised to tell her how the big night had gone. So I sent her a short text message on her cell phone: "He's the one."

Mrs. Goldfarb knocked on my office door and then walked in before I had a chance to get up from my desk. I hadn't seen her for a week; the bookstore had only reopened that morning after being closed for Passover.

"Benjamin," she said with a tone more urgent than cheerful. "Come with me. We have to go to Holy Cross."

Remembering what the rabbi had told me about her smoky car, I offered to drive. Sitting in my passenger seat, Mrs. Goldfarb cracked a window and, without asking, lit a cigarette, blowing the smoke outside. On the way to the hospital, she told me what had happened: Irene had called the store that morning. The rabbi had suffered another attack that morning after davening, probably another stroke. An ambulance had taken him to Holy Cross on a stretcher, unconscious, with Irene riding alongside him. Irene had asked Mrs. Goldfarb to give me the news.

The rabbi hadn't regained consciousness. When we arrived, he was breathing on his own, but his eyes were closed.

Irene hugged us both. Her eyes were red, but she was not crying. "He's not going to make it," she said.

"What do the doctors say?" Mrs. Goldfarb asked.

"Another stroke," said Irene. "Very bad."

"Isn't there anything they can do?" I asked.

"He didn't want any heroics," she replied. "It's time. He knew it. I know it."

In the time he'd had Irene with him, the rabbi had gotten all his personal papers in order. Per his explicit wishes, the rabbi was never hooked up to machines. And although Irene sat and held his hand for hours by his bedside, he never moved, or spoke, or squeezed her hand back.

Mrs. Goldfarb and I had already left the two of them alone when the end came. Another stroke. Cardiac arrest. No heroics. Call the shul—they have a committee.

According to Jewish law, nobody needed to sit shiva for the rabbi. He didn't have any children and his wife and siblings were dead.

Irene sat shiva anyway. "Let them try and stop me," she said. Even though she'd grown up Reform and raised her kids—at her husband's insistence—as Conservative, after living in North Beach for a few years among the Orthodox, she was used to *frum* people telling her how things should be done, so she had no problem telling them where they could stick their rules.

Every evening for a week, she had a small gathering at the rabbi's house. Mrs. Goldfarb led a short service. I came, with Jamie. (Irene insisted.) The owner of the bakery came. The rabbi's next-door neighbors, who were not Jewish, brought dinner for Irene so she wouldn't have to cook. A handful of people from B'nai Tikvah came—far fewer than had come a year earlier when the rabbi sat shiva for Sophie; these few came out of respect for their stalwart fellow congregant, but when they saw that a woman would be leading the mourners' service, they made their apologies and left.

When the week ended, I drove to the rabbi's house to pick up Irene and take her to the airport. The azaleas were in bloom in every front yard. The street had never looked lovelier.

Irene's suitcases were packed and waiting by the front door. The house was still, lifeless, vacuum cleaner tracks visible in the carpets. She motioned for me to come upstairs with her.

"The synagogue is going to pack up all of his things," she said, two steps ahead of me.

"That's nice of them," I said, genuinely surprised. I couldn't imagine Congregation Beth Shalom doing that.

"Nice, *shmice*," she said. "It's the least they could do. He left them all his money."

"Wonder what they'll do with it," I said.

She reached the top step and turned to me. "They're going to buy a Torah in his memory."

I shrugged a shoulder. "Sounds about right."

She shrugged back and waved dismissively.

"They can do whatever they want with the money," she said. "But he left you something, too."

We walked into the study. Irene flicked on the light and pointed to the top left bookshelf. A Post-it note hanging from the shelf read, in shaky block letters: "Benji, start here." I walked up to the bookcase to get a closer look. That shelf contained what might be called Jewish 101 books: basic information about holidays, rituals, history, scripture. From there the shelves grew progressively more advanced.

"He worked on this for weeks," she said as I ran my finger across the spines, reading title after title. "Rearranged all his books, just for you. So you could keep studying after he was gone."

I stood in stunned silence.

Irene gave me a minute to take it all in before she reminded me that she was on a tight schedule.

"Once those synagogue people get here, they're going to take everything," she said. "So you need to pick up some boxes and come back tonight with Jamie and take these books. He wanted you to have them."

Without turning away from the books, I nodded.

"Now let's go, dear, or I'll miss my flight."

We didn't talk much on the drive to the airport. It was only when we arrived at the terminal and I was helping Irene with her bags that I realized I might not see her again. I'd spent so much of the previous week thinking about the rabbi that I hadn't stopped to think that I'd be losing Irene, too. She had come into my life so unexpectedly, and suddenly—and just as suddenly, she was leaving.

As usual, though, Irene seemed to be able to read my mind.

She gave me a kiss on the cheek and touched my face with her hand, letting it linger for a few seconds.

"No good-bye," she said. "I expect to see you for the White Party. And bring Jamie."

I don't know if I believe that each of us has a *bashert*—someone we're supposed to spend our lives with. But I do believe that certain people are fated to meet each other, to teach each other something essential, or show each other something important. I can't believe it's all a coincidence.

Jamie and I live together now, in the apartment I used to share with Michelle. And the rabbi's books line the walls of our study—the room that used to be Michelle's bedroom.

She and Dan bought a little house in Rockville, not far from my parents. "It's really almost Potomac," she told me with a knowing wink when they moved in. Sometimes, on weekends, Jamie and I go to visit Michelle and Dan—"the newlyweds," as we will probably *always* call them. She's pregnant with twins and she's already talking about sending them to my old elementary school.

Jamie and I have expanded our family, too. We adopted a cat. He's black and white, and his name is Zisel. Appropriately enough, he naps on top of the bookcase in our study, gazing down on us as we read and discuss the rabbi's books.

It'll take years for us to get through all of them, but we're in no rush.

The night that Jamie and I went to the rabbi's house to box up those books, I also grabbed a few little things to remember him by: the photo in the alligator frame from his mantel, the pillow that sat on his sofa, his old Allan Sherman records. And the two framed needlepoints that used to hang outside the upstairs bathroom: We sent the one with the flowers to Irene in Florida. The other one, with the apple tree, we hung over our bed.

It still hangs there today.

The rabbi explained the apple tree the last time I saw him, four days before he died.

It was the middle of Passover and I'd stopped by with a box of kosher-for-Passover chocolates.

Irene had cleaned the house for the holiday. The piles of books that had cluttered the dining room table had been reshelved. The rugs had been shampooed. A clutch of orange tulips adorned the coffee table. Spring had arrived and the windows in the living room were open.

Irene was in the kitchen, beating eggs for a sponge cake.

"I can't seem to find my glasses," the rabbi said, checking the end table next to the sofa. "I left them right here."

I got up and asked Irene. "I must have put them upstairs when I was cleaning," she said. "They're probably in his study."

I ran upstairs and into his study—which at the time was also serving as Irene's room. But every day, she folded up her bed and turned it back into his study, so as not to disturb him. And months after arriving, she continued to live out of her suitcase, as if she might need to leave at a moment's notice. There was hardly any evidence that she'd been living there.

As I left the study, the needlepoints outside the bathroom caught my eye. The apple tree and the flowers. I assumed that Sophie had made them, but I didn't understand what they represented, and I couldn't read the Hebrew on the bottom of each picture.

I came downstairs and asked the rabbi.

"Those are from the Song of Songs," he said. "Some of the most romantic poetry ever written."

"In the Bible?" I asked.

"Wait, I'll show you."

He stood up and went to his bookshelves, taking a copy of the Bible and flipping toward the back.

He read to me, in Hebrew, and then he translated: "Like a lily among the thorns, so is my beloved among women. Like an apple tree among the trees of the forest, so is my beloved among men."

"It is *romantic," I said.*

"I told you, the Bible is more than rules and regulations," he said. "It is also about love."

I wanted to tell him about my love, my romance, the man I had finally found. But how to approach the subject? We had avoided getting too specific in our discussions about gay life up to this point, but I thought he was ready to hear about Jamie, if only I could back into the discussion somehow.

We sat back down in our usual places and I figured out how to tell him about Jamie. I'd start with something he could relate to.

"How was your seder?" I asked.

"Very nice," he said. "Just Irene and me. She made a delicious meal. Last year, you know, I was all alone for Passover. Some people from the shul invited me to their seder. But it wasn't the same. This year, I have a home of my own again. Thanks to Irene."

He was looking into the kitchen, where Irene was mixing batter. Then he snapped back to reality and asked me how my seder had been.

"Wonderful," I said.

"Why wonderful?"

"For the first time, I brought someone to the seder with me," I said. "A man I've been seeing."

He was silent, realizing he'd been tricked into talking about men who loved men, rather than something he'd be more comfortable dis-

cussing—like slavery in Egypt or wandering for forty years in the desert.

"His name is Jamie and he's a flight attendant."

He bit into one of the Passover chocolates.

"I've told him all about you and he really wants to meet you."

Was this too much? Was I going too far?

"Why?" he asked.

"It's funny," I said, thinking I shouldn't have started this conversation, but realizing it was too late to stop now. "I never would have met him if it wasn't for you."

The rabbi cocked his head. "I don't understand," he said, probably stunned that he might have unwittingly played homosexual matchmaker.

"Well, we met on the plane to Miami over Thanksgiving, when I went to stay in your condo. He was working on that flight. If you hadn't given me that birthday present, I never would have met him. So, in a way, you're the reason that we're together."

The rabbi took a deep breath and took off his glasses. He sat back on the couch and tried to absorb what I'd told him. I wasn't sure what was coming next: Would he ask more questions or change the subject? Tell me to bring Jamie over or tell me, once again, to get out?

After a moment, he leaned forward, furrowed his brow, and looked me square in the eye.

"Tell me, Benji," he said. "This flight attendant. He is Jewish?"

Please turn the page for a special Q&A
with Wayne Hoffman!

How did this story come to you?

One day several years ago, when I was working as managing editor at the *Forward*, an English-language Jewish newspaper, an editor from the *Forverts*—our sister newspaper, published in Yiddish, with whom we shared a newsroom—came in and asked if one of his employees could rest on my couch. I didn't know this employee, didn't know his name, and didn't even know if he spoke English. But he was very ill and clearly needed to lie down and my office had the only couch in the newsroom, so I said yes. I looked over at this bearded, observant man, who was probably eighty years old, in poor health, as he slept. And I wondered who this man was, what the two of us could possibly have in common, how a conversation might go between us. And that turned into the opening scene of *Sweet Like Sugar*. I've spent many years thinking about being gay and being Jewish, and how those two identities intersect or complement each other or come into conflict, so it was only natural that as I continued thinking about what a conversation with this man on my couch might sound like, these are the subjects that became the core of the story.

Is this story based on true events?

Although there are elements in the story that are based on things that happened to me, or to people I know, the story is fiction. However, the larger issues that underpin the story—how people are brought together by fate, how religion unites and divides us, how communities can welcome or exclude people, how personal connections can help us get past our deep-seated prejudices—are true in a broad sense, if not a particularly personal one.

Are the characters based on real people?

The only character who's based specifically on a real person is Irene; I named her after my great-aunt, who died shortly after I finished writing the book. Aunt Irene had a keen sense for cutting through the bull and getting to what was really important and she had a strong belief in fate and forces beyond our control. She was never in the situations that I describe in this book, but when I was writing Irene's scenes, I had my great-aunt in mind the whole time, trying to figure out how she'd react if she were in her namesake's place. There's also a tiny piece of my maternal grandfather in Benji's grandfather: He died when I was six years old, so, like Benji, I only remember him from my early childhood. In fact, like Benji, one of my strongest memories of my grandfather was of him leading a Passover seder while my grandmother nagged him from across the table. Most of the other characters are not based on specific individuals. My own parents are much more fun to be around than Benji's, I am much closer to my sister than Benji is to his, and unlike Benji, I have a brother—who, ironically enough, is a Conservative rabbi, one far more broad-minded than this book's Rabbi Adler. I don't have a roommate like Michelle, but I do have women in my life who have played similar roles; that's true for lots of gay men.

Much of the book takes place in suburban Washington, D.C. How do you know this area?

Even though I've spent most of my adult life in New York City, I know this area firsthand. I grew up in Silver Spring, Maryland, very close to where the book is set—that's where I went to Hebrew school, attended synagogue, learned Israeli dance, worked at the JCC, and spent summers at a Jewish camp. My parents still live there, so I visit frequently. I am well acquainted with how the Jewish community operates there and how the gay community does, too. Parts of the book are set decades ago in Jersey City, which is where my mother grew up in an Orthodox household, so I know that area during that period, as well, secondhand.

Has your spiritual journey been different from Benji's?

I grew up Conservative, like Benji. And I, too, felt alienated from a young age, despite feeling a certain sense of connection to individual parts of that tradition. But I haven't wrestled in the same way; I found a place in the Jewish community where I feel comfortable many years ago.

SWEET LIKE SUGAR

Wayne Hoffman

ABOUT THIS GUIDE

The suggested questions are included
to enhance your group's reading
of Wayne Hoffman's *Sweet Like Sugar*.

DISCUSSION QUESTIONS

1. Even though Benji feels alienated from his Jewish-ness, Jewish holidays play a large part in his story: His memories of Passover appear in the first and last chapters, and in the middle, he goes to synagogue for Rosh Hashanah, attends a Hanukkah party, bakes hamantashen for Purim, and flashes back to Shabbat services from his childhood. What role do holidays play in maintaining Jewish identity—even for people who feel disconnected from traditional Judaism?

2. How much of the story is unique to Jews? Could a similar story play out with non-Jewish characters? How might it be different?

3. As Rabbi Zuckerman and Benji get to know each other, there are several opportunities for Benji to tell the rabbi that he is gay or for the rabbi to ask. Why doesn't it happen sooner? Do you think it was a mistake for Benji to bring it up how and when he did? Did the rabbi react inappropriately? How might both men have handled it differently?

4. Irene implies that the rabbi sent Benji to Florida to meet her—that their meeting was not an accident or even something the rabbi feared. Do you agree? Why might the rabbi have wanted Benji and Irene to meet?

5. If Irene hadn't played intermediary, do you think Benji and the rabbi could ever have repaired their relationship? If Benji hadn't intervened, do you think the rabbi and Irene would ever have reconnected?

6. From what you know about Sophie, how do you think she would have reacted to the rabbi's relationship with

Benji? How would she have reacted to finding out that Benji is gay?

7. Rabbi Zuckerman tries to teach Benji about Judaism, while Benji tries to educate the rabbi about gay life. Who has the harder job? The rabbi, who must overcome Benji's negative experiences from the past if he is to succeed where others have tried and failed? Or Benji, who is likely the first person to speak to the rabbi about the realities of gay life from a personal, rather than religious, perspective?

8. Do you believe that people are destined to be together? Does that only apply to romantic couples, or to other kinds of relationships, too? Is it possible for one person to have more than one *bashert?*

9. Some of the closest relationships in the book defy simple categorization and familial labels: Irene and Rabbi Zuckerman, Benji and Michelle, Benji and the rabbi. How do the characters in the book build their chosen families and how do they try to ensure that they endure?

10. Fast-forward a few years from the end of the novel. Where do you think the characters are? Are Benji and Jamie still together and still studying? Are they still in touch with Irene? Do Benji and Michelle still see each other often? How has Benji's family changed?

WITHDRAWN